The Lure Of The Witch

The Lure Of The Witch

'Hawkman Series #11'

Betty Sullivan La Pierre
Cover Art by Author, Paul Musgrove

2008

Copyright © 2008 Betty Sullivan La Pierre
All rights reserved.
ISBN: 1-4392-1104-3
ISBN-13: 9781439211045

Visit www.booksurge.com to order additional copies.

The Lure Of The Witch

Others in 'The Hawkman Series by
BETTY SULLIVAN LA PIERRE
http://www.bettysullivanlapierre.com

THE ENEMY STALKS
DOUBLE TROUBLE
THE SILENT SCREAM
DIRTY DIAMONDS
BLACKOUT
DIAMONDS aren't FOREVER
CAUSE FOR MURDER
ANGELS IN DISGUISE
IN FOR THE KILL
GRAVE WEB
THE LURE OF THE WITCH

Also by Betty Sullivan La Pierre

MURDER.COM
THE DEADLY THORN

I want to thank Author, Paul Musgrove for the beautiful covers
he has designed for my books throughout the years.

THANK YOU, PAUL

I'd like to dedicate this book to two of the most wonderful witches I know.
Anne and Selma
They've cast their spells on this manuscript to make it a great story.

CHAPTER ONE

Hawkman sat at the desk in his Medford office, poring over the ledger containing case expenses and bills to maintain his private investigator business. When he finally finished, he let out a sigh, put the checkbook away, stacked the bills in a pile and leaned back in the chair. He sure missed Jennifer's help when the end of the month rolled around. But since she'd signed a contract for her mystery series, she had enough on her mind, and he didn't feel right asking her to keep his books.

Just as he rose to get a cup of coffee, the phone rang. He reached across the desk and punched the speaker button. "Private Investigator, Tom Casey."

"Hello, Mr. Casey, my name's Greg Willis. I'd like to set up an appointment to meet with you as soon as possible."

The name rang a bell in Hawkman's mind, but he couldn't place it. "May I ask what about?"

"My teenaged daughter, Sarah, has disappeared and I need your help in finding her."

"Have you filed a runaway or missing person report?"

"Yes, but the police are dragging their feet and have come up with nothing, not even a single clue." He let out an exasperated breathe. "I can't stand not knowing whether she's dead or alive."

"Didn't I read something about this case in the paper?"

"Probably."

"If I remember right, the girl is sixteen years old and you're divorced. Does this child come from that marriage?"

"Yes."

"I'm assuming your ex-wife doesn't know her whereabouts either?"

"No. Though she disappeared while staying with her."

"And the police told you they have no leads?"

"Right."

Hawkman checked his appointment calendar. "How about tomorrow at one?"

"I'll be there."

After hanging up, Hawkman called his good friend, Detective Williams of the Medford police force. "Hey, Williams, how's it going?"

"Not good, I've lost a couple of my best officers."

"How?"

"Better pay offers. I can't blame the men. They have families and need higher salaries. Know any rookies looking for a job?"

"Not off the top of my head, but if I hear of anyone interested, I'll send him or her your way."

"Thanks. I'm sure you didn't call to hear about my troubles. What can I do for you?"

"Greg Willis, the man whose daughter's missing, just gave me a ring."

"Oh, yes. He's about driven me nuts, but I understand how anxious he feels. However, he doesn't seem to understand I can't use my whole force to search for her. Usually these kids show up eventually, once they're tired of eating out of garbage cans. Does he want to hire you to find the little urchin?"

"I gather that's his plan. Have an appointment with him tomorrow afternoon, so wondered if I could drop by the station and get the rundown on what you've collected on the case?"

"Sure. Come on over. I can tell you right now, there's not much. Just don't have the man power to pursue a runaway kid."

"Any information will help."

"Okay, I'll pull the file."

Hawkman turned off the coffee urn and picked up the stack of mail from the desktop, which he'd drop at the post office on his way. When he reached the police station, he parked in the visitor's lot and strolled to the door. As he passed the front desk, everyone waved and congratulated him on solving the cold case, which they'd dubbed 'Grave Web'.

"Thanks, guys, appreciate it," he said, smiling as he went down the hall to the detective's office.

He gave a quick knock on the jamb as he turned into the room. Williams glanced up with a twinkle in his eye. "Have a seat. I've got something to ask you."

"Yeah?" Hawkman said as he pulled up a chair.

"Several of my cronies thought it worth my time to ask if you'd be interested in joining our force. We could use a man with your knowledge and abilities."

Hawkman reared back in the seat. "You're kidding, of course."

The detective shook his head. "No. We'd be honored to have you."

Leaning forward, Hawkman placed his elbow on the desk and looked Williams in the face. "You know I'd go nuts. I like to work in the field on my own time. I don't want orders about which shift I have to work and I couldn't handle sitting at a desk signing papers. I'd go mad." He pointed a finger. "On top of that, wearing a uniform would make me grouchy."

The detective guffawed. "So you're telling me, there's no way."

"You got the picture."

"I told the men, I'd never be able to talk you into it. They suggested I give it a try. I've done my duty, so now we can get down to the Sarah Willis case." He pulled a slim file from under some papers on his desktop, and opened it. Removing a photo, he slid it across the desk. "Here's a picture of the missing girl."

Hawkman picked it up and studied the photo. "Is this a recent shot?"

"Yes. The father said they had her portrait taken a few months ago and this is one of the proofs."

"Very beautiful young lady. Big brown eyes, long hair, nice features and clear complexion." He handed it back to the detective. "How tall is she?"

Williams flipped though some of the papers. "She's about five foot, weighs approximately a hundred pounds, and has a small tattoo on her right shoulder blade."

"What's the design?"

"A butterfly."

"Any birthmarks?"

"No, but she does have an appendectomy scar below the bikini line." The detective rolled his eyes. "Those are the father's words. I can't imagine a dad worrying about where the scar is when your kid has appendicitis at four years old."

"What role has the mother played so far?"

"Not much. She's so emotional when we talk to her, it's hard to get any facts. Maybe you'll have better luck."

"Does Sarah have a boyfriend?"

"Good question. The folks say she doesn't, but when you look at the picture, it's hard to think there are no boys involved in her life."

"Have you questioned any of her girlfriends?"

"Not yet. We hoped to embark on that task this coming week."

"Obviously, with her reported as a runaway or missing, the description has gone to the National Crime Information Center."

"Oh, yeah, went out immediately."

"Good." Hawkman stood. "This information at least gives me a start. Could I get a copy of the picture and the initial report?"

"Sure." The detective picked up the file and crossed the room to the copy machine.

Hawkman left the police station and returned to his office where he reread the information. It appeared the parents lived in separate apartment complexes. He wrote the addresses on a separate sheet of paper and decided he might cruise by to get an insight on the neighborhood where this young girl lived. He pulled a folder from a new package and shoved the report inside. Since he wasn't sure Willis would hire him, he didn't label the file.

When he arrived home that night, he stayed in the garage so long, Jennifer finally came out the front door. "Hawkman, are you okay?"

"Yeah. Just looking through the recent newspapers to see if I can find the article I read about a missing teenager."

"The Willis girl?"

He shot a look at her. "I know you're psychic now."

She laughed. "I have it in by my computer. I thought I'd cut out the piece as it might be good stuff to keep for future stories."

He stacked the papers back up in a neat pile and followed her into the house. Jennifer picked up the publication and pointed at one of the front page columns. It had a photo of Sarah Ann Willis, with the details below.

"Why are you interested?"

"Her father called me today. I think he wants to hire me to find his daughter. Said the police weren't doing their job. I dropped by the station and talked with Williams, he gave me the initial report which had the parent's addresses listed. Coming home I swung by their apartments and they live in respectable neighborhoods. So the girl does have a decent place to stay."

Jennifer leaned on the kitchen counter. "Kids don't think on those terms. Anyway, I have a feeling the police can't afford to go running around trying to find some sassy teenager, who probably ran off with a boy or is staying at a girlfriend's house."

"You sound like Detective Williams. Oh, by the way, he offered me a job today."

Her mouth dropped open and she stood up straight. "What!"

"They've lost a couple of men and are shorthanded."

"I hope you told him you weren't interested."

Hawkman turned away as a grin formed on his lips. "I told him I'd think about it."

She marched up to his side and grabbed his arm. "Tom Casey, don't you even consider it."

CHAPTER TWO

The next morning on the way to Medford, Hawkman thought about how he'd teasingly tried to convince Jennifer he should accept a job with the police force. He probably shouldn't have continued the needling so long, as it did upset her. Tonight, he'd stop by the candy store and buy a box of those dark chocolates she liked so well.

He pulled into the alley behind his office and headed up the stairs. Fortunately, he'd eaten a light breakfast and the aroma of Clyde's wonderful donuts didn't intrigue him quite so bad. He booted up the computer, put on the coffee pot and scooted a chair to the front of the desk in anticipation of the appointment with Mr. Willis.

Sticking a toothpick between his teeth, he gnawed on it while doing a background search on Gregory James Willis. He found nothing but one minor violation. Mrs. Catherine June Willis happened to be another story. She had several speeding tickets, one DUI and three minor traffic accidents. They were all dated several years ago, and it appeared she'd escaped being arrested as he found no police record on either one of the parents. He glanced at the ages of the two adults and discovered quite a difference. Greg was fifty-three, ten years older than his ex-wife. It shocked him to think they'd ended an eighteen years marriage. He had a feeling the separation had happened recently, which might explain Sarah's running away. This, he'd find out quickly, if Willis wanted to hire him.

Hawkman jotted down notes as questions entered his mind. The report stated Greg Willis worked as a highly qualified big rig truck driver, and worked for a very reputable company.

He obviously had an excellent record, and doubtless made good money. Greg's wife probably didn't like all the time her husband had to spend away from home. Hawkman leaned back in his chair and tapped the eraser of the pencil against his chin, then glanced at his watch. He sat up straight, as it startled him to see the time. Mr. Willis would be here any minute.

Suddenly, the door opened and a short burly, balding man, dressed in jeans, flannel shirt, carrying a baseball cap which he immediately plopped on his head, stepped inside. "Mr. Casey?"

Hawkman stood and extended his hand. "Mr. Willis, I assume."

Greg pumped it vigorously. "Yeah, that's me. Man, I hope you can help me."

"Have a seat." Hawkman gestured toward the chair near the desk.

Sitting down, Mr. Willis wiped a fist across his mouth. "I'm a nervous wreck, Mr. Casey. I don't know what's happened to my Sarah. She could be in terrible danger."

"What makes you think she might be in jeopardy?" Hawkman asked, as he took his seat. "You know kids sometimes get tired of their own place and just take off to a friend's. They soon return when they find out it just isn't as good as home."

He shook his head violently. "My Sarah wouldn't do that to me, and we've checked with her friends. If she ever thought about leaving her mom's, she knew I'd always welcome her at my digs." He peered up at Hawkman with tears in his eyes. "Mr. Casey, I'm scared to death something terrible has happened to my little girl."

"Do you have any reason for feeling this way?"

"No, just my gut."

"Have you or your ex-wife received any threatening phone calls or ransom demands?"

"Nothing."

"Okay, before we get more involved, I need to talk to you about my fees and contract. Then if you decide to hire me, I'll ask you more questions, and get to work on locating your daughter."

After discussing the financial arrangement, and reading the agreement, Greg Willis glanced up at Hawkman. "I've done some research and you're the best. I can only pay you five hundred up front, but I have a couple of good jobs ahead, so it won't be a problem if you don't demand more right now."

"That's just fine," Hawkman said.

Willis took the pen off the desk, wrote out a check and signed his name to the contract. "Okay, let's get moving on finding my little girl."

Hawkman peeled off Willis' copy and handed it to him, then moved a yellow legal pad toward the center of the desk. "Once I have the names and addresses of all persons involved in your girl's life, I'll get into more personal stuff, and it's important I know the truth. So, don't hold back anything."

The man nodded. "Understood."

"Your full name."

"Gregory James Willis, but everyone calls me Greg."

"The girl's mother?"

"Catherine June Willis. She goes by Cathy."

"Your daughter's full name."

"Sarah Ann Willis."

"When did Sarah disappear?"

"Three days ago."

After Hawkman had the initial information, he flipped over a sheet of the tablet. Do you have a recent picture of your daughter?"

He pulled his billfold from his back pocket, took out a photo and stared at it for several moments, his eyes watering. "This is the last picture I have of her, and I sure want it back. I gave the other one to the police."

"No, problem. I'll make a copy." As Hawkman walked toward the machine, he turned. "She's very pretty."

Greg bowed his head. "Thank you. She's the light of my life and I can't bear the thought she's gone."

Hawkman returned the snapshot and slipped his copy into the folder. "I need a full description, down to tattoos, birth marks, scars and any other identifying marks on her body."

Willis took a deep breath, then exhaled. "She's about five foot, weighs close to a hundred pounds. Has a small butterfly tattoo on her right shoulder blade." He shook his head. "Her mother gave her permission, though I opposed the idea of her marring such lovely skin."

"Scars?"

"Appendectomy at four years old, but they made the cut below the bikini line."

Hawkman recalled Detective Williams' comment and resisted smiling. "Ears pierced?"

"Yes."

"Any other piercings?"

"None I know about."

"Birthmarks?"

"No."

"Have you checked with the grandparents?"

"I checked my side. They haven't seen or heard from her in a long time."

"Where do your folks live?"

"Only my mother is alive, and she's in an assisted living home in North Carolina. I spoke with my sister who lives nearby."

"Is she close to your daughter?"

"No."

"How about your ex-wife's parents?"

"They also live on the East coast and Cathy hasn't spoke to them in years. Family thing."

"Does Sarah know where they live?"

"I don't think so."

"Check with Mrs. Willis about this matter. Your daughter might have seen her grandparents as a salvation and gone there."

"I doubt it, but I'll ask her."

"I'll speak to your ex-wife soon, but do you know if Sarah took any clothes or personal stuff from the house?"

"Yes, she took a duffle bag and told her mother she was spending the night with her best friend, Cindy."

"And you talked to this friend?"

Willis nodded. "They'd made no such plans."

"Can you give me this girl's name and address?"

"I figured you'd want to know some of her friends, so I made a list with their addresses and phone numbers." He pulled a folded sheet of paper from his shirt pocket.

"Good." Hawkman glanced through the names. "Is Cindy Jackson the girl you're speaking about?"

"Yes."

"I notice there are no male names. A girl as attractive as Sarah must have a boyfriend. She's certainly old enough to date."

"If she had a guy, we didn't know it."

"Didn't boys call her or come by?"

"Not to my knowledge. She never spoke of any calls. That doesn't mean there weren't."

Hawkman thought this odd, but decided not to pursue the subject. He figured he'd get more information from Sarah's girlfriends on this matter. "You have any thoughts on why your daughter ran away? Did you have a quarrel?"

Willis leaned back in his chair and exhaled loudly. "I didn't, but she and her mother fought constantly. I offered to have Sarah stay with me, but Cathy wouldn't hear of it. Said the girl needed to be with her mother. I agreed. I'm out of town a lot with my job. It's not good to leave a young girl alone."

"Were you able to support the three of you without Cathy having a job?"

He nodded. "I wanted to make sure my daughter always had supervision. But Sarah found work the minute she turned sixteen, so she could have some extra money."

Hawkman raised a brow. "Interesting. Have you checked with her employer?"

"She worked at a sandwich place a few blocks from her mother's apartment. When I questioned them, they said Sarah had quit a week after she started."

"You didn't know this?"

"No, neither did Cathy."

CHAPTER THREE

Hawkman jotted the name of the Mom and Pop's sandwich house on the pad. "These next few questions might make you uncomfortable, but I need to know the truth."

"I understand."

"How long have you been divorced?"

"A year this month."

"What caused the separation?"

Greg crossed his arms across his chest and frowned. "I don't rightly know. One day, when I got home from a long trek across the country, Cathy told me she wanted a divorce. She called it irreconcilable differences." He shrugged. "All I can figure out is she didn't like me being gone so much."

"Do you think she had a boyfriend?"

He threw up his hands. "I don't think so, but to be truthful, I haven't the vaguest idea."

"How did Sarah respond to this split up?"

"She didn't like it. Told us we were ridiculous and silly. One minute she'd cry and the next, she'd walk the floor waving her hands, ranting and raving."

"Does Sarah spend much time with you?"

"Every weekend I have off."

"What activities do you participate in when you're together?"

He shrugged. "We go shopping at the mall, maybe take in a movie. I even cook when she stays with me."

"When kids reach Sarah's age, they tend to want to hang around with their peers on the weekends. Did she seem restless, especially lately?"

Willis scratched his chin. "I didn't notice anything different."

Hawkman smiled. "Dad's aren't as observant as moms. Sarah might have seen it as a relief in getting away from her mother."

Greg chuckled, then grimaced. "Cathy did tell me the last time I picked up Sarah..." His voice caught and he pulled a handkerchief from his pants pocket. "Sorry, this whole thing upsets me."

"I'm sure it does, but the information is important."

After blowing his nose loudly, Willis continued. "She said Sarah had been very obstinate and talked back to her several times. Even to the point where Cathy slapped Sarah's face. This shocked me as we'd never used physical force on our daughter. Most of her discipline came from 'time outs' or restrictions. Never hitting or spanking."

"Did she mention the reason or what the girl said?"

Willis shook his head. "No. Sarah never said a thing about it either."

"Has your daughter ever mentioned being afraid of someone? A relative, friend or classmate?"

"Nope."

"Does she have a computer?"

"Yes, a desktop and a laptop she carries everywhere."

"Did she take it with her?"

"She must've. We can't find it, and have searched both apartments."

"Does she use it for studies, e-mailing friends, surfing, or shopping?"

"I couldn't tell you. I only have a small knowledge of computers."

"What about a cell phone?"

He nodded. "Yes, she has one of those too."

"Have you tried to contact her?"

"Several times, but all I got was the recording to leave a message. I left several, but received no responses. Then one day I couldn't get anything and assumed her battery had died."

"You sure she had it with her?"

"I'm assuming she does, as Cathy and I couldn't find it in either of our places."

"What about a credit card?"

"No. She doesn't have one."

"You're sure both you and Mrs. Willis still have yours?"

"Yes, one of the first things we checked."

"How much cash do you think Sarah had when she left?"

"Cathy and I discussed this. We figure she could have taken close to a hundred dollars."

"What made you come to that figure?"

Greg bowed his head. "I hate to admit it, but I keep a close eye on Sarah. I can't get Cathy to search her room, because she says it's invading her privacy. Periodically I'd go over when Sarah wasn't home and make sure she didn't have cigarettes, pot or booze tucked away. I found her stash of about seventy-five dollars just before she disappeared, and now it's gone. We figured she'd saved it from her job. Then I'd given her twenty-five to buy a new top she wanted. I'd just given it to her the week before she vanished."

"Does Sarah know how to drive?"

Willis took another deep breath and his shoulders shook. "She was just learning."

Hawkman observed the man's deep emotion and decided he'd questioned him enough. He placed his pencil on the yellow pad. "Mr. Willis."

He waved a hand in the air. "Please, call me Greg."

"Okay, Greg. Let's call it a day and I'll have a good start with the information you've supplied. If I have any questions I'll give you a call."

"I always carry my cell phone. It'd be best if you used that number. Please contact me the minute you have any sort of a lead."

Hawkman took down the number, then gave Willis his card. "I'll keep in touch on a regular basis. If you think of anything that might pertain to your daughter's whereabouts, call me immediately. The longer she's away, the harder it will be to find her."

Greg fingered the edges of his jacket, his voice quivering, "Mr. Casey, be truthful with me. What are the chances of finding my daughter alive?"

Hawkman looked into his face. "I can't answer such a question. We have no idea what has happened to her. We don't know if she left of her own accord, or was abducted. Until we have some answers, I have no conception."

Greg shuffled to his feet and held out his hand. "I appreciate you taking on my case. Godspeed."

Rising, Hawkman shook his hand. "Tell Mrs. Willis to expect a visit from me very soon. Could even be late this afternoon."

"I'll do that. I'll give her a call when I leave here."

After the man left, Hawkman immediately entered Greg Willis' phone number into his cell, then went over the notes he'd taken, and again studied the picture. A beautiful girl, but obviously troubled. Did the divorce of her parents upset her so much, she didn't want to be with either of them? The spat Sarah had with Cathy didn't bother him. Girls and their mothers were at odds during this time of their lives, so he doubted it had anything to do with her disappearance. She still had her dad nearby and would have gone to him if the situation became unbearable.

Hawkman leaned back and tapped the pencil eraser against his chin. Holding the yellow pad in his hand, he reached over and circled the word computer and cell phone. These two items bothered him with all the news he'd heard about young females being talked into meeting some weirdo at a faraway place. Another nagging item was the fact there seemed to be no boyfriends in Sarah's life. Of course, the parents might not know since she used a cell phone. Not like the old days when parents knew every time a girl got a call on the landline.

Hawkman put the yellow pad into his briefcase and placed the new digital voice activated recorder he'd just purchased into his pocket. He picked up the briefcase and decided, no time like the present to make a call on Mrs. Willis. He needed to move on this case. The girl had been missing for three days without a word, which made him nervous, and if she was still alive, a hundred dollars wouldn't last long.

He pulled into Cathy Willis' apartment complex and parked in one of the visitors' slots. Double checking the number of the flat, he spotted one zero four immediately. Advancing toward the front door, he could see a light glowing through the drapes. He pushed the button at the side of the door and heard the soft tinkling of chimes.

"Coming," a voice called.

The door opened and the woman's appearance took Hawkman aback. She stood about five foot, hundred pounds, dark brown eyes, with a lovely face framed with heavy, straight brown hair cropped to the jaw line. She could have passed as the identical twin of Sarah, except for her mature features. "Mrs. Willis?"

She smiled. "And you're Mr. Tom Casey, right?"

He touched the brim of his hat. "Yes, nice meeting you."

"Greg called and said you'd be stopping by. Please come in." Stepping to the side, she held the door for him to enter, then gestured toward the couch. "Have a seat and I'll get us some coffee."

Hawkman sat on the edge of the cushion, flipped on the recorder, placed his briefcase at his feet, then surveyed the small living room. The walls were a soft off white which fit nicely with the colors of the light beige couch and matching chair. A tall fake Ficus tree snuggled in one corner. The large screen television stood at one end of the room, with a straight back chair on each side. Magazines and a couple of books graced the coffee table. Pictures of Sarah in different poses rested on the end tables.

He glanced up when Mrs. Willis entered the room juggling two empty mugs and a carafe. Hawkman jumped up and took the tray from her, placing it on the coffee table.

"Thank you. I'm so jittery since Sarah disappeared."

"No problem," he said, pouring them each a cup.

She settled in the matching chair across from him. "I'm very worried about my daughter." Her eyes welled with tears. "I'm so happy Greg decided to hire a private investigator. We were getting nowhere with the police."

"Mrs. Willis, I will certainly try to find her, but can't make any promises. I need to ask you some questions, and I'd like to see your daughter's room."

She nodded. "Please, call me Cathy. Mrs. Willis sounds so formal." She stood. "Why don't I show you Sarah's room first? Then I'll answer whatever questions I can."

Hawkman removed a notebook and pen from his briefcase, then followed her down a short hallway, where she opened the door displaying a definite teenager's abode.

"I don't care for the way she has it decorated, but I know at this age they have strange ideas, so I tried to keep my opinions to myself."

Hawkman glanced at the walls which were adorned with large posters of rock bands, a lei of artificial flowers hung over a picture of Sarah in a grass skirt with a young man in a flowered shirt and shorts. He crossed the room and pointed at the photo. "Is this Sarah's boyfriend?"

"No," she said emphatically. "He's just a friend. A photographer took that shot at a Hawaiian Luau sponsored by the school last year."

"Did she attend many of the school functions?"

"Quite a few."

"Since school's out for the summer, what does she do for entertainment?"

"Mostly gets together with her girlfriends."

"Do they come over here?"

"Sometimes, but most of the time Sarah goes to their houses. Probably because we live in this small apartment. They feel I can hear every word they say."

He raised a brow. "Do you?"

She tried to refrain from smiling, but the corners of her mouth twitched. "Yes."

Hawkman pointed to the desktop computer sitting on a small white sturdy table. "Mr. Willis tells me Sara also has a laptop. Does she use this computer too?"

"Yes, she uses the laptop at school and takes it when she goes to her friends. I'm assuming she has it with her now." Her voice choked up and she covered her mouth. "Wherever she is."

"May I turn it on?"

"Of course."

Hawkman checked to make sure the plug was secure, then booted up the machine. He pulled out the card table chair and sat down. Once the monitor lit up, he went immediately to the bookmarks, and jotted down the url's of each web site. He then went to her address book and wrote down each of the names along with their e-mail addys.

Cathy stood next to him, her arms folded across her chest. "Are you finding anything that might help locate her?"

He glanced up. "Won't know until I check out this information."

She threw her hands in the air. "I know nothing about computers. I don't even know how to turn on the thing. Guess I should take the time to learn."

"They're an amazing piece of technology, but many people can't operate them or don't even try." He glanced up from the monitor. "Did Sarah ever get letters from people in the regular mail?"

"Sometimes. If one of her girlfriends went on a trip, she might receive a postcard."

"Did she ever correspond with any of the opposite sex?"

Cathy ran a hand across her forehead. "About three years ago, she went to a church camp and met a boy from a neighboring town. I read one of the letters Sarah received from him, and it really ticked me off. He sounded much older, so I put a stop to the letter writing."

"Do you remember the boy's name?"

"Yes. Derek Shaw."

"Where was he from?"

She put her fingers against her temples. "I've drawn a blank, but if I remember I'll let you know."

"Would Sarah by any chance still have those letters?"

"I don't know." Cathy gnawed her lower lip. "I haven't gone through her stuff. It just upsets me too much."

Hawkman frowned. "Cathy, I want you to search this room with a fine tooth comb. Any names, even if they're written on a scrap piece of paper, address books, diaries, anything that might help us locate your daughter. We need all the clues we can get. Don't throw anything away until you check with me. You need to do this as soon as possible."

She hugged herself. "I'll feel like I'm invading her privacy."

"Mrs. Willis, do you want to find your daughter?"

CHAPTER FOUR

Cathy Willis stared at Hawkman a few seconds, then suddenly burst into sobs. "Of course, I want to find Sarah. I feel so lost not knowing what to do."

"It's time to get a hold of yourself and concentrate on the job at hand. Each passing day makes it harder. I'm sorry to upset you, but if you want to help me, you have to do as I ask."

She grabbed a tissue from the box beside the bed, blew her nose and wiped her eyes. "I know what you're saying and you're right."

Hawkman stood. "Good. Tomorrow I'll expect to hear from you about the items you've found that might help in our search." He patted her on the shoulder and headed back toward the living room. "I'm returning to my office for a couple of hours. If you find anything of interest, call me immediately. Here's my card. You can reach me by my cell phone at any time. Don't hesitate to call, even in the middle of the night."

She nodded as she took the card. "Thank you."

"Get busy searching your daughter's room. If I don't hear from you this evening, I'll get in touch with you tomorrow."

Hawkman left Cathy's apartment a bit frustrated with the woman. How could any mother let her child be gone this long without tearing that room apart to find some hint of where she might be? It surprised him Greg Willis hadn't already ripped the place to shreds. "To hell with a kid's privacy," he mumbled climbing into the SUV.

He stopped at the candy store on the way to his office, and picked up the box of dark chocolates for Jennifer. The days were warm and he dared not leave it in the vehicle or it would be a melted mess by the time he got home. Carrying the sack and his briefcase, he hurried up the stairs, eager to see what he could find about the web sites he'd found on Sarah's PC. Slipping the candy into the small refrigerator, he warmed up a cold cup of coffee in the microwave, then nudged his computer out of sleep mode. The first few web sites showed women's clothing and places to shop for shoes. As he continued surfing, he found some rock band's web sites, singers, and a couple of actors. When he got near the end of the list, his interest piqued when he opened a porn site. Unfortunately, he needed a password, and had no idea what Sarah would use. He bet somewhere in her room there would be a clue.

When he finished going through the sites, he'd discovered four he found questionable. He sat back in his chair and thumped the pencil on the desk, then pulled his cell phone from his pocket.

"Hello, Greg. Tom Casey. I'd like to bring your daughter's desktop computer to my office."

He listened a moment.

"Great. Since you're there, bring along any notebooks you find in her room or anything that appears to have strange words written in it."

After hanging up, he dragged a small folding table from behind the couch and set it up next to his desk. Ripping off a paper towel, he wiped off the top and grimaced. "Damn, how'd this get so dusty," he muttered. Tearing off another sheet, he dampened it in the bathroom, and gave it a few more swipes. Satisfied, he glanced out the window to see if Greg Willis had arrived, as he might need help carrying the computer up the stairs. He had no idea what type of vehicle the man drove, but he figured he'd spot him in a minute. A gray diesel, late model, Chevy pickup, with a crew cab, drove into the lot, and Hawkman grinned to himself as Greg jumped out of the driver's side. He'd have bet, since the man was a big rig driver, that type of vehicle would've been his choice.

Hawkman headed down the stairs and hurried toward the truck. "Can I help you?"

Greg had opened the second door and was bent over trying to wrestle a large box off the seat. He turned with a scowl on his face. "Man, I've had a time with Cathy. She told me you wanted her to search Sarah's room, so I went over and started piling stuff into boxes, but she kept spouting we're intruding upon our daughter's privacy. I finally yelled at her and explained we were never going to find Sarah if we didn't hunt. So, I'd worked in Sarah's room for at least three hours before you called. I came up with a couple of boxes full of stuff you might find useful."

"Good going," Hawkman said, reaching into the pickup and hauling two boxes toward him. He stacked them one on the other and led the way back to his office, with Greg trailing, loaded down with the computer paraphernalia. Once they reached the office, they placed the PC on the table, and the boxes underneath.

Greg dusted off his hands and took a deep breath. "Boy, that machine is heavier than I expected."

"I appreciate you letting me have it for a while. There's a possibility I might find some leads hidden inside."

"No problem. It's not getting used at the house. I'll do anything to find my girl."

"By the way. I forgot to ask. Have there been any visitors to either of your homes? Girlfriends, lovers, relatives, etc., say in the last six months?"

Greg scratched his head. "No one at my place. Cathy's brother dropped by her apartment for a couple of nights about four months ago."

"What's his name?"

"Blake Hunter."

"Single, married?"

"Divorced."

"Anything you'd like to tell me about him?"

"He's a good guy. Maybe a bit on the wild side."

"Does he have children?"

"No," Greg snickered, not any I know about. He's a workaholic, and had a business conference out here, so he stayed at Cathy's."

"Does Sarah like him?"

"She thinks he's a kick, and hated to leave his company to spend the night at my place so he could use her room. They got along real well and laughed a lot."

"Does he drop by often?"

Willis shook his head. "No. I think it's the first time in a couple of years. Cathy was so excited to see him."

Hawkman glanced at the boxes. "Do you feel like you went through everything in Sarah's room?"

"No. I'm going back tomorrow. My job has assigned me to drive across the country this coming weekend and I won't be home for approximately a week. Sure hate to leave, but got to keep food on the table and pay your bill." He sighed. "There are more nooks and crannies in that girl's room than I ever thought. I just wish Cathy would quit bawling and mumbling about disturbing Sarah's privacy. She's no help at all."

"I don't understand her thinking either. If she isn't going to help, just tell her to go to another part of the house." Hawkman pointed a finger at him. "Be sure to check the underneath side of drawers, jacket pockets, inside shoes, between mattress and bedsprings. Remember, kids are con-artists and can hide stuff in the craziest places. Now, don't get me wrong, most of the things they conceal are innocent, but others could lead them into danger, and they want to keep them from parents' prying eyes. She may have unknowingly hidden something that will give us a clue."

Willis looked up at him with sober brown eyes. "I understand. I'll bring you every scrap of paper, if it will find my girl." He pointed at the cartons. "I loaded up her school notebooks, an address book and some scraps of paper with names scribbled across them."

Hawkman nodded. "I'll look through those first, then get to work on the computer and see if it has any hidden secrets."

CHAPTER FIVE

Once Greg left, Hawkman wrote the name, Blake Hunter, on the yellow pad. He wanted to get in touch with Cathy's brother and ask a few questions. He sat down and rolled his chair toward the computer table, opened one of the boxes, lifted out several of Sarah's soft backed scratch pads, and placed them on the desk. A few pieces of paper floated to the floor, which he immediately recovered. Glancing at the bits and pieces, he pulled some envelopes from the desk drawer and labeled each one individually: names, numbers, possible passwords, and miscellaneous.

Before he could approach people about Sarah, he needed to know more about the girl's pastimes and how she thought. It appeared from talking with Cathy and Greg, their daughter showed no interest in boys. Hawkman considered this far fetched or wishful thinking on the parents' part. Sarah's beauty wouldn't go unnoticed by the male high school population.

He sorted through the scraps of paper and found nothing that looked like a password or code, so slid them into the respective envelopes. Then he turned to the school notebooks. The kids had only been out of class for three weeks, and if Sarah had made contact with someone over the internet, she might have scribbled his name on one of the pages. He opened the first binder which had the word English written across the front. He scanned each page in hopes of finding some off handed note Sarah might have written in the margin or at the end of a page. Finding nothing, he went through the Math, History and Art handbooks. He turned each one over and searched the backs and inside covers. He exhaled and stacked them on the floor, then dug back into the box.

This time he pulled out a small address book which looked very intriguing. When he thumbed through it, his interest piqued immediately. It appeared Sarah had listed all her classmates' phone numbers and home addresses. This would save him ample time. He plopped it onto his desk to study more thoroughly a little later, and reached back into the container. The remaining items were small pieces of paper with page numbers, such as where to find an answer to a question. He slipped them into the right envelope and opened the next box.

Inside he found more school workbooks, one called themes or short stories. Many times kids wrote about their lives. He'd look it over a bit more carefully and placed it on the desk. As he dug deeper, he lifted out a small volume and raised his brows. "I'm really going to invade your privacy now, Sarah. You'll have to forgive me, but maybe it will tell me something," Hawkman mumbled, laying the small diary beside the address book.

He emptied the second box and pushed the two aside. Rolling his chair up to the table where he'd hooked up Sarah's desktop computer, he hit the on button. While it booted up, he picked up the diary and went to the last page, dated the night before she disappeared.

Not finding any indication the girl planned to leave, he read backwards for several days and could tell unhappiness filled her life. He set the small book aside to go through later and turned his attention to the computer. After working on the machine for a couple of hours, he leaned back and stretched his arms above his head. Fortunately, he'd found a list of passwords buried in the hard drive, which he'd apply to the questionable web sites. This could take several days to match the right one, as sometimes they only gave you a couple of chances to enter. If you didn't hit it in two or three tries, they'd block you for several hours. He'd analyze the words and try to match them up with a specific site before applying. Maybe he'd come up with the correct one.

Also, Sarah had a couple of files that required a special code to open. They looked very interesting. He might have to get his friend, Jacob, the computer guru, to help him unlock them. Glancing at his wristwatch, he couldn't believe the hour. He shut down the machine, gathered up his notes and stuck them into his briefcase. Possibly, he'd have time to sort through some of the items tonight at home. Tomorrow, he wanted to talk with Cindy Jackson, supposedly Sarah's best friend.

Thursday morning, Greg Willis, shifted from foot to foot, as he waited for Cathy to open the door. When she swung it open, she still had on her night robe, and glared at him for several seconds with a sour expression.

"Why are you here so early?"

"I've a lot to do tomorrow to get ready for the long haul. I want to gather as much information as possible for Mr. Casey before I leave. I think this man will find our Sarah. He's digging in with both heels and we have to help."

Cathy moved back and rubbed her arms. "I hate mauling through Sarah's personal things. It makes me feel horrible."

Greg stepped inside, shut the door and took hold of her shoulders. "Cathy, look at me. Dammit, look at me."

Putting fingers on her lips, she finally peered at him with moisture filled eyes.

He shook her gently. "Sarah's not here. If she's been taken against her will, she'll be happy to know we searched her room to find any clues. If she's dead, it won't make any difference."

Cathy pulled from his grip, gazed at the floor and hugged herself. "Don't talk like she's gone forever."

Greg's hands dropped to his side. "Look, we have to face reality. I know it's not easy, but there hasn't been a word from her all week. We have to prepare for the worst. Meanwhile, we've got to do everything in our power to help Mr. Casey find our daughter. Will you please help me?"

She nodded. "You go ahead and I'll be in when I get dressed."

He walked down the short hall and opened the door to his daughter's bedroom. His heart raced as he glanced around the walls. "Where are you, my baby girl?" he whispered, as he crossed the room to the dresser.

Cathy walked in as he placed the last drawer in a pile on the bed. "What are you doing?"

"Mr. Casey told me to check the bottom side of every drawer in the room and to check between the mattress and box springs. Any place a kid might hide something."

"Sarah wouldn't hide anything from us."

He threw his arms up. "Cathy, she's a kid. All kids hide stuff. It's their nature. We didn't follow her around twenty-four hours a day. You even said yourself, she didn't like inviting her friends over here because you were so close by. So get it through your head. Kids hide stuff. Girls giggle and talk about boys. They don't want you to hear what they're saying."

"Stop!" she interjected. Just explain what you want me to do?"

"I want you to list everything Sarah took the day she disappeared. Describe the clothes she had on; jot down garments and shoes missing." He raised his arms in frustration. "That type of thing."

She left the room, and returned shortly carrying a pen and paper pad. Soon, she busied herself going through the closet and taking notes.

Greg knelt down in front of the skeleton of the dresser, ran his hands around all the sides. He found a receipt or two which had worked their way down the edges to the floor. Not wanting to throw anything away, he dropped them into a brown paper sack. He dumped the contents of each drawer and meticulously went through each item, checked the underneath side, then removed the tacked lining inside. After examining each garment, he tenderly folded and placed them neatly back in the drawer, then pushed the square box into its groove in the dresser. "Well, nothing in these."

He then lifted the mattress to check between it and the box springs, and spotted a small black box on the floor behind the bedside table. Dropping the heavy burden, he leaned over, and picked up a transformer. "She won't be able to charge her cell phone without this." He placed it on the pillow. "Make a note for Mr. Casey." He let out a sigh and placed his fists on his hips. "How are you doing?"

She turned from the closet and glanced at him with a puzzled expression. "She took more than I originally thought."

Greg stepped up beside her and glanced at the list. "What do you mean?"

"When she left that night to go to Cindy's, she only had the small duffle bag she always carried for an overnight. It couldn't have held all the outfits I've found missing."

He furrowed his brow. "That's odd."

She bit her lip. "Very."

"How many pieces of luggage did she have?"

"Four. They fit one inside the other."

"Where does she keep them?"

She pointed toward the closet. "In there."

He hauled out the large suitcase and plopped it on the bed. Enclosed they found the smaller piece, but no middle sized bag or duffle.

Cathy's eyes grew wide. "I would have seen her dragging that bag. I distinctly remember Sarah carrying only the laptop, duffle, and her shoulder purse; nothing else."

Greg crossed the room to the window, shoved up the sash, and leaned out. He immediately noticed the screen propped against the side of the house. Drawing himself back inside, he flopped down on the bed. Tears rolled down his cheeks. "She pushed the suitcase out the window and picked it up later. Our daughter left of her own accord."

CHAPTER SIX

The same morning, Hawkman drove to the residence of Cindy Jackson, which stood in a nice middle class area, with well groomed lawns. The homes were older, but he recognized the construction as being one of the better built tracts in the area. The Jackson dwelling sat nestled between huge redwood trees, which afforded much shade. He walked up the slightly curved sidewalk to the front porch and rang the bell.

A woman about five foot, four, in her late thirties or early forties, answered the door. She had on jeans, sweat shirt, and her long blond hair hung from a ponytail high on her head.

"Hello."

"Mrs. Jackson?"

"Yes."

"I'm Private Investigator, Tom Casey." He displayed his badge. "I understand your daughter Cindy is a good friend of Sarah Willis."

Her dark blue eyes lit up. "Has she been found?"

"No, unfortunately. I've been hired by her father to look into her disappearance and would like to talk to Cindy."

"I'm not sure she can tell you anything, but I'll get her."

"Thank you."

Hawkman waited on the front porch, and flipped on his recorder. Soon, the two females came around the corner of the entry.

"Forgive me, Mr. Casey, please come in."

She led him to the living room, and gestured toward a large leather couch. "Please, have a seat." Then she turned to the young girl beside her. "This is my daughter, Cindy. Cindy, this is Mr. Casey, a private investigator, helping Mr. Willis look for Sarah."

Hawkman quickly rose and held out his hand. "Hello, Cindy. It's a pleasure meeting you."

When she smiled, her blue eyes, similar to her mom's, sparkled. "I hope you find Sarah soon. I really miss her."

They sat on a matching couch opposite him.

Hawkman dropped back down on the cushion, then waited until the women were situated. "I'm going to do all I can, and maybe you can give me some insight on Sarah and what she might have been thinking the last few days you were together."

She glanced at her mother. "Should I tell him everything?"

"Yes, it might help find her."

Cindy shrugged her shoulders and glanced up at Hawkman with a slight frown. "Sarah wasn't happy about her folks divorcing. She hated going back and forth from one house to the other. Her mom drove her crazy, and she really loved being with her dad, but didn't want to hurt her mom. She seemed really mixed up."

He nodded. "Very typical of a young girl or boy, put in that position. Did she ever mention running away?"

Picking at her hands, Cindy concentrated on her fingernails. "Not seriously. She made a comment or two saying she wished she had a home like mine, where both parents still loved each other."

"Did she ever tell you why her folks divorced?"

Mrs. Jackson took hold of Cindy's wrist. "Pay attention to Mr. Casey."

She sat on her hands, and grinned. "Sorry. I asked her one day what happened between her parents, and she told me her mom hated being alone. It didn't make much sense, because she's more alone now than ever before. I told Sarah how I felt, and she agreed. She thought their divorce was really dumb."

"Tell me what you girls do when you get together."

Cindy rolled her eyes. "Oh, brother, we do lots of stuff. Sometimes Mom allows us to go shopping at the mall, or we go to my room where we listen to music, talk and giggle a bunch."

"How many girls in your group?"

She counted them out on her fingers. "Let's see, me, Sarah, Janet, and Nikki. Our other friend Ann tries to come over when we get together, but she has a job now, so she doesn't have much free time."

"You girls have boyfriends?"

She wrinkled her nose. "Sort of. We have our favorite guys, but none of us date anyone special."

"How about Sarah?"

Cindy rocked back and forth on the couch. "Every boy in school would like to go out with her. She's so pretty."

"Who's her special guy?"

She looked uncomfortable and eyed her mother.

"Go ahead and tell him."

"But I feel like I'm snitching."

"That's stupid, Cindy. Sarah's life might be in danger and Mr. Casey needs to know anything you can tell him that might shed some light on what's happened to her."

The girl pulled her shoulders up and made a face. "Well, only if you promise not to tell her mom or dad."

"Why?" Hawkman asked.

"Sarah said they'd have a fit if they thought she had a boyfriend."

He leaned forward and put his arms on his knees. "Cindy, her parents knowing is not important at this stage of the game. I need to check out every person who had contact with your friend before she disappeared. It could be a matter of life and death."

Cindy immediately sat straight and her eyes grew wide. "Are you serious?"

"Very."

She turned and grabbed her mother's arm. "Mom, you mean Sarah might be dead?"

Hawkman intervened. "We're assuming she's alive, and we hope to find her before anything happens. So tell me about this boy."

She stared at the floor. "He's older, and goes to college."

"How long has she known him?"

"Not long. He didn't come from our school."

"Otherwise, you'd have recognized him, right?"

She smiled. "Yeah."

"Have you ever seen him?"

Cindy nodded. "I was with Sarah when she met him."

"Where?"

She again glanced at her mother.

"Continue Cindy."

"One Friday night at the bowling alley."

"Tell me about it."

She exhaled, raked her fingers through her long blond hair, forcing the strands out of her face, and peered at Hawkman. "It's no big deal. We didn't do anything wrong."

"I'm not saying there's anything bad about meeting a boy at the bowling alley. It's probably very innocent, but I have to investigate Sarah's whereabouts before she disappeared. The only way I'll find out where she's been, is talking to her friends. Somewhere along the line I hope to get a clue of what's happened."

Cindy took a deep breath and hugged her waist. "There were four of us girls sitting behind the bowlers waiting for an alley to open when these three guys walked up to us and started talking. We just sort of joked around and then they called our name to announce an opening, and we left. Shortly, the lane next to us became free and the three guys took it." She threw up her hands. "One thing led to another and we were all laughing and joking. When we finished bowling, we all gathered at the concession stand and had a coke. Before Mom picked us up, Sarah had exchanged phone numbers with the guy."

"Do you remember his name?"

"Glen Carter."

"What college does he attend?"

"I don't know. Sarah told me he's out for the summer and hoped to be with him a lot more. He must live around here, because he's taken her out a few times."

Hawkman frowned. "How'd she manage a date without her parents' knowledge?"

She looked at her mother, again. "Sorry, Mom, I know you've told me never to be a part of this type of thing." She turned back toward Hawkman and let out a sigh. "Sarah would tell her mom she was coming to my house to spend the night, but instead met Glen down the block. She told him she had to be here by midnight or she'd get into a lot of trouble. So, I'd watch for them to drive up and quietly let her in."

Hawkman glanced at the mother. "Mrs. Jackson, how did this set with you to find Sarah here the next morning?"

She stared at her daughter. "I had no idea this was going on or I'd have put a stop to it." Then she glanced at Hawkman. "Cindy always had a story for me when I'd find Sarah here in the morning. It always sounded logical, I never questioned the reason."

"What would she tell you?"

"Due to a baby sitting job, Sarah wouldn't be able to come over until midnight. Another occasion, she said Sarah had to work late at the sandwich shop to help get the place cleaned up for the next day. I never thought much about either time."

He nodded. "Both excuses sound easy to believe." He gazed at Cindy. "How many times did this happen?"

"Only those two. She only met Glen a couple of months ago, and school was still in session. Guess he'd come home for the weekend. Then he got out for the summer sooner than us, so she did this with a couple of our other friends."

"Who?"

"Janet and Nikki."

"Did those girls use the same excuses for Sarah's lateness?"

Cindy looked at the floor. "Yeah."

"What kind of girl is Sarah?"

She jerked up her head. "What do you mean?"

"Did she always tell people the truth? Or did she spin lies like these so she could get what she wanted?"

Cindy grimaced and waved her hands in the air. "No, no. She's very thoughtful, and would do anything for her friends.

That's why we were all willing to help her. We knew she had a miserable life."

"What else do you like about her?"

"She's very cute, has a great personality and sense of humor. When she walks down the halls at school, the guys melt. She's just all around fun. We laugh and giggle a lot."

"Does Sarah make good grades?"

"She used to make better than me, but since her folks split up, her heart isn't tuned to hitting the books."

"Mrs. Jackson and Cindy. I won't keep you any longer and appreciate your time. You've been a lot of help." He stood and held out his hand. "Mrs. Jackson, don't be to hard on your daughter for telling some little white lies. At least, she came out with the truth, and it definitely helps me in this case."

She shot a grin at her daughter. "She salvaged herself by being candid with you. Right now that's very important in helping find Sarah."

"Please notify me if you think of anything that might be useful." He handed her one of his cards. "You can reach me here, night or day."

Hawkman headed for his SUV. His cell phone had vibrated against his waist several times, but he didn't want to interrupt the interview with Cindy. When he pulled away from the curb, he glanced at the caller I.D. and realized Greg Willis had made the calls.

CHAPTER SEVEN

Hawkman punched the button on the cell where he'd stored Willis' number. When he heard Greg's voice, he sensed the urgency and pulled to the side of the road. He waited until the man finished his story before responding. "Do you still want me to try to find Sarah?"

He listened, then spoke. "I think you've made a wise decision. You need answers. Yes, of course, I'll stay on the case."

Hawkman had no more hung up, than another call came through from Jennifer. "Hi, hon. You're where? Yes, I'll be there in a few minutes." He hung up wondering why she wanted to meet him at the office.

He spotted her vehicle in the parking lot and dashed up the steps. When he opened the door, it surprised him to find his wife in jeans and a tee shirt, sitting in front of Sarah's computer. Her short curly locks bounced slightly as she concentrated on the girl's web page.

"What are you doing?"

"I want to work on this case," she said, without looking away from the monitor.

"Honey, you don't have time to fiddle with a teenage runaway."

She glanced at him. "I'll make time. Tell me what you've found out so far."

He exhaled and flopped down behind his desk. "Not a lot. I just finished interviewing Cindy Jackson, Sarah's best friend. Found out a few things. It's all on the tape." He placed the recorder on the desk.

"Did you read Sarah's diary?"

"Only a little, didn't see much that indicated why she ran away, except being upset with her folks."

Jennifer pulled the small book from her purse. "You left this in your office at home, and I decided to read through it. There's a few clues I think you've missed."

His interest piqued, and he sat up straight. "Really?"

"Yes, you don't understand the workings of a young girl's mind. I do, I used to be one."

"Yeah, but you weren't rebellious."

"Sarah isn't either."

"How do you know?"

She held up the volume. "She pours her heart out in here."

"I didn't feel she said much at all."

"See, you don't understand teenagers, especially a young woman. Most men don't. That's where I can help. I'd also like to speak with her mother."

"I've already addressed the situation with her."

"Find out much?"

Hawkman shrugged. "Nothing more than she hated going through Sarah's room, because she felt she'd invaded her privacy."

"I can get more."

"Just received a call from Greg and they've discovered Sarah left on her own accord and they're devastated."

"How did they find out?"

Hawkman told her what the girl's father explained in the phone call. "So Sarah must've been set on leaving."

"No, she's scared and searching. More than likely it was an impulsive move. Someone gave her the opportunity and she jumped on it."

Hawkman shot a look at her. "Huh?"

She turned and gazed into his face. "Will you let me work on the case?"

He smiled. "I think you've convinced me I could use your help. However, you've got to promise if any event turns dangerous, you'll back off and let me handle it."

She threw up a hand in a mock salute. "I shall be very careful and try to obey."

Hawkman shook his head and chuckled. "Okay, how do I explain you to my client?"

Her eyes twinkled as she reached beside the computer and held up a small case. "I'm your photographer. I'd like to get some shots of Sarah's room and where she lived. You'll need to give Greg a call and tell him to give Cathy a heads up about me. I intend on stopping there today."

He raised a brow. "Sounds like you planned your day in advance."

Jennifer grinned, jumped up from the computer, threw her arms around his neck, and gave him a big kiss. "This case requires a woman's touch. I prayed you'd see it my way."

He patted her on the butt. "You realize you won't get much writing done if you're going to get involved?"

She nodded. "I know, but for once I'm ahead of schedule, so I've got time. Just think of all the great information I can gain for my next book by actually working with you."

"You're definitely a schemer."

Laughing, she sat back down at Sarah's computer. "Give Greg a call and enlighten him about your new partner, then either you or he set up an appointment for me to see Cathy Willis about two this afternoon."

"Yes, ma'am."

While Hawkman set the plan in action, Jennifer studied Sarah's MySpace site. She pulled a notebook from her purse and wrote down several items, then turned toward him when he got off the phone. "You'll be happy to know, as of this morning, it appears Sarah is alive and well."

Hawkman rose and stood behind her. "How can you tell?"

She pointed to the date next to her profile. "Unless she's been phished, she came online to check her site."

"What were you writing?"

"Sarah's website address, plus the names of her top friends. I'm going to check each of their sites, then run through her comments to see if I can find any clues. I can do this job at home from my own computer. I'll be able to tell quickly if her site's been jeopardized."

"When did you become a computer guru?"

She grinned. "It just comes naturally."

He threw back his head and laughed. Putting his hands on her shoulders, he kissed the top of her head. "No wonder I love you so much. I think you're going to help me solve this case rather quickly."

She checked her watch and stood. "Is everything set for me to go see Cathy?"

"Yep. You want her address?"

"I already know where she lives."

"You've been snooping."

"Isn't that what a private investigator does?" She slid the notebook into her purse, threw the strap onto her shoulder, and picked up the camera.

"Oh, wait a minute. I need you to get some information from Cathy. Ask her for Blake Hunter's phone number."

Jennifer frowned. "Who's he?"

"Her brother, and he's visited within the past few months. I want to call and talk to him about Sarah attitude during that time."

"Okay, will do." She headed for the door.

Hawkman followed and called to her as she hurried down the steps. "You want to meet back here at the office or later at home?"

She waved. "Later."

"What a woman," he chuckled, as he closed the door.

CHAPTER EIGHT

Jennifer felt giddy as she drove to Catherine Willis' apartment.
The butterflies in her stomach reminded her of the first time
she'd met her husband. She smiled to herself. It'd been a long
time since she'd helped Hawkman on a case. Now, to live up to
what she'd promised.

She pulled into a visitor's slot at the complex, scanned the
numbers and quickly spotted one zero four. Shouldering her
camera case, she climbed out of the van and strolled toward
the door. The drapes were open, and the woman Hawkman
had described, sat in a chair reading a magazine. When Jennifer
punched the doorbell, she glanced up, placed the journal on the
side table and headed toward the entry.

"Hello, you must be Mrs. Casey?"

"Yes, but please call me Jennifer."

"I'm Cathy Willis. Do come in." She gestured toward the
couch. "Have a seat."

"Thank you."

Once they were both settled, Cathy clenched her hands
tightly in her lap. "I don't know what else I can tell you about
Sarah. Greg told Mr. Casey what we discovered."

Jennifer placed her purse and camera case beside her.
"Yes, but your husband wants him to stay on the case until your
daughter's found."

Cathy hugged herself and frowned. "Now that we know
she left on her own accord, I'm not sure I want her back."

Jennifer leaned forward and looked into Cathy's face. She
noticed how red the woman's eyes appeared, probably from
many shed tears. "I don't think you mean that. Sarah is probably

upset because you and your husband aren't together. She might even think it's her fault."

Her chin trembling, Cathy changed the subject and pointed to the camera. "Greg said you wanted to take some pictures. What in the world do you want to photograph?"

"First, I'd like to take some shots of Sarah's room."

"Good grief, we've been through her stuff with a fine tooth comb. What good would photos do?"

Jennifer removed the camera from the case, and fiddled with the buttons. "You'd be surprised what one can miss sitting in plain sight. With pictures we can go over them a dozen times without bothering you."

She nodded and rose. "Makes sense. Come with me and I'll show you where she kept to herself most of the time."

Jennifer perceived the sarcasm in Cathy's voice as she followed her down the small hallway. Once inside the room, she snapped photos of the posters on the wall, the bookcase, bed, and stood back to catch the layout of the furniture. She then walked over to the window, took some pictures, opened the sash, leaned out and focused on the screen resting against the wall of the building. Later she'd get a couple of shots from the outside. When finished, she turned to Mrs. Willis. "May I take some pictures of the rest of the apartment?"

Cathy shrugged. "Is it necessary?"

"It might help us to get an insight on Sarah's personality."

"I doubt it, but go ahead."

Jennifer made sure she got Cathy in a couple of the photos, then closed her camera and returned it to the case. "I hope my coming by on such short notice didn't interrupt any of your plans."

"Not at all. Is it possible you could you stay a few minutes? It'd be wonderful to talk to a woman for a change."

"Sure."

"I'll get us a cup of coffee? I have a pot made, or if you'd prefer, a soft drink?"

"I'd love a cup. Black, please."

Cathy hustled into the kitchen and soon returned with two steaming mugs. "I hope it's not too strong."

Taking a sip, Jennifer smiled. "Perfect."

"Do you have any idea about where my daughter is?" Cathy asked, as she took a chair.

"No, but Mr. Casey is working feverishly on the case. Not many clues have surfaced." Jennifer leaned back on the sofa. "Did Sarah confide in you about her friends?"

"Very little. I met a few of the girls who occasionally came home with her. They would only stay long enough for Sarah to pick up her laptop or duffle bag."

"When school was in session. Did you ever talk with Sarah's teachers?"

She shook her head. "No, Greg took on the responsibility of the conferences."

"Why didn't you go with him? Usually, both parents are welcome."

Cathy stared at the floor. "I didn't want to hear anything bad about Sarah."

Jennifer frowned. "Has someone said something objectionable about your daughter?"

"A couple of years ago, Sarah's teacher told me she didn't apply herself and could do much better."

"What kind of grades does she make?"

"Mostly A's and B's, and an occasional C".

"Those sound like excellent marks."

"I thought so too."

"Tell me about Sarah's friends. Does she have a boyfriend?"

Cathy jerked up her head and stared at Jennifer. "No. I wouldn't allow her to date."

"Why? She's old enough."

She threw up her hands. "And have her come home pregnant one night."

Jennifer put the cup on the coffee table. "What about her girlfriends? Do they date?"

She shrugged.

"I noticed a picture of Sarah and a boy at a Hawaiian Luau on her wall."

Cathy waved a hand in the air. "They're just friends. We've known the family for years. Greg took the kids to the school and Mark's folks picked them up and brought Sarah straight home."

"Do you know the parents of her girlfriends?"

"No. If Sarah's going to their house, I take her word one of the parents is home."

"Have you ever checked up on her?"

She furrowed her brow. "Of course not. I trust my daughter."

Jennifer gathered up her belongings and rose. "I want to get some shots of the outside before I leave, so I better get going." She snapped her fingers. "I almost forgot, Mr. Casey asked me to get the phone number of your brother, Blake Hunter."

Cathy frowned. "What in the world for?"

"Didn't he visit you a month or so ago?"

Cathy shrugged. "Well, yes, but he knows nothing about Sarah's disappearance."

"Haven't you called and informed him she's missing?"

"No, but if Mr. Casey is going to call him, I guess I better give him a ring. Hold on a minute and I'll get his number."

She disappeared down the hallway and soon returned with a slip of paper. "He'll be hard to catch, as his job keeps him on the road a lot."

Jennifer took the information and slid it into her purse. "Thanks for the coffee. After I've checked through these pictures, I might want to come back and chat some more. If that's all right."

"Sure, any time. I'm always home."

She left out the front and strolled around the building, snapping the lens as she went. After taking several photos of the window Sarah had supposedly pushed her suitcase through, she felt she had enough to keep her busy for a while and climbed into her van. Driving away, she shook her head, wondering how this mother could be so naive as trusting everything her daughter told her to be the gospel truth. Teenagers could be taken on their word about as far as you could throw them. No one knows what kind of mischief Sarah conjured up behind her mother's back. When she spoke with Mrs. Willis again, she'd carry a recorder. Trying to remember everything discussed with the voice inflections proved to be a challenge. Also, Jennifer felt taking notes in front of Cathy Willis just might intimidate her.

She headed south on Interstate 5 and soon turned off at Hornbrook, then drove the last leg toward Copco Lake. When she pulled into the driveway, it surprised her to see Hawkman's vehicle parked in front of the open garage. She steered past him and jumped out, eager to download the pictures onto her computer so she could study the results.

Hawkman stood by the kitchen counter and smiled when she entered. "How'd it go?"

"Good, but Mrs. Willis is very naive."

"You came to the same conclusion I did. By the way, did you get Blake Hunter's phone number?"

"Yes." She rummaged through her purse and handed him the paper.

"I'll give him a call right now, maybe I'll catch him eating dinner."

"You're so ornery," she snickered. "While you're in your office, I'll load the photos onto the computer."

He gave her a thumbs up as she scooted behind her desk and proceeded to set up the camera.

It didn't take long before Hawkman strolled back into the room. "I reached Mr. Hunter and asked him a few questions about Sarah. He found her a charming, giggly teenage girl. He said Greg had called about her disappearance and wanted to know if he'd heard from her since his visit. Cathy hadn't called, but he made the comment his sister lived in a fantasy world, so it didn't surprise him."

Jennifer placed an elbow on the table and rested her chin on her folded hand while listening. "You know, I agree with him. She's very gullible."

Hawkman sat down at a chair near the computer center. "Tell me about the interview."

After going through the dialog between herself and Mrs. Willis, she threw up her hands. "I've got to use a recorder so I can remember everything."

He laughed. "I have an extra. I'll rig it up for you tonight and you can carry it in your purse."

"I'd like to meet Greg Willis. It would help me analyze this family."

"You'll have to do it tomorrow, as he's leaving early Monday morning on a haul across the country and won't be home for a week."

"Do you think he'd mind if I dropped by?"

"I'll give him a heads up."

"Okay, you do that, and I'll finish downloading these pictures."

"His number's in my briefcase." He headed down the hallway again, mumbling as he went. "Sure wish they'd get a tower up here, so I could use my cell."

Jennifer soon had the pictures displayed on the monitor. She enlarged them one by one and studied the photos for clues. Suddenly, she focused on a shot from Sarah's room and zoomed in on the bookshelf above the bed. She grabbed a pen, yanked a sheet of paper from a notebook and scribbled some notes.

About the time she'd written everything down, Hawkman sauntered up beside her. "Greg said he'd love to meet you and to come by between two and three tomorrow."

"Perfect."

Hawkman glanced at the screen. "What've you found?"

"First, let me show you the shot of the window Mr. Willis described. You can see how Sarah placed the screen to the side."

He nodded. "Looks like she must have planned this for some time."

She pulled another picture toward the center of the monitor, and used the zoom feature. "I find this very interesting. I'm assuming these are Sarah's reading materials, since they were on the bookshelves in her room."

He frowned as he leaned closer to the screen. "You're kidding. This could put a whole new light on things."

CHAPTER NINE

Hawkman studied the images Jennifer had enlarged on the screen. "You think you could borrow these books for us to look over?"

"Probably, but wouldn't it be easier to go the library?"

"What if Sarah wrote notes in the margins?"

She nodded. "True. I'll drop by Cathy's first thing in the morning."

"Be sure to give her a receipt. I think the woman's very leery of our removing items from her daughter's room. I'm sure she had a fit when Greg brought the computer and boxes of stuff to my office. I have the feeling he ran the household when they were together, so now she does a lot of bawling, hoping it will sway Greg from taking Sarah's things from the house. Maybe It will ease her mind, if she knows we'll return them."

Jennifer rummaged through her desk drawer, removed a small receipt book, filled it out with the book titles she could see on the monitor, then picked up her handbag from the floor beside her feet. "I'll stick this in my purse, so I won't forget it."

"Find anything else of interest in those pictures?"

"Haven't been through them all yet. Any news on your end?"

"I talked with Cindy Jackson, and checked with several of Sarah's girlfriends. I thought it sort of uncanny as they all seem to have the same stories."

"What do you mean?"

"Why Sarah's parents divorced, and the boyfriend. Each girl sounded like she'd rehearsed her lines."

"You think they know something and aren't telling?"

"I'm really suspicious. I checked the phone book for this Glen Carter, who the girls claim is Sarah's boyfriend. I discovered a couple of Carters listed, and tried to call, but didn't reach anyone, not even an answering machine. I drove to the addresses, but found no one home at either place. I'll try again Monday."

Jennifer screwed her face up into a thoughtful expression. "Hmmm."

"What does that mean?"

"I know kids form cliques and really hang tight. But it's hard to believe the girls would jeopardize Sarah's safety by keeping quiet, unless they know she's okay. Discovering she'd visited her MySpace site today makes me think there's something fishy going on. Definitely interesting. Did you find any clues on her computer?"

"Not anything relevant, except she's visited a few porn sites. What kid hasn't? The minute you tell them they can't, they do."

Jennifer winked at him. "Hope you didn't hang out at those for long."

He grinned. "To tell you the truth, I find them a bit far out. I still haven't cracked the code on how to get into a couple of Sarah's files. It's one of my next missions. I'll probably find the password in the stuff Greg brought to the office. If not, I'll hire Jacob, the computer guru, to help me out."

"Good luck." She hit a key and brought the computer out of sleep mode. "I'm going to search through the rest of these pictures and see if I find any more interesting tidbits." She retrieved her notebook from her purse. "Then I'm going to see if I can find some of her buddies' sites and give them a look."

"Okay, I'll talk to you later. I'm going to check on Pretty Girl, then go back to my office and read through some of the stuff Greg brought over. Maybe I'll find a few clues."

The house turned silent as Jennifer focused on the computer. Miss Marple jumped upon the chair next to her and purred loudly as she batted at the cords protruding from the machine. "Hush, you're making too much noise," she scolded.

Jennifer zoomed in on the pictures and went over every inch of the surface. After taking a few notes, she went to Sarah's MySpace page. Thank goodness she hadn't set the site to private. She didn't know the password to get into Home, but figured she wouldn't need it for a while. Hawkman had found a few stray words in Sarah's stuff that might work. She'd give them a try when the time came to retrieve messages or e-mails. Right now she just wanted to check out the girl's friends.

She placed the list of people Hawkman had interviewed in front of her and began the search. Sarah only had fifty friends displayed, so it shouldn't take too long to figure out which ones came from her school or nearby, but it would require going to each person's pages.

Pulling a clean notebook from one of the desk drawers, she flipped it open in preparation to record each name, leaving spaces between them for notes. She first listed the small group of girls Hawkman called 'Sarah's little gang', and placed a star beside each of their names. Afterwards, she moved to each site, dragged their pictures to her desktop, lined them up on one sheet, then printed the page. She cut the photos apart and made individual folders for each girl: Cindy Jackson, Janet Ross, Nikki Phelps, and Ann Stewart. Right now she'd keep her heaviest investigation focused on those four girls. "Now let's check the rest," she mumbled.

Miss Marple twitched her ears and immediately stood up on the chair.

Jennifer chuckled. "I didn't mean to disturb you, my pretty kitty. You can lie back down. I don't need you in my lap at this moment."

As if she understood, the Ragdoll cat, stretched, yawned and curled back up on the seat.

While scanning Sarah's other friends, Jennifer suddenly stopped. "Oh, my gosh!" She jumped out of the chair, hurried toward Hawkman's office, and poked her head into the room. "Come see what I found."

Hawkman followed her back to the computer center. "Didn't you say Sarah's supposedly boyfriend's name was Glen Carter?" she asked over her shoulder.

"Yeah."

"I think I've found his picture. Might find even more information when I go to his site."

Jennifer moved around to the front of her computer and pointed. "It says his name is Glen Carter." She clicked on the picture and his site appeared. "You think this is the guy?"

"Wish I'd been a little more thorough with Cindy. I didn't get a description." Hawkman leaned forward and studied the profile. "He claims to be nineteen, which would make him the right age. Says he's from Medford, Oregon; so far, so good. What do the stats say?"

She scrolled down. "Single, here for friendships, straight, Medford is his hometown, five foot ten inches with an athletic body type, white/Caucasian, Christian, Libra, children someday, college student, and student as his occupation."

"Anything about where he's attending college?"

Scrolling down further, she shook her head. "No, it doesn't look like he filled out the rest of the form."

"Can you get the picture off?"

"Yes."

"Print out a copy. I'll check with Cindy and see if this is the guy."

"Will do."

She enlarged the photo as much as possible without it becoming blurry and made two copies. Hawkman stood by the printer as the photos slid into the tray.

"I'm going to make a file on him too. Even though I'll leave the males for you to investigate, I might need his picture."

"Good idea." He handed her the other sheet. "He looks like a clean cut kid. Nice smile, but I can't tell the color of his eyes."

"They could be any hue with the dark brown hair."

"If this is our boy, we'll find out eventually." He meandered over to the kitchen bar and probed in the box of chocolates he'd brought her. She glanced up and grinned as she continued going through the sites of each of the girls. While jotting down notes about Janet's page, she noticed the girl popped online. She wrote down the time and quickly logged back to Sarah's site. It showed someone on her site also. Switching back and forth from Cindy's, Nikki's and Ann's profiles, she found all five girls online at the same time. Then suddenly, Sarah went off, but the others stayed on. Jennifer slumped back in her chair and stared at the screen. "Now, that's odd," she mumbled. Her fingers flew across the keyboard as she quickly went to the comments on each page. Nothing recent caught her eye. These girls knew those could be read by the public. "Darn, I'd give my eye teeth to read their messages or e-mails," she grumbled.

Hawkman glanced at her as he headed for the refrigerator. "You talking to yourself again?"

"She laughed. "Working on a case makes a person nutty. I just had an interesting event occur."

"Oh, yeah?" he said, as he popped open a beer and approached her area.

"You know what I think?"

"No. Don't keep me in suspense. Out with it."

"I think Cindy has Sarah's password, and is keeping an eye on her site."

"How did you reach such a conclusion?"

She pointed at the screen. "Cindy came online about eight fifty-five, and a few seconds later Sarah's online signal came on. Then shortly afterwards, Sarah went off, then Janet, Nikki, and Ann popped on at nine o'clock sharp. Why would Sarah go off, if she was really there? Don't you think she'd want to speak with her other friends?"

Hawkman raised a brow. "Woman, you never cease to amaze me."

"I think I'm going to have a private talk with Cindy. See if I can arrange it without her mother present."

"Good luck. The parents of these girls are going to be very alert since Sarah has disappeared."

CHAPTER TEN

Jennifer tapped her finger against her chin. "Could you talk with Mrs. Jackson and let her know I'm your assistant, and I'd like to speak to Cindy?"

"I can do that, but don't count on her not being in the room."

"If I word things right, it might not matter. I could save you a trip and show her the picture of Glen Carter while I'm there."

"Fine with me. When do you want to do this?"

"Tomorrow."

"You're packing a lot into one day."

"I know, but this case needs to come to a head soon. Williams had it for a couple of days before you took over, so Sarah's been missing for almost a week. Each hour sends the percentages down on finding the girl alive."

"True." He glanced at the clock. "It's only a little after nine-thirty. I'll give Mrs. Jackson a call right now. What time do you want to schedule your visit?"

She checked her appointment book. "I'll run by after I meet with Greg Willis, say around four. If it's too late for her, I could go by in the morning before going by Cathy's to pick up the books. Or, between the Cathy and Greg interviews."

Hawkman chuckled. "I'll figure it out with Mrs. Jackson." He went back to his office, flipped open Sarah's address book, and punched in the number on his desk phone. After several minutes, he came back into the living room. "Mrs. Jackson said one o'clock would be fine."

Jennifer sat staring at the computer screen as if in a trance.

"What's the matter?"

"It just dawned on me. It's Saturday night and it seems odd all these girls are home. They're old enough to date and you said they were all cute girls. I can't imagine any teenager staying home on this night."

"Maybe they're at one of the houses having a sleepover. Or maybe the mothers are getting a little protective since Sarah's disappearance."

"If they were together, how could they all be on one computer at the same time?"

"Guess I forgot to tell you. These kids all carry laptops, or cell phones with internet access, wherever they go. So you can't be sure they're home just because they've all showed up on MySpace."

She nodded. "That explains why they can all get on at a given time. Boy, technology moves so fast it's hard to keep up."

"Now, to repeat what I said. I told Mrs. Jackson you'd be there around one o'clock."

She quickly jotted down the information. "Perfect."

"I'm hitting the sack. I have a full day tomorrow."

"Okay. I'm right behind you, as soon as I bookmark this stuff."

❧

The next morning, Hawkman accompanied Jennifer to the door. "Hope you have good luck. Give me a ring on the cell when you have time."

"What are your plans?"

"After making a few phone calls, I have more items from Sarah's room I want to go through before heading for town. If I find someone home at the Carters, I'll stop by there, then on to the office to work on those locked files and anything else I might find on Sarah's computer."

"Okay, I'll check in with you after lunch." She gave him a kiss, then headed toward her van.

He waved as she backed out of the garage and drove down the driveway. Hawkman closed the door, poured himself a cup of coffee and went to his office. Miss Marple followed close at his heels. He glanced down and grinned. "I guess you're bent on tormenting me, since your mistress isn't here."

He settled behind the desk, then opened his briefcase, and dumped the remaining contents onto the surface. The beautiful Ragdoll kitten couldn't stand the temptation and immediately hopped into Hawkman's lap and batted at the fluttering pieces of paper, sending them flying to all parts of the room. "You little scamp," Hawkman laughed. "I should have known better than to pull such a stunt with you in the room." He placed Miss Marple on the floor and retrieved the bits and pieces of paper. After a few minutes of searching the area, he went to her toy box, grabbed the cat's favorite stuffed rabbit, tossed it beside her and sat back down. "Now, you play with your own toys and leave me alone."

He again made a call to the two Carter residents he'd found in the phone book. No answer on the first call, but on the second number an older male voice came over the line. Hawkman punched on the speaker phone and picked up a pencil.

"Is this Mr. Carter?"

"Yes."

"My name's Tom Casey, Private Investigator. I'm trying to locate Glen Carter. Does he by any chance live there?"

"May I ask what this involves?"

"I'm investigating the disappearance of Sarah Willis and understand he knew her. I'm trying to contact everyone who had any association with the girl."

"Glen is my son, but he's at work right now. I have no idea if he knew the young lady. You'll need to talk to him."

"When's the best time to call? Or I can leave my number."

"Hold on just a moment and let me get a pen."

Hawkman could hear the muffled voices of a man and woman in the background, and soon the noise of the phone being picked up.

"Okay, Mr. Casey. Give me the number. I'll have Glen contact you when he gets home from work. It'll probably be after five o'clock."

"That's fine. This is my cell phone number where he can reach me any time, even if I'm in an area where there's no coverage. The number rolls over to my home or work phone." He recited the digits. "Thank you, and I appreciate your cooperation."

After hanging up, he focused his attention on the remaining items piled on his desk. Since Jennifer had joined him on this case, he decided to type out what he thought were possible passwords and give her a copy. He read each piece of scrap paper, recording any interesting information. The last tidbit piqued his interest. A large red heart drawn on a piece of paper with the letters GC and JO in the middle. An arrow pierced the center and little hearts surrounded the bigger one. It appeared the abbreviations were traced over and over, until they were a much brighter color than the rest. Hawkman figured the GC stood for Glen Carter, but wondered if more than one boy had stolen Sarah's heart. He'd have Jennifer check the MySpace sites for a boy with the initials JO.

CHAPTER ELEVEN

Jennifer decided to make a surprise visit to Mrs. Willis' apartment. She didn't want to give her the opportunity to remove any of the volumes from Sarah's bookshelf. She crossed her fingers, and prayed she'd catch the woman home. When she knocked on the entry, and the door swung open, she had to catch herself from staring as she'd obviously caught a busy individual, hair in disarray and a tea towel slung over her shoulder.

Cathy quickly ran her fingers through the loose strands hanging in her face and pushed them behind her ears. "Oh, Mrs. Casey, I didn't expect you."

"I'm sorry I didn't call, but didn't know what time I could come by. One of my errands brought me close to your place, so I decided to take my chances, and hoped to catch you here."

"Please come in. Excuse my mess, I'm doing some cleaning."

"No problem. I'll only stay a minute."

Cathy frowned. "Why are you here?"

"I need to borrow some of Sarah's books."

She looked confused. "Greg gave Mr. Casey all of her school stuff."

"These are ones I spotted from the pictures. They're on a shelf in her room."

Cathy jerked up her head. "I can't let you take Sarah's personal things."

"I'll itemize a list, give you a receipt, and promise to return them within a couple of weeks."

She shook her head. "I'm really uncomfortable about letting my daughter's private items go out of the house."

Jennifer placed a hand on the woman's arm. "Do you want to find Sarah?"

Her chin quivered and she turned away. "Of course. What if she returns and discovers these things gone?"

"You tell her how you and Greg were doing everything possible to find her. She'll understand, and be grateful you cared that much." Jennifer pointed toward the entry. "If Sarah walks through that door this afternoon, everything will be returned immediately."

Cathy flopped down in a nearby chair, used the corner of the tea towel to wipe her eyes, then wadded it into a ball in her lap. "I know you're right. My heart is broken, especially knowing she felt so unhappy, she left on her own initiative."

"May I get the books?"

She nodded.

Jennifer hurried into the girl's room before Cathy changed her mind. She quickly removed the prepared receipt from her purse, and added a couple of titles she couldn't make out from the picture. Then she loaded them into her arms, and walked back into the living room. She handed Cathy, who hadn't moved from the chair, the piece of paper with a carbon back. "Here's the list of items I'm taking from Sarah's room. Please check them against the receipt, then sign the bottom."

Cathy moved like a robot, took the sheet and pen from Jennifer's hand, wrote her name without even looking at the books, and rose. She turned away and headed for the kitchen. "Goodbye, Mrs. Casey."

Jennifer, sensing the miffed woman's feelings, left the carbon copy on the table, folded the original and stuck it into her purse, then exited out the door. When she reached the van, her mind reeled with the unbelievable behavior she'd witnessed from Mrs. Willis. She climbed into the driver's seat, placed the books in a satchel, and turned the key.

As she drove toward the Jackson home, she couldn't shake the feeling of how Mrs. Willis could switch her attitude from cold to hot in a matter of minutes. If she treated her daughter in this manner, it's no wonder the girl ran away. She looked forward to meeting Greg Willis later today.

She pulled in front of the Jackson home, and the clock on the dashboard read ten minutes until one. "Perfect," she whispered, picking up her camera from the seat and sticking it into her briefcase. Hawkman had told Mrs. Jackson, he'd hired his wife to help with the Sarah Willis' case, and she might want to take a couple of pictures. Then Jennifer snapped her fingers as she remembered the recorder. She stuck it in her jacket pocket and flipped it on as she walked toward the front of the house.

She rang the bell, and immediately recognized the young girl who opened the door. "Hello, I'm Jennifer Casey. My husband called and made an appointment for me to meet Mrs. Jackson and Cindy this afternoon."

"Hi. I'm Cindy." She turned her head to the side and yelled, "Mom, Mrs. Casey is here." Then she stared at Jennifer. "I never dreamed you'd be so pretty."

Jennifer felt her face flush. "Well, thank you."

Mrs. Jackson came scurrying around the corner, and held out her hand. "So nice to meet you, Mrs. Casey." Then she furrowed her brow. "You look so familiar; have I met you before?"

"I don't think so, but you might have seen my picture on the back of one of my books."

Mrs. Jackson stepped back, her mouth dropped open. "Of course, you're the mystery/suspense writer. How could I have been so stupid? I own the whole series and love them. I must have you sign one while you're here."

Jennifer smiled. "Sure, be happy to."

"Oh, my," she said, taking Jennifer's arm, "excuse our manners. Please come in."

The three females went into the living room and sat down.

Cindy leaned forward. "Wait until I tell my friends I've met an author. They won't believe me."

"I'll tell you what, I'll give you one of my cards and sign the back. Will that help?"

The girl's eyes lit up. "Yes." She jumped up from her seat and flopped down next to her.

Mrs. Jackson arose and hurried down the hallway. "Cindy, entertain Mrs. Casey while I find one of her books to autograph."

Jennifer reached into her briefcase, pulled out the picture of Glen Carter and placed it on her lap. She then continued searching in the bag until she brought out a small box of business cards. Out of the corner of her eye, she watched Cindy's reaction when she spotted the picture, as she signed the card and handed it to her. "There, that should prove you met me. I wrote 'To Cindy' on it."

"Thank you so much." Then she pointed at the photo. "I know him. He's Sarah's boyfriend."

Jennifer held it up. "Are you sure?"

"Positive."

"What's his name?"

"Glen Carter."

"Have you seen or talked to him lately?"

She shook her head. "I didn't really know him." She told the story about how they all met at the bowling alley. "That's the only time we talked."

"You never saw him bring Sarah here after a date?"

"No, she just hopped out of the car and ran to the door."

"Did Sarah like any other guys?"

"Before Glen entered the picture, she had a crush on Jerry."

"Tell me about him. What's his last name?"

"Olson. He's really cute and is a star football player at our school. Unfortunately, he goes steady with one of the cheerleaders, so Sarah didn't think she had a chance."

"I see."

"Tell me about Sarah. What did you two have in common?"

"We liked the same music, traded clothes, and even decorated our rooms alike."

"Oh, really. Can I see yours?"

"Sure."

Jennifer picked up her camera and followed Cindy down the hallway, almost bumping into Mrs. Jackson.

"Where are you two going?"

Cindy waved a hand. "I'm going to show her my room."

"Oh, dear, I hope your bed is made."

Cindy giggled. "Don't worry Mom, I actually cleaned it this morning."

Mrs. Jackson rolled her eyes. "Miracles never cease. I'll meet you two in the living room."

When Cindy opened the door, Jennifer let out a gasp. "Your room looks almost identical to Sarah's. Can I take a couple of pictures?"

"Sure."

"I can't get over this," Jennifer commented, as she photographed. "Did you girls shop together so everything matched?"

Cindy laughed. "Yep. We all went."

Jennifer looked puzzled. "Who's all?"

"Janet, Nikki, and Ann, along with Sarah and me?"

"I can't believe you all have identical rooms."

"Almost."

"I guess you girls all have MySpace sites too?"

"Yep."

Jennifer laughed. "Is it fun?"

"Oh, yeah. We keep track of each other at night. We all go online at the same time."

"What if you're on a date?"

"We use our laptops, if we have them with us; otherwise, our cell phones."

"Did Sarah participate in this ritual too?"

Cindy's expression turned sad. "She used to. I really get lonely when I don't see her online."

"I can imagine." Jennifer decided not to push too hard, and changed the subject back to the camera. "Well, since all you girls have similar rooms, I better have you in a few of these snapshots so I know this one is yours. She tapped her finger on her chin. "Why don't you stand next to the bookcase. Then I'll get another of you at the foot of your bed." After several shots and zooming in on several items without Cindy's knowledge, Jennifer turned off her camera. "I think we better go join your mother. She's probably wondering what's happened to us."

They walked back into the living room where a platter of cookies and three cans of Pepsi drinks sat on the coffee table.

"Why, thank you, Mrs. Jackson," Jennifer said.

"Please, call me Rachel"

"Rachel it is. I can't get over these girls decorating their rooms all alike."

"They had a ball doing it. However, I don't think Sarah's mother took to the idea too much."

"Oh. Why not?"

"She's a strange woman. I didn't talk to her, but Cindy did."

Jennifer glanced at the girl. "What did she say?"

"She thought we should be individuals and do our rooms separately. Later, Sarah said if we hadn't done it, her room would never have gotten changed at all."

"Mrs. Willis appears strict."

"In an odd sort of a way," Rachel intervened. "She did a lot of negative raving at Sarah, but the girl did what she darn well pleased, although she wasn't ornery about it. It's hard to explain. I'm not sure what kind of power she held over her daughter. I just pray you find Sarah unharmed."

Jennifer checked her watch. "Oh, my, I've got to run. I've got an appointment at two, so I better get going. Thank you so much for the cookies, soda and great visit."

She gathered her stuff and rose, then glanced at Rachel who had a couple of her books resting on her lap. "Let me sign those for you." Afterwards, she handed her a business card. "If you hear anything unusual about Sarah or hear from her. Please, let my husband or me know immediately."

"Don't worry, we will. Thank you for the autographs."

Jennifer left the house, much more enlightened by this visit than the one with Cathy Willis. Of course, she had to realize this mother had her daughter by her side.

Now, to meet Greg Willis.

CHAPTER TWELVE

Jennifer parked in the visitor slot in front of Greg Willis' apartment complex. She had a few minutes, so decided to change the tape in the old recorder Hawkman had found in his dresser drawer. After breaking a fingernail, she finally got it in workable order, and vowed to get a new digital one the first chance she had. "Fooling with tapes is a thing of the past," she mumbled, shoving it into her jacket pocket.

She glanced around the area and it looked secure enough, but she didn't relish the possibility of having her camera stolen, so she slipped it into her purse. Hopping out of the van, she flipped the strap over her shoulder, picked up her briefcase and searched for apartment two zero six. She lucked out and found the number on the second floor right in front. Climbing the steps, she crossed to the entry, took a deep breath, turned on the recorder and knocked.

"Be right there," a mail voice called.

She could hear rustling noises from inside and finally the door swung open.

"Hello. Mrs. Casey, I presume?"

"Yes, and you're Greg Willis?"

"Sure am. Mr. Casey should have told me how good looking you are. I'd have splashed on a bit of cologne," he laughed.

Jennifer ducked her head. "Thank you."

"I didn't mean to embarrass you. Please come in." He waved a hand toward the small living room. "Excuse my mess; I'm having to do all my laundry now and I'm getting ready to haul a big truck load across country, so I need at least a week's worth of fresh clothes."

"No problem. I understand."

He moved some shirts draped across a chair and tossed them onto the couch near an open suitcase. "Here you go. Have a seat. Can I get you something to drink?"

"A glass of water would be nice."

He nodded and waved a finger in the air. "I shall return."

Jennifer took a mental note of Greg as he traipsed into the kitchen. Even though he stood only about five foot eight inches, he threw back his broad shoulders like a man full of pride with a mission. Smile wrinkles had started to form around his mouth, giving a very pleasant appearance. Jennifer also liked the idea that he looked you in the eye while talking. He appeared to be a man with nothing to hide. She approved of him immediately.

He returned with a tall glass of ice water wrapped in a paper towel. "Figured I better put a napkin around it, so it doesn't sweat and drip on your clothes."

"Thanks."

He flopped down on the edge of the couch next to a pile of folded underwear. "Now, what can I do for you?"

"I'd like to ask you a few questions about Sarah."

He sighed. "Okay."

Jennifer removed the picture of Glen Carter from her valise. "Before I get started, do you know this young man?" She held the photo toward him.

He studied it for a few seconds, then handed it back. "No. Don't think I've ever seen him before. Does he have something to do with Sarah?"

"We're not sure yet. Did she have a boyfriend?" she asked, bending over and placing the photograph back in the case she had resting against the chair.

"Not that I know about. Cathy couldn't stand the thought of our beautiful daughter hanging around with a guy. I never understood her reasoning."

Jennifer folded her hands in her lap. "What were your wife's thoughts on the subject?"

He grimaced and rubbed the back of his neck. "Scared Sarah would come home pregnant. Which I thought ridiculous.

I figured if you taught your child about sex, and then with the school's classes, she'd learn not to give in to her whims. I never could understand why her mother worried so much. On the other hand, Cathy hardly let me put my arm around her until we were married. Since Sarah turned out such a beauty, I prepared myself for every guy in the school to be pounding at our door. But it never happened."

"Do you think Sarah might have sneaked out and dated on the sly?"

Willis laughed. "Wouldn't surprise me. I know a guy would find a way."

Jennifer grinned. "I know this won't be easy, but could you tell me about your daughter. Did you two get along?"

Greg took a deep breath, his eyes glistened. "Yes, I miss her something terrible."

"Did you ever argue?"

He shook his head. "No, but she squabbled enough with her mother. I wanted the little time we had together to be pleasant."

"What did they fight about?"

He threw up his hands and let them drop onto his thighs. "Everything. Cathy fussed at Sarah about cleaning her room, doing homework, taking care of chores, and not talking on the phone so long. I'd swear the girl couldn't even breathe right." Greg stared at the floor, then rubbed a hand across his face. "To tell you the truth, I can't blame my daughter for running away. Her mother nagged her constantly."

"Why didn't Sarah come live with you?"

"I'd have loved it, but my job sometimes keeps me away for weeks at a time. I couldn't have my daughter stay by herself. Kids get too many ideas, and if some pervert found her alone, who knows what might happen." He shook his head. "As much as I'd have liked her with me, it wouldn't have been a safe situation. She had to be with her mother."

"Did Sarah understand?"

"I think so." He raised a finger. "Don't get me wrong. She loved her mother very much and she knew Cathy loved her.

They just drove each other crazy. Especially, after Sarah matured into a young woman."

"Did Sarah defend herself?"

Greg rolled his eyes. "Oh, yeah. They'd get into screaming matches. These started before we divorced. About the time Sarah turned into a teenager." He pointed at Jennifer. "Not physical battles. I'd have stepped in if they had. Cathy and I didn't believe in that type of thing. But, oh my, they could yell at each other. I didn't like it, but didn't know how to stop them."

"I gather Sarah liked to hang out with her girlfriends. Did Cathy approve of them?"

He grimaced. "Somewhat. She didn't like their low cut jeans showing their belly buttons," with his finger, he drew an imaginary half circle on his chest. "nor the short cropped, low slung tops."

"When Sarah stayed with you, what did she wear?"

Greg threw back his head and laughed. "Anything she damn well pleased."

Jennifer chuckled, and thought, this girl has her dad wrapped around her little finger. "Did she ever want to go to her girlfriends' when she stayed here?"

"Most of the time, I'd pick up the whole bunch and take them to the pizza house, roller skating, movies or wherever they wanted to go."

"Did you accompany them?"

He reared back and made a face. "Oh, my goodness, no. They didn't want the old man around. So I'd set a time, go grocery shopping, or run errands, then pick them up."

"Did these events occur at night or daytime?"

"Mostly early evening. It's just been the past six months or so the girls have started dating and Sarah doesn't see them as much at night."

"How do you know this?"

"Cathy told me."

Jennifer studied his face, and realized the man believed it. "I see." She shifted in her seat. "I'd like to ask a few personal questions."

"Have at it. I'm not bashful."

"What caused the divorce?"

Greg shrugged. "Cathy filed and claimed irreconcilable differences. Whatever the term means, it's why we divorced."

Jennifer looked him straight in the eyes. "Mr. Willis, I don't mean to sound brazen, but you must have had some inkling things were going amiss."

He folded his arms across his chest and let out a sigh. "Yeah, you're right."

After a few moments of silence, Jennifer said, "Mr. Willis, what changes did you see in your marriage?"

Greg stood. "Many arguments, and unfortunately, Sarah happened to be the reason we fought so much."

"What do you mean?"

He paced and continuously hit his fist into the other hand. "We disagreed on her curfew, dating, clothes. You name it, we argued about it. Cathy seemed bent on smothering the child. I told her if she didn't let up, Sarah wouldn't hang around. I'm afraid my prediction came true."

"Where do you think Sarah may have gone?"

Willis flopped down on the couch and dropped his head into his hands. "I haven't the foggiest notion. I've wracked my brain trying to remember anything she might have said to give me a clue. And haven't come up with a thing." He raised his face and stared at Jennifer. "I hope you and your husband find her soon. I fear she's in the hands of some idiot she's interacted with on the internet."

"Cathy stated she knows nothing about a computer. She told my husband she didn't even know how to turn it on. You said you know a little. How much is a little?"

"The company I work for is switching over to using computers to track our cargo and where we're routed. I had to take a course on the fundamentals. So it gave me a little insight on the workings of the machine. I don't have an inkling on how to surf the web like these kids do nowadays."

"Have you witnessed her using her laptop?"

"Yes, and it amazes me how her fingers fly over the keyboard."

"So what was she doing when you watched?"

"Before school let out for the summer, she and her girlfriends had decided to set up their own MySpace sites. She showed me hers and I was impressed, yet concerned. I questioned her about the site, and she gave me the 'oh, dad' routine."

"What makes you think Sarah might have had contact with an unsavory person?"

He exhaled and stared at the ceiling. "One night when she stayed with me, I busied myself cooking dinner while she sat at the kitchen table with her computer. She got up to go to the bathroom, and I glanced over at what she had up on the screen. It shocked me to discover a chat room and I sure didn't like the comments I saw coming in."

"What were they? Did you notice the name of the site?"

He rubbed a hand over his mouth. " Things like 'hey sugar baby, what's your measurements? Where do you live?' Unfortunately, It made me so upset I didn't notice the site name."

"Did you question Sarah?"

"You bet I did."

"How'd she respond?"

"Not to worry. She never answered their smutty questions."

"Did you explain how dangerous some of these sites can be?"

He nodded. "I gave her a lecture, which I seldom do, but thought it important at the time."

"Did she take it seriously?"

"I thought so, but now I'm not sure."

CHAPTER THIRTEEN

Jennifer left Greg Willis' apartment and headed home. Her mind buzzed with the information she'd gathered from the three interviews. She felt Greg scored better in his parenting skills than Cathy, but also understood the predicament of how his job forced him to grant almost full custody of his daughter to his ex-wife. The woman had a strange sense of what she felt was best and didn't want to admit Sarah had grown into a teenager. Like many parents of today, she didn't think her daughter would embarrass her by doing something wrong or stupid. Cathy refused to understand how important Sarah's peers were at this time in the girl's life. Jennifer thought the woman needed to enroll in a course or read some books on how to raise teens. She wondered how she could suggest such a thing without making the woman furious?

Turning into the driveway, she noticed Hawkman hadn't returned. More than likely, he'd be late, since the appointment to talk with Glen Carter would be after the boy got off work. This should give her time to go through the recordings, take a few notes from the books, and scan the pictures she'd taken of Cindy's room. She hoped they could find some clues, giving them an avenue to pursue on locating Sarah.

Miss Marple followed at Jennifer's heels, as she piled books, camera and recorder on the computer desk. When the cat let out a loud meow, she jerked around and noticed the cat's empty food bowl.

"I bet you're hungry," she said, picking up the feline and cuddling her. After satisfying her pet's needs, Jennifer sat down at the computer and downloaded the pictures from her camera.

Once she'd scanned them, she enlarged the one of the bookcase, and quickly opened the satchel of stuff she'd taken from Sarah's room. Zooming in on Cindy's volumes, she removed the book called, 'Bygone Country Living' out of the bag and compared the spines. It matched. She flipped through the contents and noticed several of the corners turned down. Short memos in the margins caught her attention. "I'll study those in depth later," she mumbled, placing the book aside.

She pulled the next book out of the bag and the words, 'The Occult' on the spine, made her mouth go dry, the same feeling she'd had when she pointed it out to Hawkman in the picture of Sarah's room. She glanced at the screen and spotted an identical book resting on Cindy's shelf. Then she noticed the words 'Beware of' were almost rubbed off on the spine of the one she held. This made her breathe a little easier, but still gave her a strange feeling. "I thought I recognized these titles. Why would these girls own this type of literature? I'm sure they weren't school assignments," she said aloud, thumbing through the pages and scanning the notes alongside the print. "Something's going on here."

She took a deep breath, closed the book, placed it on top of 'Bygone Country Living', then pulled out the next text, turned through the pages and saw check marks by certain paragraphs. "I sure don't like what I'm smelling." She glanced up at the screen, and searched through the array of bindings on Cindy's shelves, but didn't spot this title.

Jennifer stacked it on top of the other two and removed the long thin narrow box, labeled, 'Map of Rural Roads in Jackson County', which had caught her eye while removing the other publications from Sarah's room. She frowned as she carefully unfolded the large sheet of colorful paper.

Hearing the front door open, she glanced up and smiled as Hawkman entered. "Hi, hon, how'd things go?"

"Not real productive. I hope you had a better day," he said, hanging his hat in the Hawkman corner.

"Hard to say. Let's compare notes, and maybe between us we'll find some connections."

"Sounds good. Let me get a beer. You want a drink?"

"Not yet."

He crossed the room to the computer, placed his briefcase on the floor, picked up Miss Marple from the chair and held her against his chest. "If you'll be still, I'll let you stay on my lap." The cat bumped his chin with her head. "I know, you love me," he said, laughing.

Jennifer smiled, folded up the map, put an elbow on the table, and rested her chin on her hand. "You go first."

Hawkman took the recorder from his pocket and placed it in front of her.

She picked it up and examined the little machine. "I definitely want to get one of these, the one you let me use is a pain."

"Didn't it work okay?"

"Yes, it did its job, but you have to remember to check the tape and make sure the batteries are charged."

He waggled his head. "Yeah, it's tough being a private investigator."

Placing a hand over her mouth, she hid a grin. "That didn't come out right." She pushed the 'on' button and Hawkman's voice boomed through the air, causing Jennifer to jump, throwing up her hands. And Miss Marple leaped to the floor.

He quickly reached over and turned down the volume as the feline scurried across the room, and hid behind the couch.

"Wow, for such a little piece of machinery, it sure has a powerful volume," Jennifer said, staring at the mini recorder.

He chuckled. "Sorry, I didn't realize it would come on so loud. I must have unknowingly pushed the volume up when I put it in my pocket."

"Is this the interview you had with Glen Carter?"

"Yes."

Jennifer listened intently as about ten minutes of conversation went on between the two men. It automatically shut off when finished. She glanced up at him, frowning.

"So he hasn't seen Sarah for three weeks. Do you believe him?"

He nodded. "Yeah. Typical college guy. As you heard, he found Sarah attractive, but very immature for his taste."

"She may have sensed this, and it gave her another reason to get away from all the stress in her life." Jennifer handed him the recorder. "Anything else of interest?"

"I still can't get into those files on Sarah's computer. Either she kept those passwords in her head or I haven't picked up on them in the pile of stuff. The chat rooms are going to take a while to penetrate. I've been able to get into three of them, but they're very edgy when I enter. Everyone tends to clam up. However, I did find something interesting." He reached down into his briefcase and brought out an envelope. After thumbing through several pieces of paper, he lifted a small piece out and placed it on the table. "Tell me what you make of this?"

Jennifer picked it up and raised a brow. "You found this in Sarah's stuff?"

"Yep."

"Obviously, she's got two boys she likes."

"I assume Glen Carter is one, but don't recognize the other initials."

"Jerry Olson."

Hawkman sat up straight. "How'd you find out?"

"I think my day has been a little more profitable. You probably asked some of the same questions to these people, but maybe, since I'm a woman, received different responses. We'll see. I'll run them in order, so sit back and listen." She placed her recorder on the table, removed the Greg interview, popped in the Cindy tape and flipped it on.

When it finished, he rubbed his chin. "I think I better add the Olson boy to my list."

"Wouldn't hurt."

"Let me see the pictures."

Jennifer brought her computer out of sleep and pointed at the books in Cindy's room. "There's something very strange going on, but I can't put my finger on it. Why would these girls have identical volumes?"

"School project?"

She shook her head. "I don't think so. Let me show you the items I brought out of Sarah's room." Placing the four in front of him, he looked puzzled.

"This is quite an assortment, yet they might fit into the puzzle if we could put the pieces together." He glanced at the monitor. "I don't see the book on disguises or the box with the map in Cindy's room."

"Me either, and I made sure I shot several different angles of the bookcase, so I could check what she had on hers."

"Wonder if you should approach the other two girls?"

"Right now, I think I'd rather concentrate on Cindy. I have the impression she and Sarah are very close."

"So, how'd it go with Mrs. Willis?"

Jennifer flopped back in her chair. "I didn't turn on the recorder since I'd gone to pick up the books, but she's something else. That woman can turn from warm to cold in a matter of seconds. I'm definitely on her blacklist. She sure didn't want me to take the stuff out of Sarah's room. I must say the receipt idea probably helped, along with my little bit about wanting to find her daughter." She waved a hand in the air. "I doubt she had any idea what I took out of there, as she didn't even look up or examine what I had in my hand. She signed the paper, got up, turned her back to me, stormed into the kitchen and said, 'goodbye Mrs. Casey'. I could feel the ice forming in the air."

Hawkman chuckled. "Did you get to see Greg Willis."

"He's the complete opposite and a delight. In my opinion, the better parent of the two. Too bad he can't take Sarah into his place, but he explained why he couldn't."

She pointed to the recorder. "Hand it to me, and I'll slip the tape in. I feel he let loose with a bunch of information. He tended to be in a talkative mood."

After listening to the conversation between Jennifer and Greg, Hawkman turned off the recorder. "You got a lot more out of him than I did. It appears the family had many loud arguments, which makes me understand why Sarah would take off. However, what I don't grasp, is why she didn't go to her dad's."

CHAPTER FOURTEEN

Hawkman picked up the books on country living and the occult.
"Give me time to skim through these two, then we're going to need a brainstorming session on what strategy to follow."

"Good. I haven't had a chance to look through them either, so take notes on the pages I should read. I'm going to examine these girls' sites more deeply, then I'll jot down some of my thoughts on what avenue I think we need to travel first. You can tell me if you feel it'll work."

"Great idea," he said, crossing to his chair by the window.

The two worked in silence, until Hawkman returned to the computer center carrying the books. Miss Marple had given up on getting any attention from them and rolled around on the floor, cuffing her tattered bunny toy.

Hawkman sat down on the chair next to the computer, placed the books on the table and picked up the one on disguises. He thumbed through it until Jennifer finally leaned back and glanced in his direction.

"Find anything?"

"Yeah, a few interesting tidbits. How about you?"

"Wish I could get into these girl's private messages. It might give me a clue, but otherwise, I'm not finding much. She suddenly raised up and grabbed the mouse. "I almost forgot, I found a picture of Jerry Olson."

Hawkman leaned over as she clicked on a picture and a page of sports items filled the screen. In the profile section, a very handsome young man, dressed in a football uniform, knelt on one leg, a helmet at his side, holding a football. He had a butch hair cut, and stared into the camera with a very no-nonsense expression.

"I do believe we're eyeing a very serious player," Hawkman said.

Jennifer pointed. "If you'll notice here at the bottom of the page, he has placed a picture of the cheerleaders. From what I understand, one of these girls is his steady. I've checked the comments and am almost sure her name is Brenda."

"Show me."

She scrolled down to the fourth one, which showed hearts surrounding a colorful little fairy which said, 'showin' some luv', signed with, 'can hardly wait to see you tonight, love, Brenda.'

Hawkman chuckled. "I'd say that's a sure sign."

"I don't think they're hiding anything, since Cindy spoke as if they've gone together for some time."

"Yeah, but doesn't it make you curious to know why Sarah had his initials in a heart along with Glen's? Do you think this Jerry guy flirted with her enough to give the impression she might have a chance?"

Jennifer cocked her head. "Possible, but I doubt it. Girls this age will swoon over a guy without a reason. Just the fact he's a football star is enough to have them dizzy with excitement. All he has to do is walk past them in the corridors at school, and they feel faint."

Hawkman stared at her. "Good grief, I'm glad we didn't have any girls to raise."

She smiled. "Girls take care of their mothers and fathers. Boys don't know how. Females dote on their dads until they have them wrapped tightly around their little fingers."

"I can see Sarah has spoiled her dad."

Jennifer frowned. "Yes, Greg is definitely devastated over her being gone. However, I get this strange feeling Cathy has distanced herself from Sarah's disappearance. I think she's hurt because Sarah left on her own accord and she doesn't want to believe it has really happened."

Hawkman nodded. "I agree. It makes it very hard to get any worthwhile information out of her."

"Have you questioned any of the neighbors about seeing Sarah leave that night?"

"Yes, but it's been fruitless. The ones I've talked to told me since the high school's only a couple of blocks away, kids are all over the area and they don't pay any attention to them unless they get rowdy. They see them coming and going all times of the day and night. Also, I discovered all of Sarah's girlfriends live within walking distance."

Jennifer let out a sigh. "Okay, what about those books. Any clues?"

He picked up the one on the occult. "I didn't realize this said 'Beware of the Occult' until I opened it. The title is almost rubbed off on the spine."

"Sorry, I should have warned you."

"No problem. It made the book even more interesting."

She raised a brow. "How?"

"Assuming Sarah bought this book new, the dog-eared pages indicate she wanted to know what to look for in case she got approached by anyone involved in the occult. If it's used, then I'm not so sure. There are a few notes in the margins that resemble her handwriting."

"What did they tell you?"

"It indicates she knows someone dealing in witchcraft."

Jennifer's eyes widened. "Are you sure?"

Hawkman referred to the piece of paper where he'd written page numbers and flipped the book open. He turned the book around and handed it to Jennifer. "Tell me why a young girl would write this in the margin."

She glanced down at the message which read, 'OMG, I can't believe this.' Then she read the passage next to it, which described and showed a picture of a necklace worn by a certain group. "Are you sure about Sarah's handwriting?"

"Yes, I have several of her notebooks. I'll compare it later, but I'd say it's hers. So what's your interpretation?"

She tapped the picture. "I'd say she's seen this necklace."

He took the book, turned to another page and handed it back. "Here's another note."

Jennifer gnawed her lower lip. In the margin were the words, 'NO, NO, NO, this can't be'. After she read the passage describing a ritual, she glanced up at Hawkman. "This is scary. I figure she's witnessed hand signals or a ritual by someone she knows."

"Those are the only notes, but there are check-marks beside some passages. We'll have to delve into those deeper. I find it interesting that Cindy has this book too."

Jennifer tapped her chin with a finger. "I think Sarah's friend knows more than she's saying."

Hawkman nodded. "Getting it out of her might not be easy."

"What do you make of the disguise book?"

"I found a couple of penciled stars on the margins of several pages, but there are many pictures showing how a wig fits with different garbs. Nothing indicating any special costume."

"I'll look at it a little later. I might have a better idea of what would appeal to a young girl." Jennifer handed him the box where she'd folded and returned the map. "Take a look at this, it's weird."

Hawkman removed the large piece of paper and flattened it out on the desk, letting parts of it drape over the edge. "Let me see the box this came in."

She handed it to him and he turned it over studying all sides.

"What are you looking for?"

"The map feels crisp and new. I wanted to see if there's a sticker telling us where she bought it."

"Find anything?"

"No." He pointed at a small dark square. "Looks like it's fallen off."

"Raising up the large sheet, he held it toward the light. "Where's your magnifying glass?"

She reached toward the cup of pencils and pens, and handed him a small round glass.

"Don't you have a bigger one?"

"Yes, I'll get it." She rose and crossed the room to the kitchen bar, pulled a larger magnifier from the pencil holder near the phone and brought it to him.

"Much better," he said, holding it a couple of inches from the paper and guiding it down a section. "Interesting."

"Hawkman, tell me what you're doing."

"Stand behind me."

She stepped over and looked down toward the map.

"Follow my finger and see if you see anything unusual."

"It looks like an erasure line."

"I don't know if it means anything. It could be an actual mistake. If so, why are there no more drawn lines?"

CHAPTER FIFTEEN

Jennifer went back to her chair. "I smell a rotten fish, but I don't know where it is."

Hawkman nodded. "You and me both."

"Let's rehash what we know to this point." Jennifer leaned back and folded her arms. "It's obvious no one forced Sarah to pack a bag and drop it outside the window. So we have to assume she left on her own accord, and told her mother a lie about spending the night with Cindy. After she left the apartment, she walked far enough so if Cathy watched, she'd assume the girl had headed for her friend's house. Then Sarah back tracked, using a different route, and picked up the suitcase. We have no idea what happened afterwards."

Hawkman scratched his sideburn. "True, but I think she kept a rendezvous with an acquaintance. It could've been a male or female."

"Have you ruled out Glen Carter?"

"Yeah."

"You also feel her girlfriends had rehearsed the answers to your questions, as if they knew Sarah was safe?"

"They definitely sounded practiced, not off the cuff."

"I had the same impression with Cindy. She put on a good show for me in front of her mother, giving the appearance she's concerned about Sarah. I had the feeling it wasn't genuine."

Hawkman glanced at her. "Why?"

"Girls at this age are very emotional. You've seen pictures of them screaming and carrying on at rock concerts, almost to the point of passing out. Also on television, their reactions to losing a colleague at school due to an automobile accident or the death of one because of illness, even if they didn't know them. They almost get hysterical. I saw none of this in Cindy, not even a hint. What about the other two friends you interviewed?"

He shook his head. "Not a tear. They were very matter of fact. When I talked with Cindy and mentioned a life or death situation, she showed a little emotion, but not enough to describe her as being an emotional teenager."

Jennifer leaned forward and rested her arms on the computer table. "I find these behaviors very odd, as this is supposedly a close friend who's disappeared. I think we're going to have to push harder."

"I agree," he said, picking up the occult book. "Before I forget, I want to scan the necklace shown in this picture. I have a gut feeling Sarah saw this on someone she knows. I think I'll ask a few people if they've ever seen anyone wearing this piece."

Hawkman headed back to his office. "Make me a copy, too," Jennifer called.

When he returned, he handed her a duplicate. She studied it for a moment then glanced up. "Do you recall seeing this type of jewelry on any of the girls you interviewed?"

"No, I doubt they'd wear it in front of their parents. Probably only with others within the group." Hawkman flipped the book pages. "Have you heard of any sort of occult clan in the area?"

"Never. It doesn't mean there isn't one. I'm sure they'd keep very private."

He plopped the volume back on the table. "I don't agree with you there."

"How come?"

"They do weird things, and word would have gotten out. I'll talk with Williams tomorrow and see if he's had any reports of such activity."

"Good idea."

"Bring up that Jerry Olson page again," Hawkman said,

walking around the table. I want to look a little closer at this boy. Think I'll try to talk to him in the next day or two."

Jennifer brought up the page and they studied the boy's site. Hawkman pointed to the picture of the cheerleaders in front of the stands.

"You think you could talk to his steady?"

"Let me check out her site." She clicked on the profile picture on the comment, and another page popped up on the screen. "There's our little beauty."

Hawkman pointed to a pinup picture of Brenda in a bikini. "Mighty sexy."

She pointed to the section 'about me'. "Her name is Brenda Thompson. States she's seventeen. It appears she and Jerry will be seniors this coming school year."

"How can you tell?"

Jennifer scrolled down to a picture of a float. "Looks like this is their homecoming parade and she's got the Junior float circled with the words 'First Prize! Yeah!'"

"Flip back to his page."

They both scanned it for any reference to his grade level. Then Jennifer clicked on pictures under his profile. A group of photos appeared. "Ah, there he is with the Junior class of football players. It says, Varsity team for next year."

Hawkman patted her on the shoulder. "Good going. He's probably around for the summer. These boys start practicing early." He went into the kitchen and brought the Medford phone book back to the computer center. "Now to find the Olsons." After thumbing through the book, he groaned. "Darn, there's an Olson listed, but no address. I'll have to do a search on my computer." He put the book in her outstretched hand. "Hope you have better luck."

"Couldn't you just call and find out the address?"

"I want to surprise him, so he doesn't have a chance to think about it. Get much better reactions that way," he said, walking toward his office.

"Don't log out until I give you the okay."

He raised a hand with the okay sign.

Jennifer opened the directory and searched for Thompson. She let out a sigh when she spotted about twenty, then smiled when her gaze rested on a 'Brenda Thompson'. Leave it to a teenage girl to finagle a way to get her own phone. She copied down the address and phone number, closed the book then went to Hawkman's office. "I got all I needed," she said, poking her head in the door.

"Great. I'm ready to hit the sack. We'll want to get an early start tomorrow."

Hawkman and Jennifer rolled out of bed before sunup and dressed.

Miss Marple followed Jennifer into the kitchen where she filled the cat's bowls with water and food, then gave the feline a pat on the head. "You be a good girl while we're gone." She then crossed over to the computer center and placed several items into her briefcase, along with the address of Brenda Thompson.

After eating a quick breakfast of dry cereal, the husband and wife team agreed to meet for lunch at a sandwich place in Medford. They then parted and drove their own vehicles toward the city. When they reached the outskirts, Hawkman turned off and headed for the police station. He needed to talk to Williams before continuing.

He rolled into the lot and parked, then made his way into the building. The door stood open to Williams' office and he poked his head around the jamb. The detective's attention seemed to be riveted on an opened folder. Hawkman cleared his throat.

Williams jerked up his head. "Hey, you've been on my mind today. In fact, I thought about calling you."

"Really," he said, scooting up a chair. "What about?"

The detective leaned back and pushed some fallen hair strands out of his eyes. "I thought it odd I've received two more reports on missing kids. Which is a bit out of the ordinary for us. Have you gotten any leads on your client's daughter?"

"No, but Jennifer and I are working feverishly. We're hoping to come up with a few clues within a day or two. The reason I dropped by today, is to ask if anyone has reported any occult activity in the area?"

Williams furrowed his brow. "You mean like finding carcasses of dead animals, killed in a ritual?"

Hawkman shrugged. "I'm not sure, as I've never done research on the different practices. I thought possibly farmers had noticed a group in a field dancing around a bonfire or some stupid thing." He waved a hand in the air. "You know, making strange gestures and wailing noises."

The detective guffawed. "I haven't received any such report. I'm not saying it hasn't happened, but I doubt the police would be notified unless someone thought it dangerous."

He grinned. "Well, I guess I can call that a relief."

Williams face turned solemn. "You're serious aren't you?"

Hawkman nodded. "Jennifer and I have come across some disturbing signs of a sorcery situation. Maybe not an abduction, but possible involvement in the high school age population."

The detective scooted forward, put his arms on the desk, and clasp his hands. "I'm interested. Tell me more."

CHAPTER SIXTEEN

Hawkman carefully related to the detective the strange things he and Jennifer had discovered. "I'm not saying occult activity is involved, but we found it odd when we ran across certain items in the missing girl's possessions."

"I can see why it concerns you," Williams said. "I'm glad you brought it to my attention. It's definitely something to keep in mind with all these reports of missing kids flying across my desk."

Pushing back his hat with his forefinger, Hawkman leaned forward. "What do you know so far about these new runaway girls?"

The detective picked up a file and handed it to him. "This one's a boy."

Hawkman raised his brows as he took the folder. "Really. That's interesting."

Williams punched his finger on the folder still on his desk. "This one concerns a girl."

Leafing through the reports, Hawkman noted that Phillip (Phil) Gray, age fifteen, had left home on foot two days ago, and not returned. He glanced up. "When this young lad left, what did he tell his parents?"

"Phil and his step-dad had an argument that evening about seven o'clock. The boy stormed out of the house, and that was the last time they saw him. The mother is beside herself and blames the father."

"How long has the man been his step parent?"

"It's slipped my mind," he pointed to the folder. "it's in there; I remember reading it."

Hawkman scanned down the page, then pointed. "Here it is. Ever since the boy turned four years. So it's not like this is a stranger stepping into the family and taking charge."

"I think the boy will come home soon. He's just hurt and mad because he didn't get his way. Let's just pray he's safe."

"I'm sure they've checked all the relatives and friends."

"Yes, we even had time to check out a few. No one has seen him."

Hawkman handed the file back. "What about the female?"

Williams opened the report and read. "Patricia Riley, sixteen years old. Left the house three nights ago on the pretense of going to babysit for a neighbor down the street. The next morning when the mother got up to go to work, she wasn't in her room. When she discovered her daughter had no such babysitting job, she panicked and called the police."

"No father?"

Williams shook his head. "Broken home."

"Did Patricia have a boyfriend?"

"Yes, we talked with him. He swears he hadn't seen her for three days."

"You believe him?"

"Yeah, his alibi's tight. He has a job at a fast food place and the employer said he worked until eleven o'clock those nights."

"Back to the girl. Did the mother go through her daughter's room and inventory any missing personal items?"

The detective flipped through the pages, reading a few notes. "Looks like she's supposed to get back to us, but hasn't so far."

"She's probably embarrassed to find out her daughter had this runaway planned."

He glanced at Hawkman. "Do you see a pattern?"

"Hard to say, until I have more information."

"I'll have one of my men follow up and give you a call."

"Mind if I make a suggestion?"

"Heck no, I can use all the help I can get."

"Send a photographer to the girl's house and have pictures taken of her room, especially of any books."

"I see where you're going. I'll get on it right away."

"I think we should keep in close touch." Hawkman stood. "We might find the Riley girl's disappearance is somehow connected to the Willis' runaway."

"Good point."

Hawkman left the station and climbed into his SUV. Before leaving, he called Jennifer on his cell, and left a message to ask Cindy if she knew Patricia Riley. He'd found several Olson families in the phone book, but narrowed it down to the school district and felt he had the right address. When he pulled up in front of a two story home, a young man cutting the lawn had just pulled the catcher off the mower and dumped it into a trash barrel standing nearby. He glanced toward the vehicle and cut off the machine as Hawkman approached.

"Hi, what can I do for you?"

"I'm looking for Jerry Olson."

"That's me."

Hawkman held out his badge. "I'm Tom Casey, private investigator, hired in the search for Sarah Willis."

"Gosh, what do you want with me?"

"I'm contacting everyone who knows Sarah. I found your name scribbled on some papers in her belongings and wondered why."

A flash of fear crossed the boy's face. He brushed the sweat from his brow with the back of his arm. "I have no idea."

"Do you have a crush on Sarah?"

He jerked up his head. "No way, man. I might have flirted with her a little. She's a cute gal. But I have a girlfriend."

"What's her name?"

"I don't think it's any of your business."

"Brenda Thompson is a very attractive girl."

Jerry's face turned crimson. "Hey, leave her out of this. How'd you find out?"

"It's my job."

"Sounds like you've been doing a bunch of snooping."

"Private investigators are known for prying into other people's lives. They get paid for it."

"Well, you can stay out of mine."

"If not me, the police will be around asking questions."

Jerry pulled off his gloves and wiped his hands down his jeans. "Look, man, I don't know anything about Sarah."

"Have you talked to her recently?"

"I haven't seen her since school let out. Just heard the other day she's missing."

"What do you think happened to her?"

The boy frowned. "I haven't the foggiest idea."

"Do you know Patricia Riley?"

"Yeah."

"She's also missing."

Jerry's eyes widened. "Hey, man. I'm going inside to get my dad. I don't like this line of questioning."

"Please do. I'd like to have a word with him too."

He drooped his gloves over the handle of the mower and hurried inside. Soon, he returned with a burly man in tow. Hawkman's gaze traveled up at least six foot four inches and a set of shoulders larger than any he'd seen in a long time. His salt and pepper hair fell across his forehead, and the deep blue eyes bore into him like a laser. The jowls were tight and he had his mouth set in a grim expression.

The boy stood to the side with a smirk on his lips and his arms crossed over his chest.

"I'm Mr. Olson and my son says you're questioning him about two missing girls from the school. Who are you and why are you talking to him about such a thing?"

"My name's Tom Casey, a private investigator, and I'm interested in anyone who has spoken to Sarah Willis or Patricia Riley in the last few weeks."

"So what, kids talk to each other all the time."

"True, but we need to question each of them in case something said would give us a clue as to what has happened to these girls. When I found Jerry's name written on some of Sarah Willis' books, it made him a person of interest."

Mr. Olson threw back his head and guffawed. "I'd imagine you'll find his name written in and on many girl's belongings. Jerry plays in all the sports the school offers, and he excels in football. Females swoon over such a guy." He turned and winked at his son. "Isn't that true, boy?"

Jerry shrugged and halfheartedly laughed. "I guess."

"I'm afraid your son misunderstood my questions. All I want to know is, when he last conversed with Sarah Willis, did she give any indication of wanting to run away? If so, did she mention any place in particular she'd go?"

Mr. Olson turned to his son. "Those are simple enough. So give the man an answer and he'll leave you alone."

Jerry shot a look at his dad, then glanced at Hawkman. "Sarah never said anything to me about running away. She seemed happy enough, just like the rest of the girls." He shrugged. " And I really didn't know Patricia very well. About the only thing I said to her was 'Hi'."

"How often did you see Sarah?"

"Before school let out. I might see her at lunch time, but we didn't always talk."

"What about after school?"

"I had practice everyday."

"Did you ever call her in the evenings," Hawkman asked.

Jerry looked at the ground and ran a foot across the grass. "I might have called her once or twice when I had an argument with Brenda."

"Did you ever take her out?"

The boy averted his gaze. "Yeah, once."

CHAPTER SEVENTEEN

Jennifer received the voice message from Hawkman about asking Cindy if she knew Patricia Riley. She decided to swing by the Jacksons before going on to the Thompson house. She parked in front and took the packet of pictures from her briefcase, stuck them into her purse, and turned on the recorder in her pocket. Rachael answered the door with a surprised expression.

"Hello, Mrs. Cascy. What brings you here today?"

"I'd like to speak to Cindy, if she's available."

She frowned. "I think my daughter's told you all she can about Sarah."

"New items come across our desk continuously, and I need to talk to her about a couple of things."

She sighed. "Okay, come in. I certainly hope this doesn't become a daily ritual."

Jennifer bit her tongue to keep a retort from exploding from her mouth.

Rachael gestured toward the living room. "Have a seat and I'll go get her."

Soon, Cindy bounced into the room, her mother following close behind. "Hi, Mrs. Casey. Mom said you wanted to talk to me."

"Yes," Jennifer said, patting the sofa cushion next to her. "I want to show you some pictures."

The girl plunked herself down and clasped her hands in her lap. "Okay."

Rachel took the large easy chair opposite them.

"Before we look at these," Jennifer said, reaching into her purse. "Do you know Patricia Riley?"

Cindy nodded. "Yeah. I heard she's missing."

"Can you tell me anything about the girl?"

"I really don't know her. She kept to herself; pretty much a loner except for her boyfriend."

"So she wasn't a part of your group?"

"No, and probably never will be. She seldom laughed or had fun."

"What's her boyfriend's name?"

"Carl Hill."

"Do you know a Bill or William Gray?"

Cindy frowned. "No. I don't think so. Does he go to our school?

"Yes, but he's probably a grade behind you.

"I might recognize the guy if I saw him."

Jennifer proceeded to open the packet with the pictures. "I took these of your room the last time I visited. I noticed a couple of books on your bookcase I wanted to ask you about." She sorted through the pictures, pulled one out of the group and pointed to 'Bygone Country Living'. "What fascinated you about this book?"

"Sarah and I had to do a report on what it would be like to live out in the country without running water, a washing machine, and the necessities we have today. So we bought the book."

Then Jennifer pointed to the one with the word 'Occult' on the spine.

"Have you read this book?"

Rachel moved from the chair to behind Jennifer and looked over her shoulder.

A flash of fear crossed the girl's face as she glanced up at her mother. "A little of it."

"What made you buy this one?"

She twisted her hands. "Sarah and I were at a bookstore one day, saw it, and thought it would be fun to read. We each bought a copy to learn what to look for if we ever ran into someone from the occult."

Jennifer reached down into her purse and pulled out the picture of the Pentacle Pendant. "Have you ever seen anyone wearing a necklace that looked like this?"

The girl's eyes grew wide, but she shook her head violently. "No!" Then she stood. "I really don't want to talk about this anymore. It gives me the chills." She took off, running toward her room.

Rachel glanced at Jennifer. "Sounds like you pushed a button. I think I better have a talk with my daughter."

Jennifer stood. "If Cindy tells you about seeing someone wearing this pendant, would you please call me?"

"You bet," she said, following her daughter down the hallway.

"I'll let myself out," Jennifer called, as Rachel disappeared around the corner.

Jennifer flipped off the recorder as she headed for the van. Her mind reeled with the possibility she might be making some sort of headway in the case. She made a U-turn and drove toward the Thompson address.

Jennifer parked at the curb in front of a very upscale two-story home, and could immediately smell money. Gardeners were working feverishly over the bushes surrounding the front lawn with their trimming shears. A pool cleaner's truck sat in the driveway and two men stood on ladders washing the tall narrow windows decorating the front and sides of the house.

She removed the pictures from her purse, as she wouldn't need them to interview this girl, put a new tape into the recorder, flipped it on and climbed out of the van. As she strolled up the walkway, she could see through the front window into a living room, dining room combination. A beautiful crystal chandelier hung over a magnificent oak table.

Punching the bell, she heard a series of chimes echo throughout the house. Soon, a young woman, with long blond hair, who had the most fascinating and penetrating green eyes she'd ever seen, answered the door. Jennifer immediately recognized her from the MySpace profile as Brenda Thompson.

She wondered if the girl wore contacts lens to get such an effect.

"Hello, can I help you?"

"Yes, I'm Jennifer Casey, and I'm helping my husband, Tom Casey, a private investigator, inquire into the disappearance of Sarah Willis. I'd like to speak to Brenda Thompson."

Her eyes immediately shadowed. "What do you want to know?"

"Are you Brenda?"

"Yes."

"Could you tell me how well you knew Sarah and the last time you saw or spoke to her."

She narrowed her eyes and stared into Jennifer's face. "I don't know her well at all and I doubt I'd speak to her if she stood in front of me."

Jennifer frowned. "You sound very bitter."

"She tried to steal my boyfriend and no one steps into my territory."

"I see. However, you said 'tried', so she obviously didn't succeed."

"Right. I hope she never comes back. I hate her."

The girl slammed the door, and Jennifer stood in shocked silence for several moments before she moved off the porch. "That girl is one little spoiled brat spitfire," she mumbled, hurrying back to her vehicle.

CHAPTER EIGHTEEN

Hawkman arrived home and stood in the kitchen for several moments in deep thought before he took the recorder from his pocket and placed it on the counter. Miss Marple wound around his ankles as he replayed the discussion with Jerry Olson and his father. He reached down, picked up the furry creature, held her in his arms, while he paced, and reflected back on how Mr. Olson interrupted, told his son he'd answered enough questions and to go into the house. "Why had he abruptly ended the interview before I had the chance to ask Jerry where he'd taken Sarah on the date?" Hawkman muttered, as he flipped off the machine.

Jennifer walked in the door just as he placed the cat on the floor.

"Hi, honey," she said, going to the refrigerator and placing a brown sack inside. "I got us a couple of sandwiches for dinner." She then went over to the computer and dropped her briefcase onto the table. "You don't look too happy."

He shook his head. "I'm not. This case is about as screwed up as any I've ever had. I'm not sure which direction to take. Something fishy's going on with these high school kids, but I can't put my finger on it."

She sighed and gave him a kiss. "I agree wholeheartedly. I picked up a lot of quirky stuff today too and am not sure what to make of it."

They moved to the computer center and sat down.

"Let's go over what we have and discuss our next move," he said.

Miss Marple jumped into Jennifer's lap as she removed the recorder from her pocket and fished for the other tape in her briefcase. "Okay, little Miss Nosey, you can stay there if you're still." She then glanced at Hawkman. "Go ahead and turn on your recorder."

"This is with Jerry Olson, the football player," he said.

She listened intently and wrinkled her forehead as it ended. "I can gather from the sound of the father's voice, he was upset with you. What does he look like?"

"Big."

She grinned. "At least we now know Jerry had a date with Sarah. So her little heart with the boy's initials inside means something."

"I would have liked to have found out a bit more." He pointed to her recorder. "Let's hear what you've got."

"This one is with Brenda Thompson, Olson's girlfriend. I've come to a conclusion about her. I'll be eager to see your reaction."

When the tape ended, Hawkman leaned back in his chair and let out a whistle.

"Brassy little dame."

"Very cocky and had the most penetrating gaze I've ever seen. I think she might have been wearing green contact lens, as her eyes didn't look normal. Her body language told me she had control, and I believe it. She definitely doesn't like Sarah. I feel she's very jealous of Jerry, which made me think she's also insecure about her relationship with the boy." She waved a hand in the air. "My woman's point of view."

Hawkman removed his hat and ran a hand through his hair. "The man's point of view thinks you're right on. You think she's brazen enough to threaten any girl who shows an interest in her guy?"

"I certainly wouldn't put it past her. But what kind of threat could she carry through?"

He drummed his fingers on the surface of the table. "Kids are arrogant and she obviously exerts power. Her responses showed she's not shy. I also thought it interesting how she claimed to hate Sarah. She must have felt intimidated or it wouldn't have bothered her. She could have easily approached Sarah and told her 'hands off'. Whether she did or not, we might never know."

Jennifer cocked her head. "I find you very observant in human behavior."

"A bit of calculating here and there," he said, brushing his nails across his shirt and blowing on his fingers.

She laughed. "Okay, quit your bragging." She removed the tape of Brenda and popped in the one of Cindy. "I think you'll find this one rather interesting too."

He leaned toward the machine and listened closely. When it ended and Jennifer shut it off, he glanced at her. "The conversation is disturbing. Let me hear it again."

She rewound the tape and hit play. When it finished, he frowned.

"Cindy sounds frightened."

"I had the same thought. When she saw the picture of the Pentacle Pendant, her expression showed fear, as did the inflection in her voice."

"How much faith do you have in Mrs. Jackson getting in touch with you if Cindy tells her who she saw wearing the necklace?"

"Rachel is a good mother, but a bit overprotective. I've never talked to Cindy without her present. If this is a factor which would cause her daughter pain or anxiety, I'm not sure she'd confide in me."

Hawkman raised a finger in the air. "I think we're getting close to a few answers. It might be time to approach the other girls in this clique again."

"As we found out before, I'm afraid it's too late to get anything out of them. Cindy will have passed on all the information and those girls will be prepared for us. We'll get nothing new. More than likely, if they had the occult book we found in Sarah's and Cindy's room, it will have disappeared from their bookcases."

"Do you have any suggestions for our next move?"

"Yes."

"Let's hear it."

Jennifer leaned back in her chair and studied her husband's face. "We've got to push Cindy harder and somehow convince Rachel her daughter knows more than she's saying. The information the girl's holding inside could be very dangerous, not only for Sarah, but for Cindy and her friends."

Hawkman nodded. "I don't want you to do this alone. We'll go as a team."

"Excellent idea. It would verify the importance of what we're trying to get across."

Hawkman furrowed his brow. "Is there a Mr. Jackson?"

"I think so. Cindy made the comment about Sarah wishing she had a home like hers, where her parents still loved one another."

"Good. Think I'll make a call tomorrow and set up an appointment in the evening, so we can speak with both parents."

Jennifer pushed the recorder to the side and stood. "Let's get some nourishment down us. I want to do a little more thinking on what I got today, but my tummy's growling louder than my brain."

He chuckled and followed her to the kitchen. Miss Marple immediately dropped her toy bunny and trailed behind.

Jennifer pointed at their pet. "You get her some food, and I'll get our sandwiches warmed."

After they ate, Hawkman exited to his office and Jennifer went to her computer. She brought the machine out of sleep, then picked up the tape of Brenda Thompson and slipped it into the recorder. After listening to it again, she clicked on the girl's MySpace site, read the new comments, then went back as far as she could and reread the old ones. Since she'd met Brenda, the words took on a different meaning.

A couple of the comments indicated a riff over Jerry about the time Sarah disappeared. Jennifer kept reading and suddenly sat up straight. She quickly highlighted the words, copied, and pasted them on a separate sheet, then printed the message.

Her fingers flying over the keyboard, she went to Sarah's site and scanned the comments. Going back a week, she found what she wanted, and printed it out. Grabbing the freshly printed pages, she headed toward Hawkman's office.

CHAPTER NINETEEN

Hawkman glanced up as Jennifer burst into his office. "From the look on your face you must have found something mighty interesting."

"I did. Brenda and Sarah corresponded on MySpace through comments, which surprisingly weren't private. However, I think Brenda did it on purpose so her friends could see she wouldn't take guff from a nobody. Why Sarah didn't delete the comment I'm not sure, but she also might have wanted people to see her response to the snotty Miss Brenda." She handed him the first sheet. "This is from Brenda to Sarah."

He read aloud. "How dare you intrude on my turf. Just because Jerry and I had a little spat does not give you the right to go out with him. You're asking for lot of trouble."

Jennifer handed him the next sheet. "Here's Sarah's answer."

"You are not married to Jerry, and if he wishes to ask me out, it's none of your business. You have no right to tell me what to do." Hawkman rubbed his chin. "Meow! Appears we have a cat fight going on between these two girls. However, from what Jerry told me, his girlfriend is Brenda."

Jennifer pointed to the date. "These were written before Sarah disappeared. I don't like Brenda's comment about 'you're asking for a lot of trouble'."

Hawkman shrugged. "It's probably an empty threat."

"When you meet Brenda, I have a feeling you'll come to a different conclusion. She's no angel."

He leaned back and studied his wife. "You think she had anything to do with Sarah's disappearance? Remember, Sarah left of her own accord."

She let out a sigh. "I don't know. It's really rather baffling and maybe I'm grasping at straws."

He shifted forward and placed his arms on the desk. "I don't think she'd leave at the advice of Brenda. These are young people with heads full of mush. I doubt they could plan a kidnapping without leaving lots of evidence."

Jennifer picked up Miss Marple from the chair, sat down, and placed the cat in her lap. "You might be underestimating these kids. Depends on their ring leader, and how much fear they instill into their rivals. They can be vicious." Then she tapped the desk with her hand. "What's the girl's name who just disappeared?"

He glanced at his notes. "Patricia Riley."

"I'm going to do a little research on her." She stood, dropped Miss Marple back on the seat, picked up the printed sheets and glanced at the small hanging clock on the wall. "It's early yet, I'm going to call Sam."

Hawkman's head snapped up. "Why?"

"I want to talk to him about the younger set."

"He's been out of high school several years and won't know any of these kids."

"I realize that. But he might have some idea about what's happening."

He rubbed his chin. "I'm not following you."

She scooted the cat over with her hip and sat back down. "Even though Sam wouldn't have had anything to do with the occult, he might've heard rumors. This type of stuff hangs around in far corners and appeals to kids who are searching for a meaning to their life. It comes out of the darkness and feeds on those suffering from trauma or low self-esteem."

Hawkman shrugged. "I'm not sure he can be of much help, but it won't hurt to get his opinion."

She pointed to the phone. "Pick up when I reach him and listen to what he has to say."

"Okay."

Jennifer headed back to her work area, grabbed a note pad and pen from the computer table, then scooted onto a stool at the kitchen bar. She pushed the memory button for Sam's number and punched on the speaker phone when it rang.

"You've reached Sam Casey's pad. Leave a message."

"Hi, Sam, this is Jennifer. If you're there, pick up."

"Hey, how's it going?"

Jennifer laughed. "What are you doing, screening your calls and only answering when it's the right woman?"

"A good looking guy like me has to careful."

"Oh, my, you sound like someone else I know."

"Don't blame me," Hawkman said from the other phone.

"What's happening? You guys usually don't call unless something's going on."

"We need your input on something," Jennifer said. She explained and condensed the situation without mentioning names. We wondered if back when you were in high school, did this type of thing ever surface?"

"Are you both working on this case?"

Jennifer chuckled. "Yes, Hawkman finally allowed me to get involved since it dealt with young girls."

"Yeah, she begged until I had to give in," Hawkman interjected.

Sam guffawed. "To answer your question. Yes, the occult stuff did show up now and then. Not like a big organization or anything, more like a group of kids getting together and experimenting. Most of the time it's harmless. But it sounds like it might have taken on a little more steam in the case you've described."

"We're not sure it has anything to do with the missing girls, but a few clues have pointed in that direction," Jennifer said.

"It all depends on who's the leader and how bold he or she is. If it's someone who's popular or has some power over the group, it could be dangerous. When I was in high school, some of the nerds took it on, and the whole thing didn't gain much momentum. We all scoffed at them, and it soon disappeared."

"Are they usually discreet?"

"Oh, yeah. They swore to secrecy. No one wanted their parents to know what was happening, even the kids who weren't involved. They stick together, regardless of their involvement."

"I certainly don't remember you ever mentioning anything," Jennifer said.

"Naw, we didn't want to get anyone in trouble."

"You've pretty much answered my questions. Thanks so much."

"Want me to come home and see if I can infiltrate their group?"

Jennifer laughed. "Doubt they'd trust you. You're not the right age."

"Sure sounds like fun. If you need me, I'm just a phone call away."

"Thank you, son, but I believe Jennifer and I can man the fort. If we need your help we'll definitely give you a ring."

After they hung up, Jennifer could hear Hawkman chuckling. She went to the computer and typed in what she figured Patricia Riley's MySpace address might be. The sparse and plain page appeared with nothing more than a picture of a lovely girl, with very long, silky brown hair, sad blue eyes, and a beautiful milky complexion. She had a solemn expression, with a slight hint of a smile at the corner of her lips. Only a few comments sprinkled her page.

Jennifer noted the girl hadn't checked her profile in approximately two weeks. Pulling off the picture, she put it onto a blank page and printed it out. She lifted the photo from the tray and studied the face. Her first impression leaned toward a troubled person. She strolled into Hawkman's office and showed him the picture.

"Is this the girl who's missing?"

He nodded. "Yeah. I should have had Williams give me a copy, but from what I remember, it's her. It looks like the same photo he had in the file. Her long hair caught my eye."

"She appears very unhappy."

Cocking his head, he studied the imprint. "Maybe she has crooked teeth and doesn't want to put on a big smile."

Jennifer rolled her eyes. "It's her orbs I noticed."

"Really, you think they look sad?"

She snatched the sheet from his desk. "You see why you need me on this case? You can't see the telltale signs of youth depression."

He glanced up and smiled. "You're right. Right now I'm more interested in finding Sarah Willis, unless you find a connection between the two girls. Now, tell me what you thought about Sam's analysis?"

"It makes sense. I still go back to my thought on pressing Cindy for more answers."

"Good. Tomorrow, I'll call and set up an appointment. So keep your evenings free, until I know which day."

She nodded and went back to her computer.

CHAPTER TWENTY

Sarah's eyes flew open and she bolted to a sitting position. The sound of the chains rattling and the grating of the hinges on the heavy wooden door sent chills up her spine. Even though fully dressed in a sweatsuit, she pulled the flimsy coverlet up to her shoulders and stared at the entry. The flickering candle cast strange shadows across the rustic walls as the girl in a black robe, with a hood framing her face, entered the room. She pushed a girl with long flowing brown hair ahead of her, then pointed to the cot next to Sarah.

"There's your bed."

"I don't want to stay here. I want to go home," the girl cried.

"Too bad, my dear. You wanted a safe haven. You're in it." The female in the robe let out a sharp shrill laugh. "Enjoy your stay." She placed the candle on the stand against the wall, and shut the heavy door, rattling the bonds as she set the lock.

Sarah again shuddered at the sound, then studied her new roommate.

The girl slowly moved her head back and forth as she scanned the contents of the unfamiliar room. Her big blue solemn eyes glistened with tears, as her gaze fell on her companion's face.

Sarah threw her legs over the edge of the cot and pushed her feet into a pair of scuffs. "I know you. You're Patricia Riley from our school. What are you doing here?"

"I ran away from home."

"How'd you end up at this place?"

"A friend told me I'd be safe here until I decided what I wanted to do."

"Did this so called buddy tell you there's no running water or electricity, and you'd be a prisoner?"

Patricia frowned. Clutching what looked like a set of linens and dragging a small suitcase, she stumbled to the extra cot, and sat down. "No."

"You may be safe from sex perverts, but this place is full of strange people."

"Where are we? It was so dark, I couldn't see a thing, but I know we took many turns, drove forever and climbed mighty high, because my ears popped."

Sarah sighed. "I wish I could tell you. The same thing happened to me. All I know is, we're a long way from home."

Patricia reached into the bag on the floor, removed a large hair pin which she put between her teeth, then twisted her long hair, which hung below her buttocks, into a bun, and secured it. "How long have you been here?"

"I think about a week. I've lost track of time."

"Who was the girl who brought me in here?"

Sarah stood and walked toward the window, where the moon beams played across her body through the bars and made her look like she had on a jail garb. She pointed out the window. "I don't know her by name, but from what I can tell, there are several hooded girls. When they leave here they always head toward the shack over by the barn."

"You mean we're alone in this building?"

"I think so. I never hear any movement once they've left me."

"Don't you get scared?"

"Sometimes, when I hear eery chanting. One night I could smell smoke and looked out the window. They'd built a small bonfire in the middle of the field and were dancing around it naked." Sarah shivered. "It's like they're worshiping the devil. I sure don't want them to drag me out there."

Patricia's eyes grew wide. "You're kidding?"

She shook her head. "It's the truth. I hope you're not into that type of stuff."

"No way!"

"Good. At least I'll have someone to talk to."

"Is there no way to get help?"

"No. They rendered my laptop and cell phone useless when they removed the batteries." She whirled around and faced Patricia. "Do you have a cell phone?"

Patricia bowed her head. "No, nor a laptop. I have an older model desktop computer at home. Mom can't afford the extra luxuries."

"Dang it. Getting help just went out the window."

"Why can't we go home, if we wish?"

Sarah slowly turned her gaze on Patricia. "Because someone wants us here. I've been told I'd never make it down the mountain alive on foot because of the wild animals."

Her blue eyes clouded with fear. "Who told you this?"

"Those strange girls," Sarah said, her shoulders drooping.

"I'm scared." Patricia said, hugging herself. "Where's the bathroom?"

Sarah gestured toward a draped bucket in the far corner. "You'll have to use the pail during the night."

Patricia's expression changed to horror. "You can't mean it?"

"Sorry. You'll have to get used to it. Don't worry, I won't watch." Sarah turned her back as Patricia walked slowly toward the grimy pail.

"This is gross."

"Try to make the best of it, it's all we've got."

When she finished, she strolled back to the cot and sat down.

Sarah glanced at the flickering light. "We better get your bed made before the candle goes out."

"Don't you have any more?"

"Oh, there's plenty of candles, just no matches. Guess they figure I might try burning the place down to escape."

Patricia smiled for the first time. "Not a bad idea."

They hurried getting the linens on the extra cot and were soon tucked into their beds before the flame sputtered and went out.

Sarah turned toward her new roommate. "We can talk at night, but during the day we have to be careful, because I'm sure the walls have ears."

"What do you do about water?"

"This place must have a well because I saw a pump in the kitchen. They bring me a bucket full every morning. The water tastes good, but is extremely cold."

"How do you keep clean?"

Sarah chuckled. "Remember, we're prisoners. There's no electricity or gas, only a big black iron wood burning stove in the kitchen. The witches know how to stoke it, and one night they brought me a warm pail of water and told me to use it for my bath. The girl left a tattered washcloth, hand towel and a small bar of soap."

"Do they do this every night?"

"No, the rest of the time the water's as cold as ice."

"Oh, great. How about food?"

"Occasionally, they bring hot soup. Most of the time it's peanut butter between crackers, or a canned meat sandwich on stale bread, and a piece of fruit with water."

"Is the kitchen in this building?"

"Yes, you'll see it when they let us go for a walk."

"Maybe we could escape."

"There's always a couple of girls who follow. Now, with two of us, they might have a few more, in case we get any bright ideas."

"What would they do to us if we tried?"

"Who knows, maybe burn us at the stake."

Patricia pulled the sheet over her head. "This is a weird place. I sure don't want to stay here."

"Maybe between the two of us, we can figure a way to get out."

"Someone must have a car. They have to get groceries up here to feed us."

"Who knows. I've watched out the window and listened, but haven't seen or heard a vehicle."

"Did you hear them coming with me?"

Sarah raised her head. "Come to think of it, no, I didn't. I was about half asleep. Did you get out of the car in front of this place?"

"Yes, I stepped up on a long wooden porch, then came into what looked like a living room, then they turned me over to the hooded ones, who brought me straight in here."

"Who's they?"

"The two guys who brought me."

"Do you know their names?"

"Yes."

CHAPTER TWENTY-ONE

The next day at the office, Hawkman opened the folder on Sarah Willis and scanned the notes he'd added from Jennifer's investigation. Before focusing on fitting things together, he decided to call the Jackson home and set up an appointment. Cindy answered the phone, and instead of identifying himself, he asked for her mother. He jerked the phone away from his ear when she yelled, "Mom it's for you."

Punching on the speaker phone, he picked up a pencil and dragged a paper pad to the center of the desk.

"Hello."

"Mrs. Jackson, this is Tom Casey. My wife and I would like to have a meeting with you and your husband."

"Is this about Sarah Willis?"

"Yes."

"Your wife really upset my daughter when she came by."

"She told me. We feel Cindy is holding back information, and we'd like to discuss this issue. Maybe a meeting without your daughter present would be best."

"I don't know. I'm really confused about this whole thing."

"I feel it imperative we talk. The police are very interested in this case. I think you and your husband would be more comfortable speaking with us rather than a detective."

"Let me confer with Dave and I'll call you back."

He could hear the anxiety in her voice. "Sounds fine."

After hanging up, he returned to the file and went over Jennifer's information. He studied the picture of Brenda Thompson, then booted up the computer. Typing in the girl's MySpace address, he examined every word on her site.

He didn't particularly like what he read or saw, but kids were different nowadays and much more brazen. This little gal seemed extremely audacious, and from what Jennifer had related, spoiled rotten. He jotted down her address and decided he needed to meet this girl in person.

Knowing he probably wouldn't hear from Mrs. Jackson for a couple of hours, he decided the best time to try to catch the sassy Ms. Brenda Thompson at home would be early afternoon. When he climbed into his vehicle, he dropped the briefcase onto the passenger seat, then removed his shoulder holster and shoved it under the driver's side.

Jennifer had given him a thorough description of the home, so he had no trouble spotting it when he turned onto the street. He parked in front, picked up his valise, locked the vehicle, and strolled up the cobblestone sidewalk.

A servant in a white uniform opened the front door and quickly put her hand to her heart when she glanced up at Hawkman. He had to suppress a smile as his eye-patch caused some women to react in such a manner.

"What you want?" she asked in broken English.

"I'd like to speak to Brenda Thompson."

"What's your name?"

"Tom Casey, private investigator."

She frowned. "You police?"

"No, private investigator."

"Oh," she said, nodding. "I'll see if Brenda's home."

She closed the door, leaving Hawkman standing on the front landing.

Several minutes passed before a tanned, slim woman appeared at the entry. She had peroxided blonde hair pulled into a side pony tail and was clad in shorts and a cotton blouse. Her green eyes stared at him suspiciously. "I'm told you're a private investigator."

"Yes," Hawkman said, showing his badge. "I'm assuming you're Mrs. Thompson."

She examined the card, then handed it back. "Yes, I'm Brenda's mother. I've heard of you. What is it you want from my daughter?"

"I'd like to ask her some questions about Sarah Willis."

"Brenda hardly knows the girl. Sarah isn't in her group of friends."

Hawkman could feel the hair on his neck bristle. "I don't care about her group of friends; I have some questions I'd like answered."

"I'll see if she has time to talk to you. My daughter's very busy."

His jaw tightened. "Mrs. Thompson, I'd advise your daughter to take the time to talk with me, or I'll send the police over to bring her to the station. She might not be very happy with such an arrangement."

She narrowed her eyes. "How dare you threaten me."

"I'm not threatening you, Mrs. Thompson. I'm telling you the facts. Sarah Willis has been missing for almost a week. We need to talk with people who had any contact with her. We have reason to believe your daughter spoke to Sarah about a week before she disappeared."

"I'll get her."

She turned abruptly, leaving the door open, and disappeared down a granite floored hallway, her heels clicking to the tune of a very brisk stride. Shortly she returned with her daughter.

Brenda's green eyes narrowed. "Hello, Mr. Casey. I met your wife the other day."

Mrs. Thompson intervened. "Are you going to leave the gentlemen on the front porch? Have you lost your manners?"

"Of course not. Please come in, Mr. Casey."

Brenda led the way down the hallway, then opened the large double doors to a magnificent study. The walls were lined with oak bookshelves and filled with more volumes than a library. "Please have a seat," she said, motioning toward a set of leather study chairs around a large highly polished wooden table. She turned to her mother. "You don't have to stay. I can talk to Mr. Casey without your help."

Mrs. Thompson backed out and stood in the hallway for

a moment, fingering the necklace around her throat. Then she pulled the door shut.

Hawkman's gaze quickly took in as many book titles as his eye could scan in the few moments he had before taking a seat. When Brenda sat down opposite him, he almost gasped aloud at the transformation of the girl's expression. Her green eyes took on an evil glow and she'd set her mouth in a firm line.

"I told your wife I hated Sarah Willis. That still stands. I have nothing to add."

"Did you speak personally with Sarah before she disappeared?"

"Yes. I told her to keep away from my boyfriend."

"What made you think she'd intruded on your relationship?"

"She went out with him."

Hawkman looked her in the eye. "Did he ask her out?"

"What difference does it make? She was trodding on my property."

"You married to the boy?"

She slapped a hand on the table. "Of course not, but the whole school knows he's mine."

"How does he feel about it?"

She glared at him. "He agrees."

"I see. Do you know a Patricia Riley?"

"Yes. She's a nobody."

"Does your boyfriend like long hair?"

Her face flushed in anger. "What boy doesn't? Not many can grow hair past their buttocks like that little bitch."

"Does it bother you she has beautiful hair?"

"Why are we talking about her?"

"Because she's been reported missing."

He detected a slight curve of a grin at the corners of her lips. "Really?"

Hawkman reached down into his briefcase and brought out the picture of the Pentacle Pendant. "Have you ever seen one of these?"

She flipped a hand in the air. "Oh, yeah. It's a witch's pendant."

"Do you own one?"

"Why would I? I'm not a witch."

Hawkman slipped the picture back into his briefcase and rose. "It's been interesting."

"Well, I hope it's the last time I have to talk to you or your wife."

Hawkman tilted his head and stared into her face. "Don't bet on it."

She stood, stuck her nose in the air and stomped toward the doors. "I hope you can find your way out. I've got things to do."

"No problem. I'm a big boy."

She tossed her head angrily and stormed out of the room.

CHAPTER TWENTY-TWO

Hawkman left the Thompson's castle, unimpressed with its occupants. He knew he'd flustered Brenda, and felt good about not falling for her sharp gazes and curt mouth. Driving away from the house, he realized what Jennifer meant, and was happy he'd turned on the recorder to catch the inflections of the girl's voice. His gut told him this young woman could be dangerous. It all depended on how much power she held over her peers or whether they saw through the hard shell she dared them to penetrate. Interesting thought.

When he arrived back at the office, he found a message from Mrs. Jackson, suggesting eight o'clock tonight would be a good time for them to meet, since Cindy had a date. He quickly called Jennifer and asked if she'd have time to drive into Medford. She did, and would meet him at his office around seven-thirty. Hawkman then contacted Mrs. Jackson and confirmed the meeting.

He'd just hung up, when the phone rang, and he jabbed on the speaker phone.

"Tom Casey, private investigator."

"Hello, Mr. Casey, Greg Willis checking in. I'm on the road and can't get Sarah off my mind. Have you made any headway in finding my daughter?"

"We're working on it night and day. So far we haven't found her."

Greg groaned. "Dear God, each day is agony. I hope and pray we find her alive."

"I've got a question for you."

"Yeah, what's that."

"Did Sarah ever mention witchcraft to you?"

"What! Did you say witchcraft?"

"Yes."

"Hell, no. I'd have blown a gasket. When did this enter the picture?"

"We're investigating every avenue. Did you ever see your daughter wear a necklace with a star pendant?"

"Definitely not. Most of the time, she wore a small gold cross I bought her a couple of years ago for her birthday. She loved it."

"Have you talked with your wife lately?"

"I call her every day, in hopes she'll have some news. All I hear are moans and groans about how Sarah planned this to punish us for divorcing."

"What do you think, Mr. Willis?"

"I can't believe it, because I don't feel in my heart Sarah would be gone this long without letting us know she's okay."

"You'll be the first I contact if we get a break in the case."

"Thanks."

Hawkman hung up and exhaled. He couldn't imagine the anxiety the man must feel with his only daughter disappearing without a trace.

He opened the Willis file and made some notes on his visit with Brenda. Reading through them again, he could see holes in the investigation, and decided his next probe would include the other three girls in the clique, along with another trip to Jerry Olson's when his father had gone to work.

Rolling his chair over to Sarah's computer, he flipped it on. While it booted up, he reached into the briefcase to remove the notepad where he'd written possible passwords. His hand brushed against the rural road map Jennifer had found on Sarah's bookcase. He pulled it out and placed it on the desk for further study.

He opened the small notebook and went down the list, trying each word on one of several files he'd had no luck opening. Just about to give up, he tried the last catalogued group of letters. The folder popped open. He breathed a sigh of relief and examined the contents. To his dismay, it appeared full of school assignments dealing with short stories. Instead of closing it, he decided to send a copy of each of the narratives to his personal computer at home and read them later. They might contain revealing clues. Obviously, Sarah didn't want anyone reading her work, since she'd locked the folder.

After he'd sent the last one through cyberspace, he glanced up when Jennifer popped in the door carrying a sack and balancing a couple of sodas on a cardboard place holder.

"Hi, hon. You're early."

"I figured you hadn't eaten, so I stopped and grabbed a couple of chicken sandwiches."

"Great. I'll tell you what happened today while we munch."

She scooted a chair up to the desk and dealt out the food. He told her about his experience with Brenda Thompson. "She's one brassy teenager. Get an earful of this." He turned on the recorder.

Jennifer listened, then flopped back in the chair. "This girl has some serious problems."

"I agree. You should have seen her demeanor change when her mother left the room. She looked like a little witch. Oh, and she might well wear green contacts. However, her mother has very green eyes too."

"Maybe they both wear them."

Hawkman nodded. "Very probable. You know what's running through my mind?"

"No. Usually I can tell."

"I'm thinking about having her followed for a couple of days. Just to keep tabs on this girl. I imagine she has all kinds of freedom, and no telling where she might lead us."

"Hmmm," Jennifer said, thoughtfully. "Let's first talk with Cindy's folks and see if they come up with anything tangible. I've also been thinking about what you said the other night regarding the other girls in this little group. I think you're right. It might be productive to interview them, as they could be getting nervous about Sarah."

"I've already got that on my schedule." Hawkman glanced at his watch. "It's about time to leave for the Jacksons'. I'd rather arrive a few minutes late, than get there before Cindy leaves on her date. I'd prefer her not to know we're questioning her parents."

"Let's just hope Rachel hasn't told her."

"You think she might?"

She shrugged. "Hard to say."

"You have any particular questions you want to ask?"

"Yes, I'll see how things go and intervene at the appropriate time." She gathered up the food wrappings, threw them into the waste basket and washed her hands before they left.

Driving down the street, Hawkman filled her in on Greg Willis' call. "I'm surprised the man can concentrate on his work, with this hanging over his head. He's worried sick and scared to death his daughter won't be found alive. I really feel for him, especially when I don't have anything positive to report."

Jennifer nodded. "His ex-wife isn't very supportive either. He certainly doesn't need her whining about Sarah leaving on her own accord. I'm afraid if I were in Cathy's shoes, you wouldn't find me moping around the house. I'd be questioning Sarah's girlfriends, making posters with her picture on them and plastering them all over the neighborhood. Anything to bring attention to the fact my daughter has been missing for almost a week. I really don't understand the woman."

"Everyone handles trauma differently. We're seeing yet another method."

She shook her head. "It sure doesn't seem healthy."

Hawkman pulled up in front of the Jacksons' home and checked his watch. "Perfect. It's five after eight. Let's hope Cindy's date arrived on time." He flipped on the recorder in his pocket as they strolled up the sidewalk.

Rachel Jackson answered the door and led them into the living room where her husband stood in front of the brick fireplace. Dressed in a dark navy blue suit, he'd removed his tie, and appeared quite casual. His thick black curly hair hugged his head in a neat cut with sideburns showing a tinge of gray.

About five foot ten, and slight of build, he held out his hand to Hawkman.

"Hello, Mr. Casey, I'm Dave Jackson, Cindy's father."

"Nice to meet you, Mr. Jackson." Hawkman turned to Jennifer. "This is my wife, Jennifer."

After the introductions, Rachel served coffee and they sat down on the couches facing one another.

Dave leaned forward, placing his arms on his thighs. "Mrs. Casey, I want to get this story straight. Rachel tells me you spotted a book about the occult in my daughter's room, questioned her about it, and it made Cindy very upset."

Jennifer nodded. "That's true. I didn't expect her reaction, and I don't think Rachel did either."

"Before we go on. Is there any word on Sarah Willis?"

Hawkman shook his head. "No."

Dave grimaced. "Maybe what we've discovered in grilling Cindy will help. She has given us a few names which left us quite surprised. We've decided, instead of going to the police, we'd tell you first, since you're involved in trying to find Sarah. We'll follow your advice, if you think it's necessary to furnish this information to the authorities."

Hawkman studied the man's face and knew he had upsetting news. "I appreciate your confidence and am assuming you've warned Cindy not to talk about this."

"Yes, she's very scared," Rachel said. "And won't be telling anyone."

Furrowing his brow, Hawkman stared at Rachel. "What do you mean she's scared? Has she been threatened?"

"In so many words, yes. As have her friends. I'm going to let my husband tell you about our conversation with Cindy. He's much better about getting things in order than I am."

All heads turned toward Dave.

CHAPTER TWENTY-THREE

After Hawkman and Jennifer spent two hours talking to the Jacksons, they rode in silence to the office, both trying to digest what they'd just learned. He pulled into the lot in front and parked next to Jennifer's van. Turning off the engine, he faced her. "Do you want to discuss this now or wait until we get back to the house?"

She let out a sigh. "It's late. I need to sort this stuff out in my brain before I can really come to any conclusion. The drive home will give me quiet time to think."

"I feel the same way. The office is locked, and I have everything I need, so no reason for me to go upstairs. I'll follow you."

She jumped out, climbed into her vehicle and they caravanned home. Once there, Hawkman went out to the aviary and tended to the falcon, Pretty Girl. She squawked and scolded for several seconds as he replaced her food and water.

"I know, I know. I'll take you out to hunt soon."

After Jennifer took care of the cat's needs, they settled in the living room with a cocktail. Miss Marple greeted her masters by rubbing her chin against their shoes, then spread out on the floor between the chairs.

"Your pet is getting smarter all the time," Hawkman said, leaning over and stroking the feline's back. "She seems to sense we don't want her on our laps right now."

Jennifer smiled. "Of course. She's a female."

He suppressed a smile. "You think it makes a difference?"

Jennifer waved a hand at him. "Let's not talk about Miss Marple right now. What's your reaction to the story the Jacksons told."

Hawkman leaned back in his chair and pushed up the foot rest. "I believed it. I think we've got a clan of young male and female witches pushing their weight around. They're scaring the other kids half to death by threatening to cast spells on them."

"How dangerous do you think this can get?"

"Damn hairy. We might even have to call in the police."

"Do you feel Brenda has so much control, she could do damage?"

"We've both met her. What do you think?"

"She's plenty arrogant, but from Sarah's comment on the website, I'm not sure she's got the control she'd like to have." Jennifer scooted forward. "What's your take on the situation?"

"I think there's an adult involved."

She frowned. "Really?"

"Yep."

"Why would someone get into witchcraft and take these kids along?"

"I've done a little research, and they might be a good witch, who thinks what their doing is okay and innocently pulled them in. Then it may have spiraled out of his or her control."

"Wouldn't the person report it if these young witches started abducting people?"

"Not particularly."

"Why?"

"It would cause too much attention and could destroy their reputations, businesses or whatever he or she is involved with in real life."

"Wow," Jennifer said, flopping back in her seat. "I never thought about an adult being the ringleader of a group of teenage witches."

"I'm not sure; I'm only guessing. The person might not even know what the kids are doing when out of his or her sight. When Sam told us this witchcraft stuff had been around for a long time, but never developed into anything, it made me wonder how Brenda could muster up the nerve to threaten Cindy and her friends with spells. There has to be a clan big enough to show it has power. My thinking is, she's displaying her nerve so she can climb the witch's ranking ladder and become a bigwig in the circle."

"What about Jerry? Dave Jackson mentioned him and said the girls were also told never to date him, as he was Brenda's property."

Hawkman nodded. "She's very possessive. I'm fearful Sarah has suffered her wrath because she actually went out with him. I'm also afraid, Jerry might have admired Patricia's beautiful hair, and she's also become a victim."

Jennifer's eyes grew wide. "A victim of what? Surely Brenda wouldn't hurt them."

Hawkman dropped the foot rest and stood. "Who knows what this girl is capable of doing? She's insanely jealous over Jerry." He shrugged. "Enough to kill? I'm not sure. My gut tells me we've got to move quickly. Tomorrow is crunch time."

She ran her hands across her face. "You've given me so much to think about, I don't think I can sleep."

"I'm going to the computer. I've got some reading to do before I hit the sack." He picked up the briefcase and carried it back to the home office. Something nagged him to read the short stories from Sarah's locked folder. Once the computer booted up, he located the files in the incoming mail and opened them up to sort by date. He read the oldest first, and found it very sobering: a young girl pouring her heart out about her sadness in experiencing her parent's divorce. She seemed to understand why they'd separated, but it didn't help.

Hawkman made a new folder, placed the first story inside, then pulled the next one forward. The next three gave him insight on the growing animosity between mother and daughter. He got up and walked into the living room where he saw Jennifer at her work center. The flickering light of the monitor showed her in deep concentration. He turned away, hesitant about interrupting.

"What is it?" she asked.

He twisted around on his heel and stepped forward. "I think you've mentioned this before, but do mothers and daughters have a rough time getting along during the adolescence years?"

"It's a stage young girls go through competing for the father's attention. They're jealous of their mothers. Why?"

"What if the father isn't present in the household?"

"I think the girl would still be at odds with her mother, just because she's female. Are you talking about Sarah?"

He twirled the pencil in his hand. "Yeah, I finally unlocked one of the files and it contained short stories she'd written. I can see why she didn't want anyone reading them; they're full of emotion on how she feels toward her mother. I've only gotten through four of the ten. So her mood may change." He raised the pencil in the air. "Oh, yes, there's something else I want to get your thoughts on."

"Okay, I'm game."

"Remember the rural map you found in Sarah's bookcase?"

"Yeah."

"Any idea why she'd have such a map?"

Jennifer frowned. "No. That has me baffled."

"I'm going to trace what I can make out of the erased line and see where it leads."

Jennifer crooked her forefinger at him. "Come here, I want to show you something."

He walked around behind her.

"Looks like we've upset Brenda." She pointed to a comment on Cindy's Myspace site.

Hawkman read it out loud. "If the private investigator and his wife come to see you, beware of a wagging tongue. You could get yourself into deep trouble."

"According to the date, it's just been posted. So more than likely Cindy hasn't even seen the note or she'd have probably deleted it."

"Wonder how many threats Brenda deals out in a day? How about the other girls in Sarah's group. Are they getting them too?"

"Hold on and I'll check."

Hawkman rocked back and forth on his boots as Jennifer clicked from one site to the other. They discovered all three girls had received the same threatening message.

"I don't like Brenda's aggressive behavior," he said. "She's getting bolder. I think we better keep a closer eye on her."

"What do you propose we do?"

"I'd like you to do some surveillance while I go speak with these girls."

"What if she recognizes my van?"

"It won't matter. Stay on the public streets and follow her if she leaves the house. Stay out of sight as much as you can, but don't worry about getting caught. There's not anything she can do, but cast a spell on you."

Jennifer grinned. "I'll do it."

"We'll keep in touch through our cell phones, so make sure yours is charged. I'll read the rest of Sarah's stories tomorrow night. I'm bushed and It's been a long day."

"I have a feeling they're not going to get any shorter."

CHAPTER TWENTY-FOUR

Hawkman and Jennifer rolled out of bed early Saturday morning.

"I've got to fill up with gas before spying on Brenda. Nothing like getting involved in a long chase on empty," Jennifer said, gulping down the last of her coffee.

Hawkman grabbed his briefcase off the counter, unplugged his cell phone and pushed it into the pouch on his belt. "I've got to stop by the office."

They grabbed a kiss at the front door, then proceeded to their respective vehicles parked in the garage. Jennifer waved as she backed out and drove down the driveway. Hawkman followed and they soon left Copco Lake behind.

Once in Medford, they parted ways as Jennifer pulled into a gas station. Hawkman parked in the alley behind his office, and took the stairs two at a time. The baker had his ovens pumped up and the aroma of baked goods swirled around his nose. A bowl of dry cereal hadn't satisfied his appetite and the donuts smelled delicious. He resisted the temptation, as he didn't have time to enjoy a bear claw this morning.

The Willis file still lay on his desk, along with the rural map he'd placed there yesterday. He shoved the map and the information he needed on the three girls into the briefcase, then slipped the recorder into his jacket pocket and left. Saturday tended to be a day of shopping and errands. He hoped he'd catch the people he needed to see at home. Since he recognized the streets where these girls lived, he didn't need the GPS. They were all within walking distance of the Willis household.

Janet Ross would be the first. He pulled up in front of an older, but modest, well-kept home. The garage door was closed, so he couldn't tell if anyone might be home. He walked up to the front door and rang the bell.

A matronly redheaded woman, dressed in slacks, and a flowered shirt, with a dishtowel draped over her shoulder, answered the door. "Can I help you?"

"Are you Mrs. Ross?"

"Yes."

Hawkman introduced himself, and showed his badge. "I'm investigating the disappearance of Sarah Willis and I understand Janet is one of her good friends. I'd like to speak with her if I may."

Mrs. Ross' face softened. "Is there any news on Sarah?"

"No, but we're working on several leads and hope to find her soon."

"That's good news. I don't know how Janet could help, but she's at her dancing class right now." She glanced at her watch. "Oh, my, how time flies. She should be home any minute, if you'd like to wait."

"Thank you. I think I will, as it's important I speak with her."

"Won't you come in?" She stepped aside and Hawkman entered the house. His nose twitched at the delicious aroma. "Whatever you're cooking sure smells good."

Her merry laugh made him smile. "I have two ovens so you're getting the mingled odors of a roast and a chocolate cake."

"It definitely caused my stomach to growl."

She motioned toward a very homey living room with overstuffed furniture. "Have a seat while I check on their progress and I'll get us a cup of coffee."

"Thank you, Mrs. Ross," Hawkman said, as he sank into the plush couch.

"Please, call me Sally," she said, as she carried a couple of mugs of coffee into the room. She set one in front of him on the marble coffee table, then carried her cup to the opposite chair and placed it on a circular shelf around a light pole.

"Now, Mr. Casey, what help do you think Janet might be in locating Sarah?"

He took a sip of the coffee. "The main thing is finding out from your daughter if Sarah by any chance gave any clues as to where she might go if she ran away. Also, maybe she could enlighten me on Sarah's demeanor the week before she disappeared."

About the time Sally started to respond, a tall lanky redheaded girl, dressed in leotards, bounded in the front door, and halted abruptly when she spotted Hawkman on the couch.

"Hi, Mom," she said, taking a step backwards as she stared at their guest.

"Come in here dear, I want you to meet someone."

When Sally introduced Hawkman, a flash of fear crossed Janet's face and her blue eyes opened wide.

"You've heard about me, haven't you?" Hawkman said.

"Yes," she gulped.

"You've also been threatened, if you talk to me."

Janet shot a look at her mother, whose mouth had dropped open with a puzzled expression. "What's he talking about? Threatened you with what?"

"Why don't you sit down, so we can ease your mother's mind," Hawkman said.

About that time the buzzer on the oven rang loudly. Mrs. Ross jumped up. "Don't say a thing until I get back. I just need to take the cake out."

Janet eased down on the fireplace hearth, biting her lower lip, her gaze nervously shooting from the kitchen door to Hawkman.

Mrs. Ross quickly returned to her seat. "Okay, what's this all about?"

Hawkman turned toward her. "In our quest to find Sarah, we've stumbled across some very strange behavior among a selected few of the high school students."

"What do you mean?"

"It appears we have a clutch of witches among us."

Sally put her hand to her mouth and stared at her daughter. "Are you involved in this, Janet?"

He glanced at the girl whose gaze was downcast, and tears trickled down her cheeks. "No."

"During the investigation, I've come to the conclusion Janet is only guilty of not speaking up."

Wiping her hands across her face, Mrs. Ross sighed. "I can't believe you'd keep something like this from us."

Janet put her hands in front her of and waved them up and down. "Mom, if I'd talked, Nikki, Cindy, Ann and me might end up wherever they took Sarah. Brenda told us we'd be in serious trouble if we told anyone."

Mrs. Ross jerked her head around. "Brenda Thompson!"

Janet nodded.

"Good grief, how could you fall victim to such a spoiled brat?"

The girl yanked a tissue from her pocket and blew her nose. "She runs the school."

"The girl's a brazen little hussy and you know it. You've told me yourself how you can't stand the sight of her."

"Tell me," Hawkman intervened. "You said you could end up where they took Sarah. What did you mean by such a statement?"

"Brenda let it be known she would cast a spell on all of us and then take us to the hills to join Sarah."

"Where in the hills?"

She shrugged. "I don't know."

"You believed her?"

"Yeah. She's scary when she looks at you with those evil green eyes and waves that witch pendant in front of your nose. And Sarah had just disappeared."

"Did you try to call Sarah on her cell?"

"Yes, but it never went through. We tried to contact her on the laptop and never got a response."

"What if I told you we suspect Sarah left home on her own accord."

Janet stared at him. "I'm not sure I'd believe it. She and her mom fought a lot, but she really loved her parents. It made her very unhappy they'd divorced. I don't think she'd leave and not come back. Unless…"

Hawkman frowned. "Unless what?"

Janet tilted her head back and blew out a stream of air. "Unless Jerry talked her into going with him."

"Are you speaking of Jerry Olson?"

She nodded. "He really liked Sarah, and Brenda got so jealous, we thought she might kill Jerry. She threatened us all with spells if we didn't stay away from her guy. Sarah told her off and that really sent Brenda into a tailspin. She wouldn't leave Sarah alone."

"What did she do?"

"All kinds of ugly stuff. Sarah told us she walked out on her front porch one day, and almost stepped in a huge pile of dog poop. Later Brenda asked her how she liked the new covering she'd put down at their entry. Another time Brenda followed us in her fancy convertible as we walked home from the bowling alley. Then she drove up alongside us real slow like she wanted to say something. Instead, she aimed a plastic catsup bottle and squirted it all over us." Janet dropped her head into her hands. "She's evil, and when she finds out I've blabbed, there's no telling what she'll do to me."

Hawkman stood. "Janet, she's not going to do anything to you, nor your friends. If she threatens you again, notify your mother, and she'll let me know." He handed Mrs. Ross a business card. "Call me immediately."

Sally escorted Hawkman to the door. "I'm still in shock."

He turned. "Don't be too hard on your daughter. Just keep an eye on her until we have this thing settled. Brenda Thompson could be dangerous."

CHAPTER TWENTY-FIVE

Jennifer topped off the gas tank, cleaned the windshield, then drove to the Thompsons' home. She found a shady spot under a large oak tree about a half block from the house, which gave her a good view of the front door and garage area. Expecting a long and boring day, she'd come prepared with a couple of mystery books, a tablet to write notes, plenty of water and a sandwich she'd grabbed from the shop next door to the station. The fanny pack containing her pistol bit into her waist, so she unsnapped the band, and placed it on the passenger seat.

She stuck a ball cap on her short hair, pushed on a pair of sunglasses, then picked up one of the paperbacks. Before she had a chance to read the first paragraph, a movement from the house caught her eye. The garage door slid open and a slick looking Saab convertible backed out. Jennifer picked up her binoculars and focused in on the young driver, who had stopped the car and let the top fold down before she continued into the street.

Tossing the book aside, Jennifer started the engine, and when Brenda rolled past, pulled into the street and pursued the silver colored Saab. She doubted the girl noticed her, but it wouldn't be long before she'd get suspicious, depending upon how often she checked the rearview mirror. Jennifer noted they were heading out of town, and hoped Hawkman would call soon. The thought had no more passed through her mind than the cell rang.

"Hello."

She listened for a moment, then smiled. "Yes, this is your one and only girlfriend, driving toward the country." After giving him the direction where Brenda was leading her, she listened to what he'd found out. "Wow! You had some interview. The next two will more than likely be comparable because Janet will get on the phone to her two buddies and prepare them for your visit. Where one goes, the others follow." Before she hung up, she warned him he might not be able to reach her if she ended up in the hills. He cautioned her to be careful.

Brenda had pulled ahead about a half mile, but Jennifer had her in sight and decided not to speed up. She figured no sense in alerting the girl she was being followed. They traveled over curvy roads constantly climbing for about forty minutes when Brenda suddenly pulled to the side of the road. Jennifer passed her and went around a curve out of sight before pulling over. She waited for several minutes and the girl never showed.

Quickly making a U-turn, Jennifer headed back the way she'd come and to her amazement, saw no sign of the convertible. Unless Brenda had turned around and headed back down the hill, the only other road she could have taken was the one dirt road leading up the mountain. Did she dare chance going up it with her van and end up getting stuck on high center? Her better judgment told her to head back and get Hawkman with his four-wheel drive vehicle.

Disgusted with herself for letting Brenda fake her out, she drove back down the mountain to check the house and see if by some chance she'd returned home. When Jennifer reached the address, she cruised by, only to discover the garage door open with no sign of Brenda's car. She hit the steering wheel with her hand. "Dang it. The little twerp outsmarted me."

Even though the shade had disappeared, Jennifer parked in the same spot and waited for Hawkman's call. He contacted her shortly and told her to meet him at the office.

Patricia Riley sat on her cot in the gloomy room. She hugged her jean clad legs, and rested her chin on her knees as she gazed at her roommate. "We've got to get out of this hell hole."

Sarah stood silently looking out the barred window. Suddenly, she straightened and frowned.

"What's the matter?" Patricia said, dropping her feet to the floor and moving to her new friend's side.

Sarah pointed toward the barn. "Something's going on. The witches are building a wood pile."

"What do you think it means?"

Taking a quick intake of breath, she gasped. "Look. You see the witch in the white hooded robe?"

"Yes. What's she doing swinging her arms and dancing in a circle?"

"She's the head honcho. Don't you recognize her?"

Patricia squinted as she gazed toward the movement. "No, who is it?"

"Brenda Thompson. She's the one responsible for us being in this place. I know why I'm here, but can't figure out why they brought you in."

"I haven't the vaguest idea. Why are you in this god forsaken place?"

"Because I had a date with Jerry Olson. He's Brenda's boyfriend. Did you have anything to do with her guy?"

She shook her head. "No, I'm going steady with Carl Hill."

"Did Carl know you were going to run away?"

"I'd mentioned how miserable I'd become at home and didn't think I could stand it much longer. He thought me crazy, but said he'd check around and see if there was a place for girls to stay while they got their heads together."

"Is he a friend of Jerry's?"

"I'm not sure, but they're on a couple of the same teams at school. They have practiced some this summer. So maybe Carl said something."

Sarah threw up her hands. "Well, you know guys. They probably teased your boyfriend and wanted to know how he caught such a babe and the word got out. Brenda probably figured Jerry had spurred it on." Sarah ran a hand across her face. "She's insanely jealous, and if she heard Jerry had talked about you in any way, she probably had you brought here too."

Patricia flopped down on her cot. "Yeah, but what I don't understand is how he knew the day I'd decided to leave. I didn't even know myself until I had a fight with my mom, packed my bag and put it outside the window. I told her I had a babysitting job and left. Then I returned after dark, picked up my suitcase and headed down the street. Jerry sat in his parked car down the road and called me over. Told me he had a safe place for me to go."

"Don't underestimate the power of Brenda. She's evil. More than likely your place had been watched day and night." Sarah glanced out the window and stiffened. "Oh, my God. The whole clan is headed toward us."

Patricia jumped up and looked out. "What are we going to do?"

"I don't know, but I sure don't like the looks of this."

The girls stepped back from the window as the group of black robed girls marched into the building. The chain on the door rattled and fear swept through Patricia and Sarah. They flattened their backs against the wall as the door swung open and the troop moved toward them.

"What do you want?" Sarah asked, shoving her hands behind her, as one girl tried to grasp her arm.

"You're invited to witness one of the rituals."

"We don't care anything about it. Just leave us alone."

"Sorry, we've been told to bring you."

Several advanced and corralled Sarah and Patricia into the corner. They kicked and fought until they were subdued by the numbers. Their hands were tied behind their backs, and when they refused to take steps, four of the robed girls, one on each side, shoved their arms under their armpits, lifted them off their feet and carried the two into the field.

Sarah scrutinized the unfamiliar area. When they'd allowed her to take a walk, the witches always directed her in the opposite direction. Not far way, she noticed a large ranch house and wondered who owned it.

Her back and underarms ached from the strain of dragging her feet, but she gritted her teeth and wouldn't give the bearers the satisfaction of not carrying her dead weight. She noticed Patricia doing the same, and it gave her courage. They soon reached the woodpile and were dropped on the ground beside the dried sticks. Both landed on their bellies and rolled over to maneuver themselves into a sitting position. They scooted close to each other as they watched the robed ones with wary eyes.

"Bind their feet so they can't escape while we're preparing the ritual," one of the girls ordered.

When one of them bent over to tie Sarah's ankles, she kicked the captor in the shoulder and sent her sprawling backwards. "Don't touch me," Sarah screamed.

Four of the robed ones converged and held her legs until they finally managed to get her feet tied together. They took precaution with Patricia and the four grabbed her before she could kick. Once they had both girls secured, they disappeared into the small building on the other side of the woodpile.

Patricia leaned forward. "Are you okay?" she whispered.

"Yeah. Just wish I had the strength of Wonder Woman. We'd be out of here."

"Hey, I think you did great. I'd liked to have given them a swift kick too, but they didn't give me a chance."

A shadow fell across the two girls and they glanced up. Patricia gasped.

CHAPTER TWENTY-SIX

The white robe rippled in the breeze and wide green eyes glared down on the two prisoners. "I need something of yours for our ceremony," Brenda said. Reaching into her pocket, she pulled out a pair of silver shears. Turning in a circle, she lifted her hands above her head, and twisted the scissors so shafts of colored beams reflected off the metal.

In horror, the girls tried to scoot away on their butts, but it didn't work. Black robes formed a barricade around them as Brenda chanted a dark rhyme. The group swayed in unison and hummed a morbid tune.

Sarah and Patricia kept their gaze on the white robe, watching every movement. Both girls jumped when Brenda dropped to her knees. Patricia screamed when she grabbed a handful of her hair and gave it a yank. Strands were caught between Sarah and Patricia, with each of them sitting on parts of the long locks.

"Stop!" Patricia yowled. "You're hurting me."

Brenda's eyes narrowed. "Then move or I'll take it off at the neck."

Sarah jerked around. "Are you crazy? Why are you doing this? You're going to end up in jail once you're caught."

"Shut up. You're not hurt. Who's going to catch me? No one knows where you are. Remember, you girls left home on your own accord. Besides, I've given you a safe place to live."

"There's nothing secure about being locked up in a room and barely fed by a witch's hive. I'd call it kidnapping and you can get many years for such a crime."

She laughed. "I'm a minor, no one's going to imprison me." Giving Sarah a shove, she pulled up the long tresses and whacked off two feet of hair.

Patricia narrowed her eyes and spat at the witch. "You're evil, Brenda Thompson."

Looking horrified, Brenda wiped her cheek, then slapped the girl hard across the face. "How dare you. Maybe now you won't go flaunting your mane at all the boys."

The ring of witches had stopped their humming and stepped back. They watched in awe at the interchange between their high priestess and the two girls.

Brenda glanced up at her troops. "It is sometimes a challenge to get the material we need for a ritual. This will make it much more meaningful." She stood, and held the handful of hair above her head. "I will now go get everything ready for the spell."

Then she pointed the scissors at the two girls. "Take them back to their room." She turned abruptly, and strode briskly toward the barn, her long white robe flapping in the breeze.

The black robed witches stood for a moment, watching her disappear. "Let's get them back to their room," said the girl in charge. She dropped to her haunches and untied the bindings around Sarah's ankles, then stepped back quickly, once her legs were free.

"Can't we untie their hands too?" another asked, as she removed the straps from Patricia's legs.

"Not until they're back in their quarters."

They helped Sarah and Patricia to their feet, then hooked their arms through theirs and escorted them back to the room. When they arrived, one of the girls bent close to Patricia's ear as she untied her wrists and whispered. "I'm so sorry about your beautiful hair. We had no idea this would happen."

Patricia looked at her puzzled. "Then why did you let it?"

The robed one put a finger to her lips. "Later."

After they left, Sarah sat down beside her friend and rubbed her shoulder. "It's horrible what she did to you. You still have a lot of hair left."

"Run your finger across my back where it ends, so I can tell how much is still there."

She did as asked and marked about midway down Patricia's spine.

Closing her eyes, Patricia sighed. "It has never been cut, only trimmed on the edges." She took a deep breath. "I guess I should be thankful I'm still alive. When she brandished those scissors, I thought she might go for my heart."

Sarah stood and went to the window. "She's evil, not to mention crazy. We've got to figure a way to get out of this place, before she decides she needs one of our internal organs for her stupid spells."

"One of the witches apologized."

Sarah snapped her head around. "When? I didn't hear anything."

"She whispered it while untying my hands. She said they didn't know my hair would be cut."

She sat down on the end of Patricia's cot. "That's odd."

"I asked her why they let it happen. She hushed me and said 'later'."

Sarah grabbed her hand in glee. "This is great news. It may be our way out of here. It sounds like Brenda's done something her followers didn't accept. This girl might help us escape." She jumped up and did a little jig in the middle of the room.

Patricia laughed. "You're funny."

Sarah put an arm around her. "You needed a laugh. You've been treated very cruelly. I'll never forget this horrible event."

Jennifer pulled into the parking lot of Hawkman's office complex, jumped out of the van and hurried up the stairs. When she stepped inside, she found her husband studying Sarah's computer monitor. The rural map lay folded in half on his desk.

"Why did you call me away from my post? Have you uncovered a clue?"

"Possibly. Grab yourself a cup of coffee and when I'm through here, I'll be eager to hear about your adventure. Then I'll let you in on what I've discovered."

Jennifer poured herself a mug of java and sat down on the small sofa. "I hated losing Brenda in the hills. If I'd been in your 4X4, I'd have taken one of those side roads, but was afraid to risk it with my van."

Hawkman twisted in the chair and faced her. "I'm glad you didn't. Nothing like getting stuck, and then discovering your cell phone won't work either. You did the right thing."

"What were you so intent on reading?"

"I wanted to finish those short stories of Sarah's after talking with the other girls. Even tried reading between the lines to see if I could find some hidden meaning."

"Any luck?"

"She mentioned Brenda in the last story."

"What's she say?"

"Called her a bitch. I don't think the girl is well liked by her peers." He put his arms on his thighs. "Now tell me what happened."

After she told him how Brenda disappeared, he took the map Jennifer had found in Sarah's room and spread it across the desk. "I've taken a soft leaded #2 pencil and traced where I could see the original markings. Is this the route you took?"

Jennifer crossed the room and ran her finger along the path. "Yes." Then she made an imaginary circle. "She vanished around this area."

Hawkman nodded. "Fits."

She looked at him, confused. "What?"

"The Thompsons' own a ranch in those hills and from what Mr. Phelps told me, I'd suspect it's in this location." He lightly drew a ring around where she'd lost Brenda.

"Who's Mr. Phelps?"

"Nikki Phelps' father. Make yourself comfortable and I'll give you my report."

She sat down on the chair in front of his desk. "Okay, shoot."

He ran through the details of the visit with Janet Ross and her mother, Sally. "I'm sure when I left there, just like you said would happen, Janet got on the phone and warned her colleagues about my visit. I also think Sally talked with the parents, because when I reached Nikki's home, her father met me at the door."

"Did he seem angry?"

"No. Concerned is a better word. He invited me in and I talked to him and his wife without Nikki present."

"How did they know the Thompsons had a ranch?"

Hawkman held up his hand. "Patience, my dear wife. Let me tell the events in order."

She ducked her head. "Sorry I interrupted. Please continue."

He smiled. "The Phelps know the Thompson family personally. He's done business with Mr. Thompson and they've been in their home on several social engagements. The Thompsons are very wealthy and hold large pieces of real estate in the area. One parcel is a ranch in the hills. He said Mr. Thompson traveled a lot out of the country and doubted he paid much attention to how his daughter or spouse ran their lives."

Jennifer reared back. "Whoa, what'd they have to say about those two females?"

"Mr. Phelps just shrugged, but Mrs. Phelps blasted them both."

"Give me the skinny."

"I have all them recorded, but jotted down some notes so I could tell you without going through all the recordings. You can listen to the interviews later." He consulted his writing pad. "Lea Thompson is manipulative, bossy and knows it all. Her daughter follows suit with those traits. Mrs. Phelps has forbidden Nikki to have anything to do with Brenda. She doesn't trust her and feels she's wild with no discipline. It didn't seem to surprise her when I related some of the incidents I'd encountered with the girl. However, it disturbed her to think Brenda had such a hold on Nikki and her friends."

"Kids at this age are very vulnerable," Jennifer said. "Brenda has scared them with the threat of spells and convinced them she's had something to do with Sarah's disappearance."

Hawkman leaned back. "I'm still wondering if an adult is involved."

"Hard to say. These kids are old enough to take things in their own hands." She took a sip of coffee. "Did you talk with Ann Stewart?"

"Barely. She had just a few minutes before heading for work and appeared visibly shaken by my presence. Janet had contacted her and she verified all the things I related. Her folks were present, but very shy about speaking with me. They didn't add anything new and wished me luck in finding Sarah."

"I have the feeling Ann is the youngest of a large family. When I checked out her web page on MySpace, she had pictures of a group of older siblings."

He tossed his pencil on the desk. "I want to have another chat with Jerry Olson, but I don't want his father there, so I'll wait until a weekday. The girl's clan has been interrogated, and I did find out a bunch of stuff. Next, I must pursue my findings." He held up his hand. "There's still another thing nagging me."

"What?"

He picked up the map and gave it a shake. "Where did Sarah get this?"

Jennifer shook her head. "Good question."

CHAPTER TWENTY-SEVEN

Patricia patted Sarah's hand. "Thank you. You're very sweet. I've always liked you." Then she gazed into her friend's face. "Cutting my hair didn't hurt, but it made me feel like I'd lost an arm. Now I'm worried about what Brenda has in store for you. Surely, she won't try the same thing."

Sarah slowly rose from the cot and moved toward the window. "It scares me too. Jerry must have just made a comment about you, but I went out with the guy. She'll probably want my blood."

Patricia jumped up and stood beside her. "We've got to get out of here."

"How?" she gestured toward the entry. "I've tried getting the door open. It's heavy and padlocked with a chain." Then she pointed at the window. "Those bars are screwed to the outside, and we can't reach them. There are no vents or loose boards any where. Believe me, before you got here, I'd scoured every inch of this room looking for some way to escape."

"Then let's make a plan to run for it when they bring us our meal."

"I've checked that out too. There's a backup of the robed ones standing outside. So it wouldn't be easy to get past the army of guards."

Patricia hit her fists on the wooden walls. "We need a plan."

Sarah sat down on the cot. "Okay, let's brainstorm."

The girls sat with their heads together speaking in hushed tones for fear of being overheard. A couple of hours passed before they fell across their cots exhausted. Then Sarah raised her head. "Just remember," she said softly, "if we get lost from one another, keep going downhill."

They both jerked their heads around when they heard the chain rattle on the outside of the door. "Must be time to eat."

Two robed witches came in carrying large paper plates with two huge sandwiches, heaped with chips, and two sodas. When they turned to leave, one of them reached into her pocket and tossed two candy bars onto Patricia's cot. She placed a finger to her lips as she backed out of the room.

Several seconds after the witches left, the two girls glanced at one another. "They didn't chain the door shut," both whispered in unison.

They hurried to the window and watched the black robes disappear into the barn, then ran to the large door and pushed it open. Sarah quickly removed the chain.

"What are you doing?" Patricia asked.

"It might come in handy for a weapon. We have nothing to scare off wild animals, and this might do the trick."

"This changes our plans."

Sarah grinned. "Yes, for the better. We'll wait until dark. Meanwhile, let's eat those sandwiches to keep up our energy, carry the candy bars, and hopefully we can find some water in the kitchen. It'll be a scary hike."

"Can't be more horrifying than staying here."

Hawkman folded the map and slipped it back into the folder. "Did you notice if any of the other members of the family left the Thompson household while you were there?"

"No one else left, but my surveillance didn't last long, as I took off after Brenda."

"Do you know if there are any other siblings in this family?"

"There's no mention or pictures of brothers or sisters on her site. None of the people we've talked to have spoke of any either. I think she's an only child."

He nodded. "Figures. Why don't we take a chance and pay the Thompsons a visit? Maybe with a little luck we'll find mother and daughter home."

Jennifer emptied the remains of her coffee. "I'm game."

They piled into Hawkman's SUV and took off. When they parked in front of the mansion, the sun had set and Jennifer pointed out the soft glow of lights coming through the drapes. "I believe we're in luck. I don't see Brenda's car in the garage."

"On second thought, I think I'd like to speak with the lady of the house alone."

"Hopefully, the servants have left for the day."

They rang the doorbell and had to wait several moments before Lea Thompson answered the door. She frowned when she saw Hawkman.

"Hello, Mr. Casey. Don't you think it's a little late to be making a business call?"

"A private investigator doesn't keep nine to five hours. He goes when he needs to get some answers." He introduced Jennifer. "May we come in? We'd like to ask a few questions."

"What about?"

"Your daughter."

Her eyes narrowed. "You've already spoken with my daughter. There's nothing else to say."

"There's another subject I'd like to talk about."

"Oh, and what might that be?"

"Witchcraft."

She put a hand to her throat. "Did you say witchcraft?"

"Yes."

"I guess you better come inside. It looks like this might take awhile."

They stepped into the foyer and she closed the door. "I think it best we go into the study." She led them into the same room where Hawkman had interviewed Brenda. "Have a seat. Can I offer you a drink?"

"No, thanks. We're fine. Could you have Mr. Thompson join us?"

"He's out of the country at this time. I don't expect him home for several weeks."

Hawkman pulled a chair out for Jennifer and they sat down.

Lea took a seat across the table. "Now what's this about witchcraft?"

"Before we get into that aspect, do you own a ranch nearby?"

She furrowed her brow. "Yes, what does it have to do with this topic?"

Jennifer scooted forward. "I followed Brenda into the hills this morning, then lost her. We've learned your property is in that vicinity."

"Brenda's allowed to go there anytime she pleases. She has a good heart and is housing some wayward girls until they get their lives in order. We told her as long as they keep the place in good order, we'll allow them to stay. She drives up and checks on them several times a week, taking food stuffs. They don't stay in the main house, only Brenda is allowed in it. The girls stay in a bunkhouse by the barn. There's a kitchen in another cabin on the property, but it only has a cistern with a pump, no running water or electricity. It's good for these girls to learn how to use a wood burning stove to cook a meal. Maybe they'll appreciate the finer things of life if they have to live in a rustic manner." Then she turned to Jennifer with a puzzled expression. "Why were you tailing Brenda?"

Jennifer met Lea's stare with one of her own. "We've received some disturbing complaints about her."

Lea frowned. "Complaints? What about?"

"How much does your daughter know about witchcraft?" Hawkman asked.

"A little. She saw a program on television a few years back, so we decided to check out some books from the library. We dabbled a little with it, did a few spells, but nothing serious. She never took it outside the house."

Jennifer pulled out the picture of the pendant from the briefcase. "Does Brenda own a necklace like this?"

"Yes, but she never wears it."

Jennifer pointed at the woman's neck. "I see you have one."

Lea placed her hand over the jewelry. "I bought this overseas and it's made with precious jewels."

"Why did you pick a witch's pentacle piece, when I'm sure there were many other styles you could have chosen?"

She narrowed her eyes. "I love beautiful jewelry and this happened to be the prettiest on display. I didn't really think about what it meant."

Hawkman leaned forward. "I find your explanation a little hard to believe. Brenda is threatening her classmates with spells, if they so much as look at Jerry Olson."

Lea threw back her head and laughed. "Brenda could have any boy she wished. Haven't you noticed, she's the most beautiful girl around? What leads you to believe such trash?"

"Mrs. Thompson, your daughter has put the fear of God into three young girls, and we've probably just scratched the surface. She's threatened them with spells like she cast on Sarah Willis, if they don't heed her warnings."

Lea abruptly stood, almost knocking over her chair. Her green eyes flashed with anger. "Those girls are lying. There's not a word of truth to what you say. How dare you come in here accusing my daughter of such deeds. I want you out of here right now. If you ever set foot on this property again, I'll have you arrested." She pointed a finger at Jennifer. "You leave Brenda alone too. Now get out, both of you."

CHAPTER TWENTY-EIGHT

Brenda turned the corner onto her street and gasped. The vehicle parked in front of the house looked like the private investigator's. She pulled into the garage and pushed the button for the big door to slide closed. Biting her lower lip, she quietly opened the kitchen door a few inches and listened. Not hearing anything, she stepped inside and tiptoed toward the hallway. Her mother's voice boomed from the study, telling someone to get out.

She quickly backtracked, slipped into the pantry, and left the door slightly ajar so she could see out and hear their words. Sucking in her breath, she spotted Mr. and Mrs. Casey hurrying toward the front entry. Her mother followed, arms straight down, and fists clenched at her sides. Brenda knew it as a sure sign of her mother's anger. What the hell had gone on, she wondered. Should she approach her mom or let her cool down?

The front door slammed and Lea stormed into the kitchen, looked in the garage, then yelled. "Brenda, I want to talk to you."

She let her mother head up the stairs before she snuck out of her hiding place and ducked into the downstairs bathroom. She soon heard her mom grumbling as she traveled down the staircase.

"Brenda, where are you? I know you're in the house. I heard the garage door close."

Flushing the toilet, she called. "I'm in here. Be right out."

When she stepped into the hallway, her mother stood outside the door, her arms crossed and the toe of her shoe tapping a rhythm.

"What's the matter? You look pissed."

Lea narrowed her eyes and glared at her daughter. "Yes, my dear, I'm very disturbed. Come into the study. We have a few matters to discuss."

Gnawing her lower lip, Brenda followed her mother and sat down at the table. "Mom, what's the problem?"

"That private investigator and his wife just left. They told me some very troubling things about you. You've been threatening people with spells. Especially girls who showed an interest in Jerry."

"It's no big deal."

"Yes, it is. Remember our agreement about how you weren't to let any of our knowledge of witchcraft go beyond these doors? Also, don't you think you're being a little presumptuous on assuming Jerry only has eyes for you? He's a young man, and his gaze will wander."

Brenda shrugged. "You sound like Sarah."

Lea stared at her daughter. "Explain what you mean."

She threw up her hands. "I confronted her about flirting with Jerry and she asked me if I was married to him."

"When did you speak to her?"

"We commented on MySpace."

"I asked you when?"

"Before she disappeared."

"Do you know where she went?"

Brenda stood. "This conversation is ridiculous. I have no idea where she is. I don't care to talk about this subject anymore."

Lea leaned back in the chair and studied her daughter. "How are the girls doing at the ranch?"

"Fine. They've kept everything in good condition, and are obeying the rules."

"I think I'll drive up there in the next day or two."

Brenda jerked around. "Uh, I don't think that's necessary. I'm keeping things in order."

"Still, I need to keep a watch over my property, since I am the proprietress." Lea rose and walked out of the room.

Brenda stared after her mother as she strolled through the door into the hallway.

Driving back to the office, Jennifer tried to analyze her husband's pensive expression. "What's bugging you? As if I need to ask."

"Mrs. Thompson is either putting on a great act, or she's guilty as hell. Did you noticed how she skirted around the questions on witchcraft? She reverted to the idea we'd lost our minds, the girls were liars, and her darling daughter would never do such stuff."

"I've been thinking about it too, and have come to the conclusion it might be a little of both."

"How could it be? Either they studied witchcraft or they didn't. I think our dear Lea Thompson might be a full-fledged witch."

"What makes you think so?"

"Tell me what woman would buy an expensive piece of jewelry in the shape of the witch's pentacle if it didn't mean something to her?"

Jennifer frowned. "You might have a point. I hadn't thought along that line."

"Her pendant had diamonds and rubies set into it. The setting and chain appeared more like platinum or white gold. Such a necklace would cost a pretty penny."

"I don't think money is a problem with this family."

"Okay, apart from the jewelry, did you notice the books on the shelves in their study?"

"No, I didn't."

"There were several volumes involving the Wiccas, and other witchcraft."

"The Wiccas are supposedly good witches."

Hawkman glanced at her. "You're saying Brenda decided to go a step farther?"

She raised her hands and let them drop to her lap. "It's very possible. Kids of this age are cocky and she definitely fits the form." Then she turned in her seat toward him. "What bearing do you think the ranch plays in Brenda practicing the craft?"

"A lot. I suspect it's very private. When I go to the courthouse tomorrow morning, I'm going to find the exact location of their property and drive out there."

"You're not leaving me behind. I'm coming with you."

"Dress appropriately, jeans and boots. We might have to do a little hiking." He pulled into the lot and stopped beside her van. "It's getting late. You're not going to want to cook when we get home and I'm starved. Tell you what, meet me at Joe's Barbecue, I'm in the mood for ribs."

Jennifer laughed as she climbed out. "Sounds great."

When they finally arrived home, the house stood in complete darkness. Jennifer hadn't left a light on for Miss Marple and immediately searched for her beloved pet. She soon found her on their bed, snuggled between the two pillows. "You are one spoiled cat." She lifted the animal from the crevice, gave her a hug, then placed her in the feline's wicker bed.

The next morning, Hawkman and Jennifer left the house early so they'd arrive at the courthouse when the doors opened. They had no trouble locating the piece of property belonging to the Thompsons.

"Look at this," Hawkman said, running his finger over two roads. "There's a couple of entries leading up to the place. Can you calculate the area where you lost Brenda?"

Jennifer studied the diagram. "I'd say about here," she pointed. "Because I drove by her when she pulled over." She tapped the diagram. "I went around this curve and waited for her to come, but she never did. The other road appears to be past where I stopped."

He made a copy of the area. "Once we get near, this will help us decide which road to take. The ranch house is defined, and there are a few outbuildings scattered across the property. We'll make a decision when we reach this spot."

CHAPTER TWENTY-NINE

Sarah and Patricia sat huddled on their cots as the moonlight gleamed through the barred window and spread eery beams across the plank walls. When the howl of a coyote pierced the air, they both jumped and glanced toward the opening.

"I hate to think about trudging through the jungle in the middle of the night," Patricia said, hugging her knees close to her chest. "There are wild animals out there and I don't want to be attacked by a mountain lion or a bear."

Sarah took a deep breath. "I hear ya, but we've got to get out of here before they make their rounds. Otherwise, we'll get locked up again. There's no way all those witches agree with the one who left the door unlocked."

"Why can't we hide in the attic or something?"

"What good will that do? They'll search this building from top to bottom. We need to get far away from this place, maybe even find a farm house with a telephone so we can call for help."

Patricia jerked her head around. "Who do you think owns the big ranch house we can see from the bonfire site?"

Sarah sighed. "Probably Brenda's folks."

"I saw wires leading into the house. Do you think there might be a phone?"

"Could be, but the house is probably protected by an alarm system."

"What good would that do out here in the boonies?"

"It could be wired to send a signal to the nearest fire station."

Patricia dropped her feet to the floor. "Hey, that might work. Especially if it's a silent one. We set it off and hide in the house until they get here."

Sarah shook her head. "Too risky. What if it's one of those that blares like a fog horn. The robed ones would have us in a minute." She moved to the window and looked outside. Her eyes were used to the darkness as her gaze moved toward the barn. Swiftly, she moved to her cot and slid the backpack underneath. "Quick, get under the covers, and pretend you're asleep. Two of the black robes are headed this way."

Patricia grabbed her blanket, and threw it over her body. "Do they usually check on us at night?" she whispered.

"Occasionally a couple take a walk after dark. I don't know why; it's possible they check the premises. I saw the flashlight beams hitting the ground, so stay quiet and maybe we'll hear them talking."

They didn't move for several minutes as they watched the window. A light flashed across the bars while both girls sucked in their breath, and listened intently.

"Sure seems quiet in there. Should we take a closer look?"

"Climb on that box and shine your flashlight in the window."

Both girls closed their eyes as the beam ran over their bodies.

"They're asleep," she said. Then she let out a yelp as she jumped down from the perch. "Ouch!"

"You okay?" the other one asked.

"I've turned my ankle, and it hurts like crazy."

"Lean on me and we'll get you back to the bunkhouse."

Sarah gave them a few seconds to get away from the window before she leaped from bed, and peered out.

"Are they going back to the barn?" Patricia whispered.

"Not yet. It's a slow go, because one of them is limping badly."

Sarah went back to the cot, reached underneath, and dragged out the backpack. "I'm going to see if I can find some bottled water in the kitchen. There must be some, since they serve it to us with our meals."

"You want me to come with you?"

She pointed to the window. "No, you stay and keep guard. Come and warn me if you see anyone coming toward the building."

Patricia got up and manned her post. "Okay. Don't stay long or I'll get scared."

"Remember it's as dark as pitch. I'll have to feel my way around."

"Light a candle."

"Are you kidding? They'd spot the glow immediately and know we're out of our room."

"You're right. Be careful."

When Sarah opened the heavy door a few inches, the hinges screeched like crazy. "I never noticed them making such a horrible noise. Let's pray the sound doesn't travel."

Patricia peered out toward the barn. "I don't see any movement."

"Good." Sarah slipped through the opening and headed toward the kitchen. Her eyes had adjusted to the darkness and it amazed her how well she could see. The clear night and the moon's glow helped tremendously. She quickly busied herself, squatting down and looking through the rustic cabinets, when suddenly a beam of light glanced off the window pane. Sarah jumped up, her heart thumping against her ribs, when she realized a car had pulled in front of the cabin. If she ran toward the room, she'd have to pass the front door, and probably get caught. Frantically, she glanced around seeking an area big enough to hide in, and spotted the broom closet. She quickly squeezed into the small area, and managed to get the door almost closed. Holding her breath, she watched through the small crack as two boys brought in what looked like sacks of groceries and placed them on the large wooden table.

They were talking in low tones and Sarah couldn't understand them. When one of them turned around, her hand went to her mouth and her elbow raked against the door causing it to open slightly. She froze for a second, then quickly hooked her finger around the edge and pulled it back toward her.

Neither of the young men appeared to have noticed and went on about their business. After they made several trips into the kitchen Sarah felt her legs going to sleep and wished she could change positions, but didn't dare move in her cramped quarters.

After what seemed like an eternity, the two suppliers finally made their last trip to the kitchen and didn't return. She heard a vehicle engine start up and drive away. Afraid to move, Sarah stayed hidden for several minutes, then finally decided they'd left and slowly opened the small door.

When she stepped out of the broom closet, her legs almost buckled, and she grabbed the counter for support. Fighting the numbness, she made her way to the table and examined the products. A parcel of water bottles sat at the end of the table. Leaning forward, she used her fingernail to cut through the plastic, then struggled to get them out of the packet. Just as she yanked out the fourth, a hand grabbed her shoulder from behind.

She swung around with the bottle in her hand and smacked the intruder in the face, knocking him against the cabinet where he hit his head and crumbled to the floor. He groaned and she knew the fall had only knocked him out, so she snatched the other three bottles off the table and ran down the hallway.

When she crashed into the room out of breath, Patricia looked at her wide-eyed.

"What's happened?"

"Come on, I'll tell you later. We've got to get out here; this is the only chance we'll have." She grabbed the backpack and threw the bottles of water inside. Heaving the straps over her shoulders, she headed for the door. Peeking out cautiously, she motioned for Patricia. "Let's go."

The two girls tiptoed out of the room and down the hallway. Sarah glanced into the kitchen and saw the silhouette of the groaning male moving around on the floor. She grabbed Patricia's hand, dragged her out the front door into the forest and darkness of night.

CHAPTER THIRTY

Nightmares plagued Brenda most of the night. She slept fitfully until early morning, then finally fell into a heavy sleep. A constant ringing brought her out of the deep fog.

"Why doesn't someone answer the damn phone?" she growled, tugging the covers over her head.

When the incessant chiming didn't quit, she pushed back the covers, forced open her eyes and glanced at the clock. "Six in the morning," she groaned. "I haven't been awake at this hour in ages."

Only then did she realize it was her cell phone on the bed stand making the noise. She grabbed the instrument, flipped it open and read the name of the caller. Instantly, she sat up. She'd instructed the girl in charge never to call unless there was a crisis. Something must have happened at the ranch. The caller had hung up, so Brenda decided to listen to the two voice messages first. One came from Jerry, telling her she better get to the ranch as soon as possible. The other came from her head girl, who asked that she call her pronto.

She pushed the reply. When the girl answered on the first ring, Brenda listened intently. "How the hell did that happen?"

Holding the phone to her ear, she flipped the covers back, jumped out of bed and grabbed her jeans off the chair. "Is Jerry okay? I'll be there within the hour." After hanging up, she ran into her bathroom, splashed cold water on her face, ran a brush through her hair, and tied it back into a ponytail. She went to the closet and grabbed a long sleeved cotton blouse and hiking boots. Quickly dressing, she placed the cell phone, a tube of lipstick and a comb into a small bag and slipped the strap over her shoulder. Draping a lightweight jacket over her arm, she picked up her car keys, then softly opened the door, peered down the hallway, then stepped into the corridor. She tiptoed down the stairs, through the kitchen and out to the garage. Cringing at the sound of the huge door gliding open, Brenda prayed it wouldn't arouse her mother. She didn't need to contend with her at this moment.

Brenda drove as fast as she dared. No need to have the police on her tail. She clenched the steering wheel until her knuckles turned white as her mind raced through what had gone wrong. How did those girls get out of the room? She'd tested it several times and had found no way of escape when everything was locked. Perhaps someone hadn't padlocked the door. She'd lectured them over and over about making sure the room stayed secure. Some of the girls didn't like the idea of prisoners on the premises, but the place didn't belong to them. She'd warned them, they either obey the rules or go back on the streets. Her threats meant little, as none of them would ever leave, not alive anyway.

When she introduced them to the witch rituals, they all appeared to love dancing around the bonfires and doing simple spells. She'd noticed they were a bit taken back when she cut Patricia's hair. "Too bad," she said, chuckling to herself. "My dear ladies, that's just the beginning of getting you prepared for bigger things."

Brenda smacked the steering wheel with her hand. Since Sarah and Patricia had escaped, her plans would be delayed. She also didn't like the idea of the private investigator and his wife snooping around. They'd aroused suspicions in her mom, which she didn't need. She'd somehow have to get things back in order.

She felt a smile twitch the corners of her mouth. Why wouldn't today be perfect for her mom to visit the ranch? Her little witches could be out searching for the girls on the pretense of looking for wild berries and herbs. They'd hide the robes and the house would be clear of any prisoners.

Brenda turned on the second road leading up to the ranch. She parked in front of the big dwelling, then hurried toward the bunkhouse. When she stepped inside, Jerry sat at the table, surrounded by the girls. They had wrapped his head in a big damp towel.

She hurried to his side and draped an arm around his shoulders. "Are you okay?"

"Yeah, just a big lump on the head."

She flopped down in a chair next to him. "What happened?"

He removed the towel and handed it to one of the witches. "When I brought the food in last night, I noticed someone hiding in the broom closet. I had Chuck go ahead and leave as we had to get the truck back to the grocery store before midnight. He'll pick me up today, unless I can ride back with you."

"I may need you to hang around and help us locate Sarah and Patricia. But first, go ahead with your story."

"I hid outside the door until I heard movement in the kitchen. When I snuck in, I discovered Sarah rummaging through the groceries. I reached over to grab her by the shoulder, she whirled around, and swatted me across the face with a bottle. It threw me off balance and I fell, striking my head on the cabinet. It knocked me out cold. When I came to, she and Patricia were gone."

Brenda glanced up at the girls. "Have you searched for them?"

"Yes, we never went to bed. We've combed every building except the big house. We did inspect all around it to make sure they hadn't crawled in a window."

"We needn't worry about the ranch dwelling. It's rigged with a very complicated alarm system which has to be turned off before entering. The whole area would have known, if they'd managed to get inside." Brenda looked thoughtful as she drummed her fingers on the table.

Jerry rubbed her arm. "What's on your mind, baby?"

"They're out there in the forest. We've got to find them. The road isn't far away, and once they locate it, they could easily make their way down the mountain."

He raised a hand. "Yes, but remember they'll be petrified of any car because it could be one of us looking for them. I doubt they'll boldly walk down the road."

Suddenly, Brenda counted heads. "Two of you are missing."

They parted and pointed at the couch in the adjoining room. "Ruth has a badly swollen sprained ankle. Christina hasn't been seen since last night."

Brenda's eyes narrowed. "You haven't found her either?"

They shook their heads in unison. The head girl took a deep breath. "We discovered the chain missing on Sarah's room and Christina had the duty of locking up last night. We think she helped the girls escape."

Brenda stood and paced the floor. "We have a few problems ahead. Mother wants to come to the ranch and see how you girls are managing things. I want you to hide your witch robes, then I want you to each take a pail or sack with you when you go searching for the three girls. I'm going to tell Mom you've gone berry picking or herb gathering. She mustn't know about our witchcraft or she'll shut us down and send you all packing. If you should return with the girls, check the cars and make sure she's not here before entering the grounds. If you don't find them, go straight to the bunkhouse. Understood?"

"Yes."

"Good, get things straightened up and out of sight. I'm going to the ranch house."

She turned to Jerry and took his hand. "Come with me."

He stumbled along beside her. "Don't walk so fast, Brenda, my head is killing me. I might have a concussion."

She opened the front door of the large abode with a code, then once inside, she disabled the alarm system. "I'm going to fix my poor baby right up," she said, leading him straight to her bedroom.

Pushing him down on the bed, she removed his shoes and unbuckled his belt and jeans, then slid them off his body.

"Aren't you worried about your mother catching us?"

Brenda laughed as she unbuttoned her blouse and slipped it off her arms, revealing firm round breasts. "Mom probably isn't even up yet," she said, as she wiggled out of her jeans with sexy little movements.

He watched her as she undressed, then swaying her hips, she slinked toward the bed. Her green eyes were full of lust as she straddled his body and rode him until he gasped for breath. "Oh, baby, you definitely know how to make a man feel better."

CHAPTER THIRTY-ONE

Sarah grabbed Patricia's hand and dragged her deep into the forest before she finally slowed her pace. Exhausted and panting, she flopped down on a fallen log.

"What happened back there?" Patricia asked, gasping for breath, as she alighted beside her.

Keeping her voice low and her gaze alert, Sarah quickly filled her in on the events. "I knew we had to get out immediately. Because once Jerry came to, we'd be locked up and never be able to escape."

Patricia glanced around the dense jungle surrounding them. "We'll never find our way out of here. I'm scared."

Sarah patted her arm. "Me, too. I'd hoped we could have waited until early morning, when some light would have helped us maneuver through this maze. But we couldn't take the chance."

They both stiffened as they spotted a light coming through the forest.

"Oh, my gosh, they're looking for us already," Patricia said, grasping Sarah's arm."

"Quick, lay down behind this log," Sarah said.

They both pressed themselves close to the big piece of wood. Then a soft voice met their ears.

"Sarah, Patricia, it's me, Christina. Where are you? I want to get out of here too. I'm the one who didn't lock the padlock. Please answer me if you're near."

They watched the young witch still clad in her robe sink to the ground. She sat there for several seconds weeping. Patricia raised up on her elbow, but Sarah pushed her head down. "This could be a ploy to find us," she whispered. "Let's give her a few minutes, then if no one else shows up, we'll let her know we're here."

The two girls stayed hunkered down for what seemed like an eternity. Soon, Christina stood and walked slowly in the opposite direction.

Sarah crawled out from behind the log and called softly. "Christina, we're over here."

She whirled around and pointed the flashlight beam toward them.

"Turn that blasted light off," Sarah demanded. "You'll give us away."

Christina flipped it off and stumbled toward them. "I'm so happy to see you," she sobbed, as she hugged Sarah.

The three sat down on the log.

"How did you know we were gone?" Sarah asked.

"Jerry stumbled into the bunkhouse and said Sarah had knocked him out. When he came to in the kitchen, he checked your room and discovered you both were gone. I knew the minute he announced your escape, I had to get away. Because when they put two and two together, they'd know I was the one who left the room unlocked. So during the commotion of running to the cottage, I cut away and ran into the forest."

"How long ago?" Sarah asked.

"Since I couldn't find you, it seems like I've been wandering for hours, but it probably hasn't been much more than thirty minutes."

"When do you think they'll start looking for us?" Patricia asked.

"They won't do anything until Brenda gives them the order."

"Is she your boss?" Sarah asked.

"Oh, yeah, if it weren't for her, we'd all be on the streets selling our bodies for food."

Sarah straightened her back. "I don't get it. Right now we really don't have time to shoot the breeze. I think we better try to find our way off this mountain. We can talk when we're safe."

Christina pulled the witch's robe off and dropped it on the ground. "I don't want this thing anymore."

Sarah picked it up and handed it back. "The nights get cold, you'll be glad you have it. Later, we might all want to crawl under it. You can discard it when we're safe."

She nodded. "You're right. I don't have much on underneath."

"Don't turn on the flashlight. It's a dead giveaway. We'll have to find our way in the dark. Let's put it in the backpack as we might need it down the way. Also, we have to keep as quiet as possible, as our voices will carry for some distance. So if you want to speak, talk in whispers."

"This is one time I wish I was an Indian scout," Patricia said. "Then I'd know which direction to take by reading the stars."

"It would be nice to have that knowledge. Right now, we'll do the best we can and move as far away as possible from this place," Sarah said, treading toward a denser area of the woods.

The other two girls followed in single file, fighting the brush and low slung branches of the trees. They swatted at bugs landing on their faces and arms. The howl of a coyote made them stop in their tracks. When a deer bounded out of the brush, they grabbed each other, scared half out of their wits.

The moon slipped behind a cloud, and it became so dark they couldn't see the figure in front of them. "Let's hold each other's hands. We sure don't want to get lost from one another," Sarah said, waving her hand behind her trying to find Patricia's fingers.

Once connected, they kept moving.

"I'm tired and thirsty," Patricia said. "We've been hiking for hours. Can't we stop and rest for just a few minutes?"

"How are you doing, Christina?" Sarah asked.

"A rest would be good."

"It's so dark, I can't see a place to stop." Sarah gazed at the sky. "Maybe the clouds will pass across the moon soon and then we'll stop. Right now I'm just praying we haven't been going in a circle. I have no sense of direction."

Patricia gasped. "Don't say such things. Surely we've made some headway."

"I wish I could assure you we have, but I can't."

"I think you're doing fine in leading," Christina said. "I feel we're going in a downhill direction. We're not climbing, and that's important."

"I'm relieved," Sarah said. "I had the sensation we were moving downward, but wasn't sure."

The moon finally peeked out, and the girls could partially see the area.

Sarah glanced around. "We're in the midst of very dense brush. Why don't we move on a little farther? There's bound to be a space with a fallen log or boulder so we can sit down."

Patricia and Christina followed as they clawed their way through the tangled web of vines.

After their heavy bout of love making, Brenda jumped in the shower. When she emerged she found her lover asleep on the bed.

"Get up, Jerry. Mother mustn't find you in here."

He groaned as he rolled over, grasped his head with his hands, and slowly dropped his feet to the floor. "I've got a splitting headache."

Brenda handed him a couple of aspirins with a glass of water. "Take these; it'll make you feel better. You can't act like anything has happened in front of Mom."

"Yeah, that's all fine and dandy. How are you going to explain me being here?"

She shrugged. "Easy. You brought up the groceries and I asked you to stay."

"I thought you wanted me to help hunt for Sarah and Patricia."

Shooing him off the bed, she proceeded to make it. "We'll do that once Mom has gone back home. Those girls aren't going to get far. There's a lot of forest out there and our best bet is to patrol the roads."

"You must be some sort of miracle worker. We only have your car up here."

She laughed. "Don't forget my clan of witches."

"My head hurts so bad, I can't even think. I'll leave the planning up to you."

Before Brenda could respond, her cell phone rang. She put a finger to her lips as she snatched it off the dresser.

"Hello."

"Hi, Mom. I'm at the ranch."

"I couldn't sleep, so decided to drive out and see how things are going. Are you coming up?"

"Okay, see you in about an hour."

She hung up and glanced out the window. "Looks like the girls are forming their search party. I'll run over and give instructions where I want them to concentrate their efforts."

CHAPTER THIRTY-TWO

Jerry watched Brenda through the window. His stomach churned as he wondered how he'd ever get out of this situation. She tantalized him with her beautiful body, but she had an evil mind, and he didn't trust her. He didn't like the idea of bringing girls up here on false pretenses. It tickled him Sarah and Patricia had escaped.

Her 'clan of witches' as she called them, were girls she'd enticed off the streets and given promises of food and shelter. They had to keep the ranch in good repair and follow her orders. Little did they realize, until they got here, Brenda had an alternative scheme. She planned teaching them witchcraft, with her as their leader. Her motives were not honorable, but these girls were tough and would do anything to keep from being prostitutes.

He remembered when he fastened the bars to the windows, how she'd lied that they were to keep out the wild animals so they wouldn't steal the food in the kitchen. All along she'd planned on using it for a prison.

When she had him bring Sarah to the ranch, she lied, telling him how sorry she felt for the girl, because she'd end up with some pimp on the streets. Since Sarah trusted him, why didn't he bring her to the ranch where she'd be safe. The same with Patricia. Now he saw through her scheme, and realized what he'd done. It made him sick to his stomach.

Brenda desperately wanted these girls back, and if she found them before they got off the mountain. He didn't know what she had in mind, but the thought frightened him. Pretty ironic one of the witches had defected, too. He prayed they'd make it to safety before Brenda got her hands on them.

Not wanting the wrath of Brenda's mother, he headed outside. He knew she didn't like him, but he doubted she'd cotton to any guy who dated her precious daughter. It surprised him she'd take a couple of spare hours to make a trip to the ranch. She had such a busy schedule with all her social engagements. Seldom did he find her home when he went to see Brenda, and he remembered the times he'd sweated it out as they made love in the bedroom. He figured if he ever got caught by her mom or dad, he'd be dead meat.

He headed toward the bunkhouse and met Brenda with her gang of witches. She pointed toward the road. "Okay, girls, I want you to search that area. I doubt you'll find Sarah, Patricia or Christina on the road, so spread out and work the sides. Jerry and I will comb the other route when my mother leaves." She turned to her head girl. "Do you have the gags and ropes?"

"Yes."

"Good luck. I hope we find them."

Jerry stood with his thumbs hooked in his back jeans pockets as he watched the troop head into the forest. Brenda turned toward him, swinging the bandanas and nylon cord she held in her hand.

"I want to put these in my car."

"If you find those girls, do you expect them to hold still while you tie them up?"

She winked and gave him an alluring smile. "I'll have my strong man with me."

"What if I decide not to help?"

Her smile turned down into a pout as she gazed at him seductively through her long, thick eyelashes. She wrapped her arms around his waist and pulled him close, then rubbed her pelvis back and forth against the front of his jeans. "You don't want to give up this, do you?"

He put his hands on her buttocks and pushed her into him. "Don't do this to me now. We don't have time for another romp before your mom gets here."

Her eyes sparkled as she backed away, sliding her hands across the bulge in his jeans. "I do turn you on, don't I?"

"I think you can see that."

Sarah trudged through the dark woods, as the other two girls lagged behind. She kept hoping to find a spot without all the brush. Finally, she stepped into a small opening where a large boulder protruded from the ground with several smaller ones scattered around its edge. She slipped off the backpack, dropped it to the ground and plopped down. Letting out a sigh, she leaned back against the hard rock. Patricia and Christina soon joined her.

Opening the pack, Sarah handed each of them a water bottle. "Go easy on the liquid; we only have one extra. I didn't expect another person."

"I'm sure I've put a crimp in your rations," Christina said.

"Don't worry. I just don't want us to waste any. We don't know how long it will take us to get off this mountain and we'll need water. I have a couple of candy bars, but we'll not touch those until we really have a need. We can live without food, but not water."

"I'm exhausted," Patricia said. "Are we going to rest here for a while?"

"Yes," Sarah said. "I'm not sure we want to fall asleep though, unless one of us stands guard."

The girls turned silent and huddled close to each other as the sounds of the forest engulfed them. Every rustle of leaves, the hoots of the owls, the crackling of dried leaves as the night creatures scurried for food, and the occasional snap of a twig, caused them to jerk their heads from side to side.

"I hate the forest at night," Patricia whispered. "I couldn't go to sleep if I tried; I'm too scared. What if a bear or mountain lion found us? What would we do?"

Sarah dug the chain she'd removed from the door out of the backpack, and laced it around her neck. "This is the only weapon we have. Let's just pray they'll be more scared of us than we are of them."

"It's better than nothing," Christina said in a low voice.

Patricia zipped up her jacket and slipped her hands into the pockets. "When we get some sunlight, not only will it get warmer, but we'll make much better time finding our way out of here."

Christina held her wrist near her eyes and moved around until she caught a streak of moonlight which reflected off her watch. "Only a couple more hours before things lighten up. It's three o'clock."

"Just remember," Sarah said. "They'll be out in full force searching for us. So we're going to have to be careful. I've been thinking about how we're going to do this and I hope we can find the road going up to the ranch. The main thing is not to walk out in the open. So we'll stay deep in the shadows of the forest and follow it down until we come to a main road. Then we'll decide what to do from there."

The girls huddled together as the chill of the night wormed its way around their bodies, and the rock they leaned against became very cold. They moved away from the stone and sat with their backs against one another, sharing each other's body heat. Christina took off the witch's robe and they wrapped it around the three of them, making sure their new friend had the bulk, as she didn't have on a jacket.

A mountain lion let out a cry in the distance, causing the girls to let out a yelp and leap back toward the rock. They clung to the large boulder for several minutes before drifting back toward one another.

"The cat is far away. I doubt he can even smell us. He's probably just letting the others know he's in his territory." Sarah said, trying to sound confident.

They grew quiet, huddling as close as they could to each other, and shivering in the cold night air. Suddenly, they stiffened and stared into the dark forest, as the definite sound of footsteps over the leaf clad ground, met their ears. Sarah slowly stood along with Patricia and Christina. They backed up to the big rock.

"Climb the boulder," Sarah whispered.

Christina grabbed a long stick, Patricia picked up a few small stones and the three girls climbed to the top. Fortunately, in its protrusion through the ground, the peak had busted off, leaving a flat area. The girls were able to get themselves situated without fear of sliding to the bottom. Their gaze shot back to the spot where they'd heard the sound.

They gasped as a black bear emerged from the dark shadows and ambled toward the rock. Sarah yanked the chain from around her neck and slapped it against the boulder. The bear, startled by the sound, rose up on two feet and sniffed the air.

"Get out of here!" Patricia yelled, and hurled a rock, hitting the furry beast on his shoulder.

Christina whacked her stick against the hard surface. "Go home!"

Again, Sarah swatted the chain against the surface. "Run away, you silly creature!"

The bear dropped to all fours, turned and ran back in the direction he'd come.

Sitting rigidly on the rock, the girls stared into the void.

"You think he's gone for good?" Patricia whispered.

"Black bears will usually run from humans, if they haven't been fed by people. I imagine this one was wild, as this area is not heavily populated." Sarah slid down the boulder. "I'm praying our voices haven't carried and given our position away."

"I think we should move on," Christina said, slipping down beside Sarah.

"Don't leave me," Patricia cried, grasping the side of the rock as she glided down.

Sarah picked up the backpack. "We're lucky the bear didn't rip this apart for the candy bars inside. He obviously didn't smell them."

"I have a feeling he was just rambling around, and didn't expect to come across three loud females," Christina said.

"Thank goodness," the other two said in unison.

The girls again trampled through the brush.

"I'll sure be glad to see the sun," Patricia mumbled.

CHAPTER THIRTY-THREE

Lea quickly dressed, grumbling about Brenda, "Why did she leave for the ranch? I really hadn't planned on going up there, even though I told her I intended making the trip. My day is full of appointments and this is only going to make it more hectic."

Her mind drifted to her husband, as she slapped on a bit of make-up. When Darek returns from his trip and finds out his daughter has been fooling in witchcraft, he's going to have a holy fit. He warned me not to teach her, but I ignored him. Hopefully, I won't find any evidence of it at the ranch. She quickly ran a brush through her hair, grabbed her purse and headed for the car.

She pushed the accelerator hard and prayed no cops were out at this time. When she got to the cut off, she decided to take the back road. Even though it was a lot rougher, it saved about ten minutes and she could use every second.

When she drove up to the house, her anger flared when she saw Jerry Olson standing out in the front yard with Brenda. She came to a hard stop next to her daughter's convertible, sending dust flying into the air.

Brenda hurried toward the car, waving her hand in front of her face and coughing.

"What's your problem, mom? You've just covered my car with dirt. Why'd you come up the back way?"

She pointed toward Jerry. "What the hell's he doing here?"

"Oh, he and his work buddy brought up the groceries in the store's van. Jerry doesn't have to be at work until later, but they had to get the truck back, so I told him I'd take him home."

"To answer your question, I came up the back way to save time. I've got a million things to do and I really hadn't fit this trip into my agenda. So I want to quickly check out the bunkhouse and cottage." She glanced around. "Where are the girls?"

"They've gone berry picking and herb hunting. It's amazing how self-sufficient they've become."

Lea snickered, as she walked briskly toward the building. "I'm sure they love the outdoor johnny."

Brenda shrugged as she skipped along trying to keep up with her mother. "They haven't complained. I think they're very happy to be off the streets."

"I hope they appreciate our kindness in letting them live up here. I don't know what they intend to do with their lives, but they can't stay here forever."

"We'll work it out," she said, opening the door for her mother.

When they stepped inside, Lea stopped abruptly, and stared at the girl with her leg elevated. "What happened to you?"

The girl gave her a nervous smile. "I turned my ankle last night while jogging."

"I see, and where were you running?"

"Back and forth from the bunkhouse to the cottage."

Lea stepped into the other room, with Brenda at her heels. She glanced into the closet and pulled out a few of the dresser drawers. Her gaze scanned the room and made up beds. "It does appear the girls keep a neat place."

"They have to with so many living in such close quarters."

"Do they all get along okay?" Lea asked, looking her daughter in the face.

"As far as I know. They've never complained about each other."

"Okay, I want to check the cottage, then I've got to get home."

They walked across the grounds and entered the small house. The groceries were still stacked on the big table.

"I can see they eat well."

"It's a little hard without a refrigerator and electricity. All the food has to be dry or in cans. They told me they enjoy fixing stuff on the big wooden stove."

"Good grief," Lea said. "How do they bathe?"

"Fortunately they have the well. They just heat it on the stove. They do prefer the bottled water to drink, so I have quite a bit brought out."

"The well water is plenty safe for them to drink; we've had it tested."

"Fine, I'll tell them. I won't have any more brought up. They can save and refill their bottles."

"That will cut down on the grocery bill," Lea said, as she brushed by Brenda and headed for the bedroom.

She opened the door. "Who's staying in here."

Brenda put her hand to her mouth as she noticed the rumpled covers on the cots and a couple of suitcases against the wall. "Oh, my, I'll have to talk to the two girls I put in charge. I told them since there were six, the two I picked to head the group could stay in here. Looks like they're expecting more out of the others than themselves."

Lea waved a hand and left the room. "Well, you can handle that situation. I've got to get going." She headed out the door and hurried back to her car. Climbing in, she slammed the door, and rolled down the window. "When are you going to get Jerry home? I really don't like him up here with all these girls. One of these days he's liable to bring up a group of his drunken buddies and we'll have a rape case on our hands."

"Oh, Mom. He's not that kind of guy."

She narrowed her eyes. "All men are alike. I'll expect you home before dark." She started the car, turned around, and headed toward the back road.

Hands on her hips, Brenda watched as her mother drove out of sight, then she strolled up to Jerry, who'd spent his time leaning against the trunk of a large oak tree, listening to the interchange between mother and daughter.

She took his hand. "Come with me."

Before she could lead him away, he pointed to the main road. "There come your girls."

Brenda jogged toward them. "Did you spot the escapees?"

"No, we didn't see another human being. Not even your mother."

"Mom came and left by the back way."

"I hope everything at the bunkhouse suited her."

"She said you girls kept a neat house."

They all clapped and yelled 'yea'.

"Where in the heck did you store your witch's robes? I didn't spot a one."

The girls giggled. "We spread them out and put them under our bedspreads."

"Great idea," Brenda said. Then she pointed to the road. "I want a couple of you to walk down there every hour and keep an eye out for our lost wanderers. We've got to get them back here. The rest of you need to go to the kitchen and put away the food Jerry brought up last night."

One of the girls stepped forward. "Why do you want to catch the runaways? They're nothing but trouble."

Brenda's eyes flashed. "They have to be taught a lesson."

The girl started to say something else, but one of the others pulled her back into the group.

"I'll check in with you later. Jerry and I will make some runs down the back road and see what we can find."

She moved away from the girls and strolled toward her boyfriend.

He put a hand on her shoulder. "I noticed you scared the girls by talking about teaching Sarah, Patricia and Christina a lesson. I'm curious too. If you catch them, just what do you plan on doing?"

"Scaring the hell out of them with a little witch magic."

Jerry stared at her. "I don't like the look in your eyes."

She swatted his arm away. "Don't worry about it. It has nothing to do with you."

"I'd like for you to take me home soon. I've got some things I need to do."

Tossing her head, she marched to the car. "Okay, but first I want you to help me."

He got into the passenger side. "Doing what?"

"You'll see."

She stopped at the cottage and jumped out. "Come on."

He climbed out. "My head is still killing me. I hope this isn't some major thing you want done."

"It's no big deal."

He followed her inside and into the bedroom she'd used to keep the girls prisoners. "I want all of Sarah's and Patricia's stuff taken out of here. I had to lie to mom and tell her it belonged to Shelby and Barbara. She said they hadn't taken care of this room like the girls in the bunkhouse, and told me to handle it."

"So what are you going to do with their belongings?"

"Put them in the attic out of sight in case Mom makes a surprise visit. You go get the ladder from the shed and I'll put everything I find into their suitcases."

It took about twenty minutes to get the room back in shape and the suitcases hidden. Brenda put the linens in the kitchen for the girls to wash. Then they left in the car and headed down the back road.

The sun finally made its way into the sky. Sarah, Patricia and Christina, happy they could now see where they were stepping, trudged through the underbrush. Once the sweat trickled down their backs, they shed their jackets and tied them around their waist.

All at once, Sarah held up her hand and moved behind the trunk of a large tree. She put her finger to her lips and gave the signal for the girls to drop to their haunches. When the noise of their own footsteps subsided, they could hear a traveling vehicle nearby.

Sarah tried to focus on the sound, and turned her head side to side. Finally, she fixed her gaze to the left and squinted her eyes as she studied the landscape. She scooted around the tree to make sure she couldn't be seen and peeked through some low branches as the noise grew louder. Her heart pounded with renewed energy when she spotted a vehicle about a hundred yards away. Patricia and Christina raised up, and big smiles creased their faces as they watched the car slowly travel out of sight. They'd finally found the road.

"We've got to be extremely careful," Sarah said. "Brenda and Jerry were in her convertible and at the slow rate of speed they were traveling, you can bet they're searching for us."

CHAPTER THIRTY-FOUR

Sarah slipped the backpack off her shoulders and let it drop to the ground. She twisted her torso back and forth, then moved her arms up and down.

Patricia stepped forward. "I'll carry the pack for a while. I'm sure it's making you ache."

"More than I thought it would. Guess I'm not in good shape." She reached into the bag. "Are you ready for a swig of water?"

They nodded.

She handed them each a bottle, took one out for herself, leaned against the tree trunk, and took a large gulp. Screwing on the lid, she placed it back into the pack. "I wonder how far we are from the main road? I haven't heard the car coming back."

Christina wiped her mouth. "They could have circled the area and gone up the other road."

Sarah stared at her. "You mean there's another way to get to the ranch?"

"Yes."

"I wonder which one we just saw Brenda and Jerry going down?"

Christina flopped down on the grass. "Since they kicked up a lot of dust, I'd say the back road, which runs by the cottage. The other one is gravel and leads straight to the ranch house."

Patricia followed Christina's lead and sat on the ground. "The back road must have been the one Jerry used when he brought me, because he stopped right in front of the little house and took me inside."

"Me, too," Sarah said. She glanced at Christina. "Have you ever been inside the ranch house?"

She shook her head. "No, we weren't allowed. Brenda told us it had a very sophisticated alarm system and she'd know immediately if we even peeked in a window."

Sarah slid down the trunk and sat on a root. "How come you ended up here?"

Christina picked up a leaf and tears rimmed her eyes. "Stupid me ran away from home. I realize now what a mistake I've made. If we ever get out of here, I hope my parents will let me come back."

"So you were picked up like us?"

She shook her head. "Not quite. Brenda found several of us on a street corner in San Francisco. After talking to us awhile, she knew we were scared, broke and lonely. She's quite persuasive and before we knew it, we all climbed into her car."

Patricia looked puzzled. "I don't get it. What the heck did she offer you that was so enticing?"

Christina wiped her eyes with the back of her hand. "A roof over our head, free food, and safety from the pimps. At first we all found it fun and exciting living like they did a hundred years ago. But when she introduced the witch stuff, I didn't like it a bit."

Sarah moved closer. "Didn't any of you have cell phones?"

"Only a couple of us did, but once the batteries died, we had no way of charging them. So we decided as long as we were safe, we'd make the best of it and go along with her crazy scheme."

"What made you change your mind?"

Christina reached over and ran her hand over Patricia's head. "When she took the scissors to your beautiful hair. That little act frightened several of us. We knew then, she was capable of doing a lot worse."

Sarah patted her on the shoulder. "I'm glad you found us. I'd sure hate to be wandering around in this forest alone. It's bad enough with the three of us." She stood. "Well, girls, I think we've rested long enough. Let's go find the road."

Hawkman and Jennifer left the courthouse and climbed into the 4X4.

"I think before we head up to the property, I want to swing over to Jerry Olson's place. I'd like to catch him when his father isn't around."

Jennifer frowned. "You don't want to push him real hard or his dad could get you arrested for harassing his son."

He grinned as he pushed the key into the ignition. "I've thought about it. What I'd like to do is scare the hell out of him."

"How would you do that, without his dad knowing?"

"I don't think he'll tell his father about our conversation."

"Are you going to enlighten me?"

"No, I'll see how it goes first. As you've probably guessed, I want you to remain in the car."

She gave him a playful swat on the shoulder. "You're so ornery."

He laughed and pulled away from the curb into the traffic. "I think Jerry is somehow involved with the disappearance of Sarah."

Jennifer glanced at him. "How do you figure?"

"I've been rolling the whole scenario through my head and trying to put myself into his shoes. The other girls in Sarah's group told us she'd had a date with Jerry. Obviously, he saw something in her he liked."

"True, but didn't he tell you Brenda was his girlfriend? So why would he have a date with Sarah?"

"They probably had a squabble."

"If a guy really likes a girl, he's not going to jeopardize his chances of getting her back by having a date with another good looking chick."

Hawkman shrugged. "Depends on how much he really cares about her."

"You're saying, he really didn't want to make up with Brenda?"

"Right. You're getting the picture."

"Then why did he take her back?"

"Because she's probably got something on him."

Jennifer put a hand to her throat. "My word, are you saying Brenda could blackmail Jerry."

"Yep."

"It's hard to believe a girl her age could have such a criminal mind."

"I think she's capable of about anything."

When Hawkman turned the corner, Jennifer suddenly sat up straight. "Don't go any farther!"

Startled, Hawkman stopped at the curb. "What's the matter?"

She pointed. "Does Jerry live on the corner?"

"Yes. Why?"

"Because Brenda just pulled up in her convertible at the front of the house."

Hawkman reached into the glove compartment, withdrew the binoculars, flipped up his eye-patch and placed the glasses to his eyes.

Jennifer watched through the windshield as Jerry fondled Brenda's breast, and gave her a long sensuous kiss. He then climbed out of the car and headed up the sidewalk. Brenda beeped the horn and when he turned around, she blew him a kiss.

"Duck below the dashboard," Hawkman said, as he watched Brenda pull away from the curb. "Never mind, she's making a U-turn."

"Wonder where those two have been?" Jennifer said sarcastically. "Certainly doesn't appear he's grown tired of her."

Hawkman chuckled as he replaced the binoculars into the glove compartment, and flipped down his eye-patch. "At his age, a boy's hormones work overtime."

Jennifer rolled her eyes. "Hers must have a similar growth pattern."

He started the vehicle and drove up to the front of the house. "I think my timing might be perfect."

She undid the seat belt, reached into her purse for reading material, and settled against the back cushion. "Good luck."

Hawkman strolled to the entry and rang the bell.

After a few seconds, Jerry opened the door, then stepped back in surprise. "What do you want?"

"I'd like to talk about Sarah Willis."

"I don't have anything to say to you."

"The police are going to be interested to know where you took Sarah when you picked her up the night she ran away."

Hawkman noticed a flash of fear cross the boy's face. "I don't know what you're talking about."

"I think you do. I have a witness who saw her get into your car that night."

"Hey, man, I just took her to the house of one of her friends."

"Which friend?"

"Uh, Janet Ross."

"Sorry, Jerry. Janet hasn't seen Sarah since she was reported missing. You want to try another guess?"

He tried to shut the door, but Hawkman stuck his boot between the wood and the jamb. "If you'd like to talk to me sometime, here's my number." He held out a business card. "If not, you might tell your dad you're going to need a good lawyer."

Jerry snatched the card from Hawkman's hand and slammed the door.

Moseying back to his 4X4, Hawkman smiled to himself. The boy was definitely involved with Sarah's disappearance.

CHAPTER THIRTY-FIVE

After closing the door, Jerry fell back against the heavy wooden slab, sweat beading his forehead. He soon headed down the hallway. "Thank God, no one's home," he muttered. "If Mom would have heard this conversation, she'd never quit nagging me. Then she'd tell Dad and I'd get hell."

He glanced down at the crumpled card he held in his hand. What does this private investigator know? His tee shirt clung to his back and he felt grimy. He'd go take a shower; maybe it would help him think straight and get rid of this annoying headache.

While the water ran over his body, tangled thoughts drifted to Sarah, Patricia and Christina. They were lost in the forest, with no food. He knew the girls had water, because the side of his head suffered from a good blow from a bottle. Surely they'd find their way to the road before Brenda stumbled across them. She'd become so evil. A shudder ran down his spine, when he realized she could twist everything until the blame for Sarah and Patricia disappearing fell on him. She'd used him and he fell for it. The only good thing was the use of her body, which she freely gave when he had the desire. Thank goodness she used birth control pills, as sometimes her teasing made him so crazy the thought of a condom never entered his mind.

He stepped out of the stall, dried and wrapped the towel around his middle. Gulping down a couple of aspirin, he picked up the business card on the dresser and flopped across the bed. He wished he didn't have to go to work in a couple of hours. He'd drive out to the ranch and search for the girls by himself.

Of course, they'd probably hide, knowing he took them out there.

"Damn!" he said out loud. "Why did I let Brenda talk me into such a crazy scheme? I could go to jail for kidnapping." He tossed the business card onto his desk, and dressed for work.

❦

Jennifer held the map they'd copied at the court house in her lap and directed Hawkman. "This is the same way I went when tailing Brenda."

When they started climbing, it wasn't long before she pointed ahead. "Brenda disappeared in this area. See that dirt road leading up the mountain? I'll bet you that's where she went." She glanced back at the map. "It looks like it's one way to get to the Thompson's ranch."

"Did she stop in this area?"

She nodded. "Yes, I'm sure she spotted me. We were the only two vehicles on the road."

"I think we'll drive around the bend and see where the other entry is located. Then we'll decide which one to try."

He drove past the curve for about a half mile when he spotted a sign in black block letters with an arrow pointing toward a gravel road, stating 'Thompson's Ranch'. "This is certainly a better way to go." He turned onto the narrow lane and steered up a slightly curvy road for about a mile, then popped out of the trees into a cleared area occupied by a lovely ranch house. Hawkman drove past the house and circled the area which consisted of several outbuildings.

She pointed out an area behind a small cottage some distance away. "You can see where the other road comes in."

"We might take it out."

"Seems mighty desolate around here," Jennifer said, snapping pictures of the area.

"You're not looking in the right direction," he said, pointing toward the bunkhouse.

She twisted her head around. "Those must be the girls Lea Thompson talked about."

"Let's stop and find out."

Hawkman pulled up close to the two girls who'd walked out to the circle drive, and rolled down his window. "Hello, we didn't expect to find anyone home."

"We're the caretakers of the ranch. May I ask who you are?"

"My wife and I are looking for property to buy. We saw the sign down on the main throughway and thought we'd just drive up to see what the land looks like with a house on it. I must say, it's a lovely place."

The taller girl folded her arms across her chest. "This property isn't for sale and you're trespassing. I'd like for you to leave."

He motioned toward the other road. "Does that lead out to the main artery?"

"Yes."

"Okay if we use it?"

"I don't care how you go, just get off the property."

As he turned around, two girls jogged up from the road they'd just used. "Wonder how many girls it takes to care for this place? Smells a bit fishy, wouldn't you say?"

"Yes," Jennifer said. Then she gasped. "Well, we've been caught. Here comes Brenda up the back way in her convertible."

Hawkman put on the brakes as the girl skidded to a halt sending dust flying in every direction. She jumped out of the car and stomped up to the driver side of the 4X4, her hands in tight fists resting on her hips. Hawkman peered into blazing green eyes.

"What are you doing here?" she spat.

"Just out for a drive."

Her mouth turned down in a grim expression. "I don't believe it."

Hawkman shrugged. "I really don't care whether you do or not."

Brenda stepped back and pointed at the back road. "Get out of here. You're trespassing on private property. If I catch you up here again, I'll call the authorities."

He rolled up the window and slowly pulled away from the irate girl. "She really likes to throw her weight around for an underaged kid. You'd think she owned the place."

Jennifer had turned in the seat and watched out the rear window as they drove away. "Did you notice her outfit?"

"Don't most kids wear jeans and boots when they come to a ranch?"

"If they have all those girls working here, why would she be in a pair of hard toed boots, as if she's going to do hard labor?"

"Remember, I have no idea how the female mind works, so you tell me."

"It seems odd. She doesn't impress me as one who would get her hands dirty. Another thing mystifying, why all girls and no boys? I'd think working on a ranch would be more of a male thing."

"Good question. I don't see any live stock, or corrals, so maybe they just do soft stuff." He glanced in the rearview mirror. "Wonder where they came from?"

"This whole set up doesn't look right to me."

"Maybe I should go talk to Mrs. Thompson again."

"I think that might be a good idea. However, how are you going to explain us being here?"

He smiled. "My wife and I were out for a ride."

Jennifer laughed. "You think she'll fall for it?"

"Probably not, but the ironic part is, it's true."

CHAPTER THIRTY-SIX

Sarah talked to the girls in a low voice as they trudged through the heavy brush toward the area where they'd seen the car. "We'll use the road only as a guide. If we walk in the open, we'll be spotted, so stay in the shadows along the side. If any vehicle comes through, drop down behind a bush and stay hidden until it passes."

"Why can't we flag down a car to help us?" Patricia asked.

"Who can we trust? We have no idea how many people Brenda might get up here to hunt us down."

"Then how are we ever going to get help?" Patricia asked.

Sarah let out a sigh. "I'm hoping there's another house nearby."

"If there is, it's probably a vacation house and no one's there," Christina said.

Sarah stopped and brushed her hair out of her face. "We might just have to break in."

Christina threw up her hands. "What if there's an alarm system? We could be arrested."

"This is a different situation from breaking into the ranch house. We'd just wait for the authorities to come. Tell them we were kidnapped and how it happened. I don't think we'd be arrested."

When they were in sight of the road, Sarah snapped her head around and immediately dropped to the ground behind a big oak tree. "Get down, there's a car coming."

Both girls plunged to the ground and rolled under a big bush.

Once it went by, Sarah stood. "It was Brenda going to the ranch."

"By herself?" Patricia asked.

"Yes."

"She'll probably get the girls together and form a search party. If we're lucky there'll only be five of them, because Ruth sprained her ankle and I'm not there. I don't think she'll have much luck talking them into separating. After hearing the wild animals at night, none of the girls would venture into the forest without another person."

Sarah turned and looked into her face. "You did."

Christina's gaze went to the ground and she kicked a pebble. "I know, but I couldn't stay any longer. I either had to run or face Brenda's wrath. I chose the forest."

Sarah jerked her head around. "I hear a car coming from the ranch. It might be Brenda with her hoard of witches. Hide!" Once it passed, she frowned. "Christina, did you recognize that light colored SUV?"

She shook her heads. "I've never seen that vehicle at the ranch. Could you make out the passengers?"

"Yes, a man with a cowboy hat and a woman."

Christina frowned. "I wonder who they were?"

"We better keep moving," Patricia said. "Otherwise, we'll never find the main road before dark." She folded her arms across her stomach. "I'm getting mighty hungry."

"At our next break we'll divide up the candy bars."

The girls trudged forward.

Brenda watched the 4X4 disappear around the turn. She whirled around and marched toward the cluster of girls gathered in front of the bunkhouse. "What did they want?"

Shelby stepped forward. "They said they were out looking at property, saw the sign pointing to the ranch and decided to come up."

She threw back her head and laughed. "Would you like me to tell you who they are?"

Shelby shrugged. "Sure, if you want."

"The man is Tom Casey, a private investigator and his wife. They're looking for Sarah Willis."

The girls gasped.

Shelby stared at Brenda. "How did they know she might be here?"

"They don't. I haven't the vaguest idea why they showed up. Right now we don't have time to discuss it. We've got to search for those three, and find them before dark. Grab a jacket and let's get going. I'll meet you at the cottage."

"Wait," Barbara yelled.

Brenda whirled around. "What?"

"I want to know what you're going to do to Sarah, Patricia and Christina if we find them?"

Brenda sensed hostility in the girl's voice. "Don't worry, I'm not going to hurt them. I'll probably take them to a big city and put them on the streets. We'll see how they like it there. I just don't want their bodies found in the forest."

"I sure don't want to get in trouble with the law."

"Oh, my gosh, Barbara," Brenda said with a wave of her hand. "No one's going to jail. Those girls are out there without food or water. If we don't find them, they'll die." She walked toward her car with a sly grin, then turned and yelled. "Meet me at the cottage in five minutes."

Soon four of the girls meandered into the kitchen. Brenda pointed at the stack of sacks on the table. "I see you girls haven't put the food away yet."

"We haven't had time. We've been going up and down the road looking for Christina," Shelby said. "If you want, Tammy can stay and clean things up."

Brenda flitted a hand in the air. "No, I need you all. Where's Ruth?"

"She still can't walk. Her ankle is really swollen. Maybe you should take her to the doctor."

"I'll check her out later," Brenda said, picking up a bottle of water and pushing past them. "I'll drive us down to where I think we should start the search." Then she stopped. "Have you got the ropes?"

The girls nodded.

"Okay, grab a bottle of water and let's go."

Brenda drove down to the main road and parked on the side. "I figure they've gotten quite a ways from the cottage, so we'll come from the opposite direction, which they won't expect."

"What if they followed the road down and headed toward town?" Barbara asked.

Brenda bit her lower lip. "Good thinking. They won't walk on the pavement, as they'd be scared I'd spot them. They'll more than likely be alongside the bank so they can keep the thoroughfare in sight, but still duck down and hide from oncoming traffic." She eyed the dense forest. "They could be on either side. We'll walk down about a half mile, then go up into the bushes and search the area going back toward the ranch. We'll meet at my car in a couple of hours."

Before leaving the convertible, Brenda put the top up so she could lock the car, and the girls started walking toward town.

Sarah, Patricia, and Christina dashed across the back road and quickly rolled under some bushes as they again heard another vehicle. Squeezed together under a clump of branches, they peeked out at the passing car.

"They're going to search for us now," Sarah said.

Christina, with a puzzled expression, watched the car roll by their hiding place.

"Where are they going?" Patricia whispered.

Once the witches had gone around a bend in the road, Sarah stood and ran her fingers through her hair. "I think they're planning to start at the bottom and work their way up, in hopes of catching us from the opposite direction. It'll make it hard for us to keep the road in sight. We've got to figure out a plan to fool them." She waved an arm forward. "Let's keep moving while we talk."

Christina had long legs and could keep up with Sarah, but Patricia lagged behind and kept having to jog to keep up.

"I'm really getting tired, and I'm so hungry," Patricia said.

"Let me have the pack, it's probably slowing you down," Sarah said, then pointed to a knoll up ahead. "Let's make it to there, then we'll rest and I'll give you a candy bar, but you shouldn't eat it all at once. You may need a bite or two later."

They finally made it and flopped down on the grass just before the crest. Sarah crawled up to the top then dropped down flat. She waved for the other two to come up, but put her finger to her lips to warn them to be quiet.

"Keep your head below the tall grass," she whispered, then pointed in a downward direction.

Christina covered her mouth and let out a low gasp.

CHAPTER THIRTY-SEVEN

Hawkman drove in silence for several minutes.

"I can hear the gears grinding in your brain," Jennifer said. "What's on your mind?"

"My gut tells me something's all wrong at the Thompson's ranch. Did you get the feeling Brenda was in control?"

"No doubt."

"Doesn't it strike you as odd a young girl of seventeen would be running a ranch?"

"Definitely. As aggressive as she is, she's still a minor."

"Let's stop at the police station and talk to Williams. I want to find out if he's had any breaks in the cases of those other two kids who were reported missing."

When they arrived and parked, Hawkman moved around to the passenger side and took Jennifer's hand as she climbed out. He put his arm around her shoulders as they walked up the steps. "You sure look sexy in those jeans and boots."

She laughed. "I feel like a lumber jack."

"No male fills out those pants like you do."

"Hawkman, stop it, we're at the police station."

He chuckled and gave her a squeeze as they walked into the building. When they reached the detective's office, Jennifer stepped in first.

When Williams glanced up, he dropped his pen and jumped out of his seat. "Jennifer! How good to see you." He gave her a big hug, then pushed her back at arms length and gave her the once over. "You're as beautiful as ever."

She waved him off. "You're making me blush."

He hooked a thumb at Hawkman. "Can't you get rid of this big ugly guy. I could show you the town and we'd have a great time."

"Afraid not," Hawkman said. "I'm not only her husband, but her bodyguard as well, so wherever she goes I tag along."

"He's no fun." He pulled up an extra chair for Jennifer. "I can probably bet my last dollar you're here on business."

"Yep," Hawkman said, as they huddled around the detective's desk. "Have you had any clues pop up over those two kids you told me disappeared. One, a boy and the other, a girl."

Williams pulled a couple of folders from underneath a stack of papers. "Phil Gray returned home over the weekend. Turns out he spent a few nights with a friend his folks didn't know. Guess he cooled off and decided the old homestead wasn't so bad after all."

"What about the girl?" Hawkman asked.

The detective shook his head. "Not a trace of her whereabouts. The mother is beside herself and calls the station several times a day."

"Does she have any idea where the girl could have gone?"

"None. No kin have seen or heard from her. The mother was devastated when she discovered the girl had packed a bag and left on her own accord."

"Sounds familiar." Hawkman leaned back in his chair. "You know Darek and Lea Thompson?"

"Not personally, but know of them. They own quite a bit of real estate in the area, and Mr. Thompson is a very successful executive."

"What about Lea and the daughter, Brenda?" Jennifer asked.

"I see their names in the paper a lot. They're quite the social butterflies." Williams frowned as he eyed her. "Why all the questions about this family?"

"We suspect they're somehow connected to the disappearance of Sarah Willis."

The detective leaned forward. "Please fill me in."

Hawkman and Jennifer told him about the events of the day, and why they thought Brenda was dabbling in witchcraft, but had no proof.

Williams listened intently, then scratched his sideburn. "You asked me earlier if I'd seen any signs of witches in the area, which I hadn't. So this all sounds mighty bizarre. Of course, if anything was going on at the Thompson's ranch, no one would know about it, because the place is way up in the hills, miles from civilization." He furrowed his brow. "I wonder what those girls are doing up there and where they came from?"

"Who knows. Supposedly, they're looking after the ranch." Jennifer said.

"Seems a bit far-fetched; tending a ranch is usually done by men. Are they taking care of the house?"

Hawkman shrugged. "Have no idea. I thought I'd go over and talk to Mrs. Thompson about the arrangement."

"Good idea. Also, you mentioned Jerry Olson. He's a high school athletic star. What role does he play?"

"Not sure," Hawkman said. "He's somehow involved, maybe no more than being Brenda's boyfriend."

"Well, you've got a case on your hands. Let me know if I can be of assistance."

Jennifer and Hawkman rose. The men shook hands and Williams gave Jennifer another big hug.

"Drop by and see me anytime." He winked as he nodded toward Hawkman. "He doesn't have to be with you."

Hawkman raised a finger. "I'm her bodyguard. Best you not forget."

Jennifer shook her head. "Would you two knock it off."

They left the station and climbed into the SUV.

She let out a sigh as she snapped her seat belt. "Detective Williams didn't have much to offer."

"No, afraid not. We pretty much have to go on our leads. I think we're on the right track. I didn't tell Williams the fright I put into Jerry Olson."

She cocked her head and looked at Hawkman. "What did you say to the boy?"

"I accused him of picking up Sarah after she left her house. Told him I had a witness. The weird thing is, he didn't deny it."

Jennifer frowned. "Do you think he could have killed her?"

He shot a look at her. "Boy, are you morbid. I'm hoping he followed Brenda's orders and took Sarah to the ranch. I'd really like to search those outbuildings. First, I need to get permission from Mrs. Thompson. If she doesn't give it, I'll have to use Williams to issue a warrant."

"I don't think we have enough evidence to obtain one from a judge."

Hawkman grimaced. "I'm afraid you're right. Which means I might have to do some sleuthing on my own."

"Not without me. I'm your partner; don't forget."

He grinned. "Didn't figure you'd let me go alone."

Christina watched through the tall grass, her hand still covering her mouth, as Brenda and her tribe of witches strolled down the road.

"Where the heck are they going?" Patricia whispered.

"Sarah's guess was right," Christina responded. "They're hoping to cut us off by coming up in front of us."

"We've definitely got a problem," Sarah said. "They'll probably split up and half will work the other side of the road. So regardless, we risk getting caught."

"What about going above them," Christina said.

Sarah shook her head. "The chance of losing our way is too great. We need to keep the road in view at all times. Also, we don't have enough water to last more than a day or two."

Tears welled in Patricia's eyes. "What are we going to do? I don't want them to catch us, but I don't want to die either."

Once the band of witches disappeared around a curve in the road, Sarah rolled over, sat up and hugged her legs. "Our best bet is try to spot them before they see us."

Christina pushed herself up off the ground. "You know they'll fan out. They're not running for their freedom like us, so it'll be hard to see them all at once."

Patricia's gaze darted from girl to girl, her expression reflecting fear. "We're going to stay together, aren't we?"

Sarah reached over and patted her leg. "Yes. If one of us is caught, we all go." She stood. "Okay, let's head out. We'll stay in the thickest brush and no talking."

She picked an extensive thicket for them to trudge through. Sarah and Christina had to continuously stop to let Patricia catch up. As they plodded along, branches scraped their arms, caught in their hair and slapped against their faces. The heat became unbearable, to the point their shirts clung to their backs and insects buzzed around their heads.

Soon Sarah stopped, took the corner of her sweatshirt tied around her waist and wiped it across her eyes, then squinted into the bushes. "Where's Patricia?" she whispered.

Christina jerked around. "She was right beside me just a few minutes ago."

Suddenly, a scream echoed through the forest. Sarah broke into a run toward the sound. Christina followed at her heels.

CHAPTER THIRTY-EIGHT

"Let's see if we can catch Mrs. Lea Thompson at home," Hawkman said, as he turned the corner.

Jennifer pointed toward the house. "You're in luck. She just pulled into the driveway. Want me to go with you?"

"No, I don't anticipate this will take long."

"True. Throwing you off the property only requires about a minute."

He grinned as he climbed out of the vehicle. Adjusting his hat, he walked toward Lea as she climbed out of her car. "Hello, Mrs. Thompson."

Her head snapped up from digging in her purse. "What do you want? I'm in a big hurry and don't have time to answer a bunch of your silly questions."

"I only have a couple this time."

"What are they?"

"How many girls are living at your ranch?"

She glared at him. "I don't think that's any of your business."

"My wife and I were driving around in the hills and came across your property. We were confronted by several females."

Her eyes narrowed. "I don't believe you just came across the ranch. It's not on a main thoroughfare. You have to drive up a private road. You were snooping."

Hawkman shrugged. "I'd like your permission to enter the premises."

Lea frowned. "Why?"

"To prove your daughter has nothing to do with the disappearance of Sarah Willis."

She abruptly stood and shouted. "How dare you insinuate such a thing. If you're caught at the ranch again, I'll have you arrested for trespassing. In fact, get off this property." Lea grabbed a jacket out of the car, slammed the door and stormed into the house.

Hawkman strolled back to his 4X4 and climbed into the driver's seat. Jennifer glanced at her watch.

"I underestimated the time. It took a minute and a half for her to give you the riot act."

Smiling, he turned over the engine. "How could you tell?"

"Her body language. You didn't make her very happy."

"No, I didn't," he said, pulling away from the curb. "These people seem very sensitive. Sure makes them appear guilty of something."

"Consider the fact you're a private investigator. No one likes having their lives disrupted by a nosey person."

"Little do they realize, I could make things easier if they'd cooperate. Especially, if they have nothing to hide." The cell phone vibrated against his waist. He unsnapped the instrument from his belt, and placed it to his ear. "Tom Casey speaking."

Jennifer could tell from his sudden rigid posture and solemn expression, this call had grabbed his attention.

The brambles lashed at Sarah's arms as she bolted toward Patricia's scream. She and Christina skidded to a halt when they spotted their friend sitting on the ground Indian style, clutching her head. Brenda stood over her, gripping a fistful of hair, holding the glistening shears in her other hand.

Her gaze pinpointed Sarah's face. "Stay where you are, or I'll cut the rest of her hair to the scalp."

Sarah breathed heavily as she glared at Brenda. "You're evil."

"Shut your mouth."

The rustle of bushes caused Sarah and Christina to glance around. Coming up behind them were two of the witches carrying pieces of rope.

Brenda motioned toward the two girls. "Tie their wrists behind their backs, then signal the others we've found them." Then she yanked up a sobbing Patricia to a standing position and bound her hands. "You're lucky your friends didn't give us any trouble or you'd now be bald." She shoved the girl toward Sarah and Christina.

After the witches bound their hands, Barbara blew a shrill whistle.

"Okay, let's get them to the car," Brenda ordered.

Their hearts heavy, and pushed ahead by the witches, the three prisoners lumbered through the thicket down to the road. They journeyed up the asphalt until they came to the convertible, where the other two were waiting. They shoved Sarah, Patricia and Christina into the car, then piled on top of them, practically suffocating the three. Brenda drove up the rough back road at quite a clip, bouncing the girls unmercifully.

They finally arrived at the cottage and dragged the three girls by their arms into the former cell. Patricia slumped down on her cot. "Where's Christina going to sleep?"

"The traitor might have to sleep on the floor," Brenda smirked.

"What'd you do with our stuff, burn it in your witch's bonfire?" Sarah spat.

Brenda stepped up right in Sarah's face, their noses almost touching. "You're a real smart aleck. Keep talking and I'm liable not to give anything back."

Sarah narrowed her eyes and stared into the evil green orbs.

Brenda shoved her away. "Barbara and Shelby, come with me, you other two guard them until we get back."

She led the two girls into the hallway, directed them to get the ladder and bring down the girls' suitcases from the attic. "I've got an extra chain and padlock in the kitchen. We'll need to secure the door again. Are your girls trustworthy enough to take care of them, or am I going to have to do it myself?"

"I'll take on the responsibility," Barbara said. "They won't escape again."

"Good." Brenda turned and headed for the kitchen as the other two carried the small ladder to the opening in the ceiling.

Shelby remained silent as Barbara climbed the rungs and handed down the two suitcases, then returned the ladder to the outside. When she joined Shelby in the hallway, she picked up one of the bags and whispered, "What's eating at you?"

"I don't like what's happening," Shelby said. "We could be in serious trouble if we're ever caught."

"We'll talk later," Barbara said, as Brenda came from the other direction, a large chain dangling from her arm.

"What about a bed for Christina?" Barbara asked.

"Oh, damn, I forgot about her, the stupid traitor," Brenda said, stopping outside the door. She tapped her forefinger on her chin as she glanced down the hall. Then she pointed to a door. "Check the closet and see if there's an extra cot."

Shelby opened the door and searched inside. "No, there's nothing in here but linens."

"Grab a set of sheets and a couple of extra blankets." Brenda grinned. "Guess she'll have to sleep on the floor after all."

They entered the room and dropped the girls' belongings on the floor, then piled the linens on the top.

Christina stared at the floor. "Could I get my things from the bunkhouse?"

Brenda rolled her eyes. "You've survived just fine without them. What were you going to do, come back and get your stuff?"

"No. I'd hoped never to see this place again. But since I'm here, I need some clean clothes."

She sniffed. "I'd say you need a bath, too. If the girls want to bring your things, it's fine with me. I'm not going to get them. You've caused me enough problems."

Brenda glanced around the room. "Looks like you'll be sleeping on the floor; we couldn't find another cot."

Christina nodded.

"Could we have some water and maybe a sandwich?" Patricia asked.

"Good grief," Brenda said. "Tammy, go get some water bottles. Oh, and I forgot to tell you girls. The water from the well is good to drink. It's been tested. So no more bottled water. Save your containers to carry some back to your quarters." Then she turned back to Patricia. "You'll have to wait until the girls fix their dinner. I'm sure they'll bring you something to eat."

Tammy came back into the room and placed three bottles of water on the dresser.

Brenda stood in the doorway. "Let's hope you've stated all your prisoner demands. Get ready for your punishment tonight."

The three girls stared at the evil leader.

Brenda stepped into the hallway and gestured toward the girls. "You can untie their hands, and we'll go back to the bunkhouse and make our plans."

The girls rubbed their wrists while gazing at the big door as they heard the rattle of the chain and the click of the padlock.

Patricia put her hands to her face and sobbed. "If it weren't for me, we wouldn't be back here."

Sarah sat down beside her and put an arm around the quivering girl's shoulders. "Don't cry. We figured we weren't going to get away when we saw the witches coming up the mountain. Like I told you, if one of us got caught, we would all come back together. Now we've got to plan our next move."

Christina handed each one a bottle of water.

"Oh, man, does that taste good," Patricia said.

Sarah went to the window and peered out. "I hope we don't have to wait long for food. I'm famished. Good, they're headed for the bunkhouse." She bent down and picked up the backpack off the floor. "You know they didn't search this." Rummaging through the bag, she pulled out what water they had left, and the candy bars they'd never had time to eat. Then with a smile on her face, she dragged out the chain she'd taken off the door. "Where can we hide this, we might need it?"

"Maybe as soon as tonight," Christina said. "I get the feeling Brenda has something malicious up her sleeve."

Sarah gnawed her lower lip in thought, then jumped up and dragged her suitcase to the cot. She unzipped the lid, flipped it back, drew out a long-tailed blouse, then glanced at the girls with a twinkle in her eye. "We'll figure out a way for me to wrap the chain around my waist and I'll cover it with this shirt. We have to make it so I can easily reach it."

"What if they tie us up?" Patricia asked.

"We'll convince them we won't cause any trouble."

"Let's hope it works. Right now let's split those candy bars," Christina said.

CHAPTER THIRTY-NINE

Hawkman's jaw tightened as he listened to the caller. "You know where it is? I'll meet you there in thirty minutes."

Jennifer watched the veins in his neck bulge. When he hung up, she frowned. "Very intense conversation. Who was it?"

"Jerry Olson. He's meeting us at the office."

Her mouth dropped open. "Really? Did he give you any reason why he wanted to see you?"

"He said, it's important. I have a gut feeling he's somehow involved with Sarah's disappearance. Maybe we're going to get to the bottom of this mess. At least get a clue or two."

Jennifer leaned back against the seat and stared out the windshield. "It really bothers me to think these underaged kids might be involved in crime." Then she glanced at him. "I take my comment back. It bothers me to see anyone involved in criminal behavior, but especially kids."

He nodded. "I understand what you're saying. It exasperates me too. I feel my hands are legally tied, as I can't go after them like an adult. I'm about ready to pull in Detective Williams."

Jennifer let out a sigh. "It might be wise."

Hawkman pulled into the alley and parked in his usual place. When they approached the stairs, Jerry stood up from where he'd been sitting on one of the steps.

"Hello, Mr. and Mrs. Casey. I'm glad you could meet me at such short notice." He ducked his head. "Otherwise, I might have chickened out."

Hawkman pointed up the stairs. "Let's go inside."

Jennifer took a seat on the couch in the small waiting alcove out of Jerry's view. She figured the boy would be more at ease talking man to man. Hawkman motioned for the young lad to take the chair in front of the desk. He studied Jerry and could tell the boy was very nervous as the minute he sat down, he clasped his hands in his lap so tightly, the knuckles turned white.

"What's on your mind?" Hawkman asked.

Jerry closed his eyes and tilted his head upwards. "Man, I think I'm in a heap of trouble and when my old man finds out, I'm done."

Hawkman frowned. "I don't follow."

"He warned me a year ago about getting involved with Brenda and I ignored his advice. He told me her whole family was nothing but trouble."

"In what way?"

"Mrs. Thompson has the reputation of being a witch." He raised a finger. "That's the real kind. Brenda learned the basics from her mom, but has gotten more deeply involved and thinks she can cast spells on people."

"So how does that involve you. Are you a warlock?"

He let out a nervous laugh and shook his head. "No way. I know this sounds cocky, but Brenda's very jealous of me. If I so much as comment about another girl, she goes into a tizzy. We got into a big argument one night and broke up. Not thinking about the consequences, I asked Sarah for a date. Once Brenda found out, all hell broke loose. After we patched things up, she made me swear I'd do anything she asked."

"I still don't see where you've done any wrong."

Jerry held up his hands, palms out. "My story's just beginning."

"I'm listening."

"On my date with Sarah, she told me how unhappy she'd become at home since her parents had divorced. Her mother drove her crazy and she couldn't live with her father because of his job, which took him out of town for days. She gave me the impression she wasn't going to hang out at her mother's much longer." He shrugged. "To make a long story short, in Brenda's cunning way, she got it out of me about Sarah's thoughts of running away. She told me to tell her she could come stay at her ranch with the other girls. It would be a safe place until she got things in order."

Hawkman sat up straight. "Are you telling me Sarah Willis is there?"

The boy nodded. "Yeah, guarded by the tribe of witches."

"Where did those girls come from?"

"Brenda picked them up off the streets of San Francisco, promising them food and a roof over their heads. All they had to do was keep the ranch in order."

Hawkman nodded. "Fits with the story Mrs. Thompson told me."

"Yeah, but Brenda had other ideas, and I doubt her mom knows what she had planned. She also neglected to tell those girls anything, until she had them settled at the ranch."

"Oh, and what were those?"

"She wanted to start her own witch clan."

Hawkman raised a brow. "Did the girls agree with this plan?"

"All but Christina. She helped Sarah and Patricia escape."

Hawkman stiffened. "Patricia who? And who's Christina?"

Jerry ran his hands over his face. "I've gotten ahead of myself. Patricia Riley is a girl from school who ran away and Christina is, or was, one of the witches until she defected."

"How'd the girls arrive at the ranch?"

He backtracked and told Hawkman how he'd waited for Sarah down the street from her house and driven her into the hills. He'd done the same things with Patricia Riley.

"How'd you know what day or time the girls would leave their respective houses?"

The boy shrugged. "Just kept my eyes and ears open. It took me a couple of nights watching their places before it actually happened. I'd overheard Sarah's friends talking one day, and they said she'd made the decision to run away. Patricia's boyfriend just flat out told me."

"So why did Brenda want Patricia out there. Did you have a date with her too?"

"No." Jerry took a deep breath and exhaled. "Like I told you, Brenda's insanely jealous. One day I remarked about Patricia's beautiful long hair. She went off like a firecracker."

"So Brenda wants to cast a spell on both those girls?"

"Yeah, and probably Christina too, since she betrayed the group. Maybe even do worse to her since she's a deserter."

"Where were Sarah and Patricia kept on the ranch?"

"There's a cottage right at the corner when you go up the back road. It has an old fashioned kitchen where the witches fix their meals. There's no running water or electricity on that place except at the main ranch house. There's a well where they can pump water."

"The girls were kept in this dwelling?"

Jerry nodded. "Yeah, there's a couple of extra rooms. Brenda keeps the prisoners in one of them. She got the door chained with a padlock and the window has bars. There's no way they can escape. I thought they'd be with the others in the bunkhouse. When I discovered they weren't, I made up my mind not to bring any more girls out there."

"How did you know they'd escaped?"

He told Hawkman about the night he caught Sarah in the kitchen and how she'd hit him with a bottle of water causing him to bang his head against the cabinet, knocking him out. "I figured the girls would be safe when they got out of there, but it's rugged country and they didn't know the area. So they could flounder for quite awhile before coming upon a road, which is obviously what happened, because Brenda's group found the girls and brought them back to the ranch, locking them all in one room."

"Do you know what Brenda plans to do to them?"

He looked into Hawkman's face. "I imagine she'll use some sort of witchcraft. I really don't know, but I'm scared she'll do something drastic. I think she's lost it. I'm hoping you'll go up and rescue those girls."

"Do you think Brenda's capable of physically hurting them?"

Jerry slapped his hands on his thighs. "Yeah."

"You realize, if what you told me is true, you're going to be in trouble for participating in a kidnapping scheme."

The boy's eyes glistened with moisture as he nodded. "Maybe with me coming to you, they'll go easy on me."

"I'll do what I can, but can't promise a thing."

He sighed. "I understand. At least I feel better."

"When do you think this witch ritual will take place?"

"No idea. Since the escapees were found today, Brenda will need time to plan her evil deed. I'd say no later than tomorrow night." Jerry stood. "I hope you can do something to save them from her wrath."

"If you're right on the timing, we can." Hawkman rose and extended his hand. "I appreciate your coming in. Stay in town."

"Don't worry, I'm not going anywhere until this whole mess is cleared up."

"By the way, do you have a cell phone so I can contact you?"

"Yes." Jerry gave him the number.

After the young man left the office, Jennifer crossed the room. "This is boiling into a scary situation."

"Very. I'm going to contact Detective Williams. He needs to know we've located Patricia Riley. Also, I'll need his assistance in gaining entrance to the ranch. Mrs. Thompson has threatened me with arrest if I set foot on her property."

"This will help convince him." She placed the tape recorder on the desk.

He smiled. "Great thinking."

"I figured you didn't want to use yours at the moment."

"It might have turned Jerry off."

He picked up the phone and punched the memory button for the detective. "When do you expect him back? Have him call me when he returns. Tell him I have information on the missing girl, Patricia Riley." He hung up, frowned and glanced at Jennifer. "He's out on a case, probably for the rest of the night. Jerry thinks it won't be until tomorrow before his girl friend conjures up some spell to cast upon her prisoners, but I don't trust Brenda. She's impulsive and will want to take out her revenge soon. Are you ready to take on the risk of getting arrested?"

Jennifer nodded. "Absolutely. We've got to get those girls out of there."

CHAPTER FORTY

The three girls snapped their heads around as they heard the chain rattle on the door. When it opened, a large black plastic bag was scooted into the room.

"Here's your stuff, traitor."

Christina dragged it to the foot of Sarah's cot and proceeded to search through her items. She pulled out several pieces of clothing and folded them neatly, stacking them in a pile. "Boy, you can tell they just threw my stuff in here. Sure shows you what fake friends they truly are."

"It's hard to say how they really feel with Brenda standing over them. They're probably scared to death," Sarah said.

Patricia lay curled in a fetal position on her bed. "I don't trust any of those witches. Their minds have been warped by the evil one."

The sun had sunk into the horizon and the room took on an eery cast of gloom. Sarah stood looking out the window toward the bunkhouse.

Christina slipped on a pair of clean jeans and a shirt. "It sure feels good having on fresh clothes. I sure envied you guys when you were able to get out of those dirty things and I had to stay in my filthy ones." She glanced over at Sarah. "Any action?"

"There's some movement, but they aren't heading in this direction."

Christina moved behind Sarah and peered into the evening dimness. "They're piling up wood to make a bonfire. I don't like it."

Sarah turned and looked at her friend. "You were involved with them for a while. What do you think Brenda has in mind?"

"Anytime she had us build a fire, she did strange things. Once she had us dance around it naked as she threw stuff into the flames. It crackled and popped, then weird laughter echoed through the air." She shivered. "Gave me the willies, not to mention scared me to death."

"What does she plan on doing with my hair?" Patricia asked.

Christina rubbed her arms. "She talked like she wanted to cast a spell on you, so you'd never be able to grow it long again."

Patricia's eyes grew wide. "How could she do such a thing?"

"That's ridiculous," Sarah scoffed. "Brenda's obviously lost her mind. What kind of power does she think she has?"

"She's done some very weird things."

Sarah stared at her. "For instance?"

Christina wrung her hands and paced the small room. "One day she brought in a lizard, and made us sit around her in a dark room. She did some chants, and moved her hands over the thing. The lizard turned onto its back, then flipped up into the air and dropped dead."

Sarah threw her hands in the air. "Good grief, Christina, you actually believe she made the lizard die?"

"I don't know. I just knew I didn't want any part of it."

"Sounds like Brenda's enthralled with herself and thinks she's got super powers. It's a bunch of hogwash," Sarah said, emphatically. "You can't let her scare you."

"Look what she did to my hair," Patricia said.

Sarah pointed a finger in the air. "She cut your hair with shears, not with magical powers. That's what frightens me the most. Brenda's capable of hurting us." She patted the chain laced around her waist. "We prepare physically to fight her off, not with some stupid witchcraft."

Patricia scooted to the end of her cot and swung her legs over the edge. "How will we do it with all those other girls helping her? They can hold us down while she does whatever she pleases."

Sarah narrowed her eyes. "For one thing, we won't let them tie our arms. We'll fight them off. There's three of us and probably only four of them, as I doubt Ruth can come, if her ankle is still swollen. Brenda will be busy preparing her big debut, so she probably won't show up to escort us to the spot." Sarah rolled her eyes. "She'll just send her servants."

"We can count Tammy and Kate out as problems. They're wimps, and will back off from any confrontation," Christina said.

The two girls continued to gaze out the window, even though the room had darkened considerably, the outside still glowed from the setting sun.

Sarah turned and gazed at them. "Tonight, we don't sleep. We'll keep watch, as I have a sneaky suspicion they'll make their move near the bewitching hour of midnight."

A sob came from Patricia. "I'm horrified at what they might do to me."

Sarah put a hand on her hip and glared at Patricia. "This is no time to be a chicken. We need you, so stop bawling. Think about Christina. No telling what they have in mind for her. She deserted the clan and they're mad."

"Aren't you worried about yourself?"

"If they so much as lay a hand on my body, I plan to give them a fight for their money."

Patricia pulled her legs up on the cot, hugged her knees and shivered. "You've got more guts than me."

Christina walked over and patted her on the shoulder. "The adrenalin will flow when you get into a situation, so don't fret. You'll strut your stuff like a banty rooster."

"What do you think they'll do to us?" Patricia asked.

Christina exhaled. "I don't know what they'll try, but we're not going to let them finish."

"I don't understand how those girls could do what Brenda wants."

"They're all lost souls. Shelby and Barbara are the mean ones. Kate, Tammy, and Ruth follow them around like whipped dogs."

Sarah crossed from the window toward the girls. "Do either of you have anything in your stuff which might serve as a weapon?"

Both shook their heads.

Hawkman and Jennifer sat at the desk in the office, making their plans. He leaned back and tapped the pencil eraser on his chin.

"I doubt any type of ritual will occur before dark, and we need to catch them in the midst of whatever they plan on doing. The bad thing about trying to rescue the girls is, they have no idea we're the good guys and might run or turn on us."

"That's right," Jennifer said, wide eyed. They have no idea who we are."

Hawkman's cell phone vibrated against his waist. "Maybe this is Williams." He held it to his ear. "Tom Casey." He glanced at Jennifer. "Get to my office as soon as you can. I'll tell you when you get here." He hung up. "Our salvation has just arrived."

Jennifer wrinkled her forehead. "Sure didn't sound like you were talking to Detective Williams."

He shook his head. "Greg Willis just rolled into town and wanted to know if we had an update on Sarah."

"I know what's going through your brain. Do you really think it's wise to have him accompany us?"

"Yes, once Sarah sees her father, she'll know we've come to rescue them."

"I understand that part, but how will he respond when he sees the situation?"

"He seems like a level headed guy. Hopefully, he'll remain calm until we get the girls to safety." Hawkman glanced at his watch. "It won't take him ten minutes to get here from his apartment."

They turned toward the door when it opened with a whoosh. Greg Willis stepped inside.

"I drove as fast as the law would allow. Have you found my girl?"

"I think so. Sit down. I'll tell you what we've discovered."

Hawkman highlighted the events of the past few days.

Greg wiped a hand across his face. "You mean my little girl is held a prisoner by a group of hags?"

"We understand Brenda Thompson leads the pack; the rest are followers. Sarah knows her from school, and dated Brenda's boyfriend, which led the girl into a frenzy of jealousy. We also learned, Sarah is not alone. Two other girls are also kept confined in the same room."

Greg clenched his hands into fists. "Have these witches hurt my daughter?"

"We don't know. The story we were told, is the girls did escape, but were captured before they made it to safety. We want to get to them before any harm is done."

"You're sure this is my Sarah?"

"My source would know, and I believe him."

Tears streamed down Greg's face. "I'm so relieved."

"I'd like you to go with us, but you have to assure me you'll obey my orders. Your daughter has no idea who we are, and considering what she's been through, she might not trust us as being her rescuers. Once she sees you, then she'll know we're there to save her."

"I'll do anything you ask. First, may I call Cathy?"

Hawkman held up a hand. "I don't expect any trouble, but one never knows. So why don't you hold off contacting her until we have Sarah safely in our hands. Then you can walk her right to the door."

Willis stood abruptly. "Let's get going. What are we waiting for?"

Hawkman motioned him to sit down. "Darkness."

CHAPTER FORTY-ONE

When Lea Thompson finally reached her daughter on the cell phone, she didn't like Brenda's tone. "What do you mean you'll be spending the night at the ranch? Is that boy up there?"

"For crying out loud, Mother, Jerry's not here. The girls and I decided to have a little party and since I brought up some wine, I don't think you'd want me to drive off this mountain if I got tipsy."

"I'm not happy with this news one bit. Those girls are all minors and if one of them gets drunk and ends up hurt, I'm responsible. Don't you realize we could be sued for everything we're worth?"

"Mom, give me a break. There's hardly enough to go around, so stop worrying about us getting wiped out."

"Maybe I should drive up and chaperone."

"No! You'd spoil the whole thing. Don't you dare come up here."

"Promise you won't get into the liquor cabinet at the ranch house."

"I give my word. I'll talk to you in the morning."

After Lea hung up, she scowled and drummed her fingers on the desktop. "That child is going to be the death of me," she mumbled. Pulling her appointment calendar toward her, she glanced at the clock and realized she'd scheduled a meeting in an hour to introduce the chosen fashion models for the upcoming show. She sighed, and headed for the shower. "Thank goodness, I don't have to dress up," she said aloud, grabbing a pants suit from the closet.

Brenda had stepped outside to answer the call from her mother. When they finished their conversation, she jammed the phone into her jeans pocket in disgust. "Mom better not come up here. It would ruin everything," she growled, stomping to the back of the bunkhouse where she'd set up a small lab in a long skinny room, which at one time served as a closet for dirty cowboy boots and slickers. She'd always kept it locked and had tacked an 'Off Limits' sign on the door. As far as she could tell, no one had ever entered her domain.

She sat down on a tall stool and turned on the battery operated lamp. The small shelf, originally used for saddle packs, functioned great as a work table. Brenda pulled the book of witch spells toward her and flipped open one of the marked pages. The corners of her mouth turned up as she read. Reaching across the space, she dragged a plastic bag full of hair toward her, reached inside and took out several strands, which she dropped into a decanter. She then mixed a concoction, and her green eyes sparkled as the mixture fizzed and bubbled, almost running over the top. Taking a pen, she wrote the letter 'P' on a label and stuck it to the outside. Covering the brew with a plastic lid, she turned to another page and went to work making two more sinister looking brews which she labelled with the initials 'S' and 'C'. She then prepared another potion and as it bubbled she raised it to her lips. After taking a couple of swallows, she stood and held the canister above her head. Her arms trembled as the green eyes narrowed, and her mouth turned down in an excruciating frown. She quickly lowered the beaker, sat down, and rested her head on her outstretched arm laying across the shelf. Beads of sweat popped out on her forehead and upper lip. Her insides quivered as the power of the potion took hold. She sat for several minutes until the feeling wore off, then lifted her head.

Wiping her face with a soft towel, she placed the containers on a tray and shoved it to the corner of the shelf. "Things are going to be quite exciting come the stroke of midnight. First, we must finish the preparations," she whispered.

Brenda stepped out of the small room, and went to her car, which she'd parked at the back of the bunkhouse on purpose.

Unlocking and opening the door, she reached into the back seat and removed a cleaner bag, which contained a long white robe. She carefully carried it back into the small lab and hooked the hanger over a nail on the wall. Turning off the light, she secured her secrets, then scurried around to the front to survey the witches' progress.

She smiled as she walked around the large stack of dried branches forming the pile for the bonfire. "You girls have done a great job. This is perfect."

The girls looked pleased.

"Is there anything else we need to do before midnight?" Barbara asked.

Brenda tapped a finger on her chin. "All of you wear your robes, and about 11:45 tonight we'll start the bonfire." A cynical smile creased her lips. "Once we have the blaze going, you girls can bring up our three escapees. They'll regret they ever left."

Shelby put her hands on hips. "I hope you've got something special in mind for Christina."

Brenda's eyes glowed and she clapped her hands. "Oh, I do. She'll be very sorry she ever deserted our clan to help those two get away." She glanced around and frowned. "Where's Ruth?"

"In the bunkhouse. Her ankle is still really swollen and she can't walk. She's in a lot of pain, and I suspect has a broken bone. We even have to help her go to the bathroom. I thought you were going to get her to the doctor," Barbara said.

She threw up her hands. "Oh, shoot, I completely forgot about it. I promise to take her first thing in the morning." Brenda walked around the pile of kindling. "Looks like we're ready for tonight. Take a break, get a bite to eat and meet me back here in a couple of hours."

After she watched the girls head for the cottage, she turned and strolled toward the ranch house. Her mind whirled with thoughts of what would happen when she had the three girls under her witch's spell. She could hardly wait. This would be a good test on her ability to create curses. Punching the security code, she entered the house and went into the kitchen. Her stomach growled as she opened the refrigerator and prepared herself a sandwich with all the trimmings. It didn't bother her in the slightest that the girls didn't have this luxury. After all, she saw to it they had the necessities and weren't starving. What more could they ask?

She thought about Tammy and Kate. Not sure she trusted those two and could see them bolting from the group like Christina. A word to Barbara and Shelby might be in order. They needed to be watched.

After finishing her meal, she cleaned up her mess, then meandered into the living room and flopped down on the couch. Her thoughts drifted to Jerry and she smiled to herself. A frolic in bed would be very pleasant right now. She picked up the phone on the end table, fearing she might not get a good signal with her cell. Punching in his number, she waited for several rings, then his voice mail picked up.

"Hello, darling. Why aren't you answering? Sure wish you were with me right now, a romp would be great. Dream about me." She hung up and frowned. "Why didn't he answer?" she mumbled.

CHAPTER FORTY-TWO

Sarah, Patricia and Christina took turns watching out the window. Suddenly, Patricia let out a yelp, and leaped toward her cot.

"They're headed this way."

Sarah hurried to the window. "She's right. However, they don't have the bonfire going. Bet they're coming down to eat."

Christina moved behind Sarah and peered out. "Wonder if they'll give us a sandwich? My stomach is really growling."

"Knowing what's ahead of us, how can you eat?" Patricia gasped.

She smiled. "We need the energy, especially if we have to give them a fight."

"There's just four of them," Sarah said. "Ruth must still be laid up with her ankle."

She then backed away from the window as the witches neared the building. Once they were inside, the girls could hear muffled voices and cabinets closing through the walls.

"Wish we could understand what they were saying," Patricia whispered.

Christina immediately cupped her hands around her ear and pressed it against the wood. When she didn't move for several seconds, the other two followed suit. They listened for several minutes and then in unison, they moved to the cots and sat down. The chain clattered and the door slowly opened.

Tammy and Kate entered. Barbara stood behind them holding the padlock and chain. Shelby brought in a candle and placed it on the small table.

"Enjoy your last meal," Barbara said, in a menacing voice. "We've even given you dessert."

Shelby ushered the two younger witches out, then turned and glared at the girls. "We'll be back shortly to take you to your deaths."

She slammed the door and the links rattled excessively as they were again locked in.

Patricia stared blankly at the closed entry.

Sarah waved a hand in front of her face. "Patricia, snap out of it and eat your sandwich."

Blinking, she gazed up at Sarah with fear in her eyes. "She said they're going to take us to our deaths."

Sarah sat down beside Patricia. "Listen to me. You heard what they said through the wall. They were going to give us a good scare. None of those girls want to go to prison, so forget the 'death' part. Now eat."

Christina finished her sandwich, and moved back to the window as she heard the witches leaving the building. Due to the flickering candle, she stood to the side so they couldn't see her wavering shadow. Once they were out of earshot, she crossed the room and sat next to Sarah. "They were carrying extra food back to the bunkhouse. Probably for Ruth. I hope she's all right. I liked her, but I've never cared for Barbara or Shelby."

"Why?" Sarah asked.

"They were always saying mean things to intimidate the rest of us. I'm sure that's the reason Brenda picked those two as the overseers of the group."

"Why was Ruth different?" Patricia asked.

"She stayed pretty much neutral. I'd watched her expressions and I don't think she cared for some of the things Brenda brought into the group. Especially about keeping you guys locked in this room. She questioned the reasons, but Brenda never gave her a clear cut answer. Ruth thought you guys should have free roam of the grounds just like the rest of us. Brenda wouldn't hear of it."

"What about the other two?"

"Tammy and Kate are followers, they don't think for themselves. Like I told you, they're wimps."

"Do you think any of those girls know Brenda has us here for selfish reasons?"

Christina shook her head. "I'm sure of it. She gave them the idea you two were evil and hurting other people in your school."

Sarah stood and ran her fingers through her hair. She glanced out the window, then turned to the girls. "We need a rough plan. Let me give you an idea what I've been thinking and then give me your input."

They both nodded.

"Okay, shoot," Christina said.

"We're going to try and persuade them not to tie us up. If they insist, we fight, taking out Barbara and Shelby. We won't get aggressive if they let us go to the bonfire without being bound. Once Brenda starts whatever ritual or spell she has in mind, we will not allow them to touch us, including her. If they try," Sarah patted the chain around her waist and narrowed her eyes, "they'll get our wrath."

Patricia stared at her wide eyed. "How could you hit anyone with a chain?"

"Think about it. If Brenda acts like she's going to cut off the rest of your hair, won't you fight her?"

She ducked her head. "Probably."

"What if she plans to throw acid on your face or body? Are you just going to stand there and let her do it?"

"Not if I can help it."

"Me, either."

"How can you be sure the chain will work?" Patricia asked.

"I learned how to crack a whip a couple of years ago. It won't have the same feel, or work the same, but maybe I can arrange to at least get in a couple of good hits."

Christina studied her hands as she doubled them into fists. "Our objective is to take out Barbara, Shelby and Brenda if things don't go right."

Sarah raised her hand and gave the 'okay' sign. "Yep, we're going to war."

❧

Greg Willis wrung his hands and paced the floor in Hawkman's small office. He kept glancing at the clock as the minutes slowly ticked by.

Jennifer finally stood and moved toward the desk. "If you'll hand me the phone book, I'll order a pizza. We're going to be mighty hungry if we don't eat a bite."

Hawkman slid the directory toward her.

"Mr. Willis, what topping do you like?"

He stopped in his tracks as if he'd come out of a fog. "Anything, as long as it has a lot of cheese."

Jennifer called in the order, then moved back to the couch.

Greg placed his palms on Hawkman's desk and leaned forward. "Is it okay if I bring my pistol? I'm licensed to carry a gun. I know how to use it."

Hawkman frowned. "I'd prefer you didn't. This is a delicate and serious situation. We need to be extremely careful. We're dealing mostly with minors, and your daughter is among them."

"Won't you carry a weapon?"

"Yes, but I don't have the personal attachment you do. You might see something that bothers you, aim and fire. Possibly killing an innocent person."

"I can't imagine who'd be innocent in this situation."

"Take my word, Mr. Willis, I think there are several blameless people involved. They just don't realize what's going on. Through no fault of their own, they've walked into a predicament." Hawkman leaned back, raised his hat and ran a hand through his hair. "I'm hoping to hear from Detective Williams before we make our move, then we'll have the authorities to back us up."

"Okay, I'll leave my pistol in the truck. What's the plan if you don't hear from the police?"

Hawkman came forward and placed his arms on the desk. "We're still going in. I want to get your daughter out of there."

Greg exhaled in relief. "Thank God. I couldn't stand the thought of doing nothing."

CHAPTER FORTY-THREE

Lea Thompson arrived at the meeting on time and sat at the head table with the rest of the committee. The models strutted their stuff in front of the panel as the women took notes on who would look best in certain styles. Lea had a hard time focusing on each girl, as Brenda's face kept flashing through her mind. This worried her, because such a phenomenon had only occurred a few times and it always meant something bad. By the time the meeting ended and the girls had been assigned their fashion outfits, she suffered a horrible headache.

One of the women approached Lea. "How about we go to the cocktail lounge and have a drink. I think we deserve it after this trying experience."

Lea smiled. "Any other time, I'd jump at the offer, but I have a horrible migraine and I don't think liquor would help."

The lady frowned, and patted her on the shoulder. "I'm sorry. You'd better go home and lie down. I hope you have a good medication. Those types of headaches are horrible and can make you sick."

"Thanks for your concern, Jenny. Yes, the doctor prescribed a good pain killer. I just don't have it with me, because I don't need it often."

The two women headed for the door, then parted ways in the parking lot.

"Take care of yourself," Jenny said, waving as she strolled toward her car. "I'll talk to you in the next day or two."

Lea climbed into her vehicle, and pushed the key into the ignition. Before turning on the engine, she massaged her temples. Suddenly, Brenda's face flashed in front of her, causing shooting pains to radiate across her head. She rubbed her eyes and muffled a moan with tight lips.

The image soon faded and Lea took a deep breath, turned on the engine and drove home. She stumbled into the kitchen, stopped at the sink and splashed cold water on her face. Her head felt like someone had hit her with a sledgehammer. Clutching her temples, she weaved toward the stairwell, grasped the bannister and pulled herself upstairs. Staggering into her bathroom, she opened the medicine cabinet and fumbled for the pain pills. After gulping down two, she dropped onto the bed and reeled with the pain. Again, Brenda appeared before her, this time in a white robe and dancing in circles around a bonfire.

Lea grabbed her head with both hands and screamed, "No!" She fumbled for the bedside phone and punched in her daughter's cell phone number.

Brenda hadn't turned on the lights yet and had a good view of the property from the living room couch. In the twilight, she watched her clan of girls making their way from the cottage back to the bunkhouse. Shelby and Barbara were in the lead, carrying wrapped plates, probably dinner for Ruth. Brenda snapped her fingers and reminded herself not to forget to take the girl into the doctor tomorrow. There could be a serious problem with her ankle and she definitely didn't want her folks liable.

Tammy and Kate lingered behind. Those two really didn't fit in with her head girls, but it didn't matter. You have leaders and followers. Those two were definitely followers without much backbone. As long as the others were on her side, the rest wouldn't give her any trouble. Especially tonight, when they see what happens to Christina; fear will forever be instilled into their minds. She watched the novice witches walk around the tall pile of branches and wondered what they were thinking. They rearranged a stick or two, then disappeared into the bunkhouse.

Brenda closed the drapes, flipped on a lamp beside the couch, sat down with one leg folded underneath her butt and thumbed through the spell book she'd brought from her small lab. After reading for close to an hour, she again went through the instructions for the ritual tonight. She closed her eyes and envisioned the ceremony in her mind. Feeling confident she'd prepared everything right, she put the book aside.

She glanced at her wristwatch and sighed. "Another hour and a half to wait," she mumbled, crossing the room to the portable liquor bar. Removing the key from the hidden compartment, she opened the doors, and glanced through the bottles of whiskey, then decided to have a shot of brandy. Why not, she thought. I won't be driving.

Removing a snifter from the cabinet, she poured in a small amount of liquid and swirled it around the glass, as she'd seen her father do many times. She replaced the bottle, closed and locked the cabinet, then sat in the large overstuffed chair in the living room. The first sip burned all the way down to her stomach.

"Wow," she exclaimed aloud. "No wonder adults only have small doses of this stuff."

Her thoughts drifted to Jerry. Why hadn't he returned her call? He'd surely gotten the message. She really cared for him. He was so handsome with his broad muscular shoulders, short hair and tight jeans. Thank goodness, he didn't wear his pants hanging so his butt showed.

She hated it when other girls ogled his body or when he flirted. It made her furious. To think Sarah and he had gone on an actual date, made her insanely jealous. She knew Jerry had probably kissed her and no telling what else they'd done. The thought infuriated her so much she wanted to kill the girl.

After taking another sip of the burning liquid, she set the glass on the table, picked up the portable phone and dialed his number again. Still no answer. This time she decided not to leave a message and hung up instead. She figured either his cell needed charging or he'd been called into work. Tomorrow would be another day.

A warm tingling sensation rose in her body and she smiled to herself. So this is how Daddy feels after having a snort of brandy. No wonder Mom always made sure they have plenty on hand. She finished off the snifter and stood, her head reeled. "Oh, my Lord," she exclaimed. "This is potent stuff."

She teetered to the kitchen sink, washed out the glass, and put it away. If she left any telltale signs, her mother would know she'd gotten into the liquor cabinet. The clock showed she had thirty minutes before joining the girls at the bunkhouse. What a night this would be. She whirled around and almost lost her balance. Reaching into the cabinet, she removed an aspirin bottle, dropped a couple into her hand, poured a glass of water and gulped them down. "Whew, I didn't know brandy would do this. I hope these help. I certainly can't stagger during the ritual." Weaving down the hallway, she decided a cool shower would help. Undressing, she stepped into the stall, put the water on full bore and let it pound her body. Her cell phone lay on the end table in the living room and she didn't hear it ringing.

CHAPTER FORTY-FOUR

Hawkman checked his watch. "I think it's about time we headed for the ranch. We'll park my 4x4 about half way up the back road, then hike in the rest of the way."

"The surprise factor is preferable in this situation," Jennifer said. Then she glanced at Greg Willis' feet. "Do you by chance have some different footwear in your truck? The landscape is rugged and it'll tear up your loafers."

He jumped up, and headed for the door. "Yes, I'll go get them right now."

Jennifer waited until Greg left, then turned toward Hawkman. "I'm taking my pistol in my fanny pack, and pray I don't have to use it."

"Fine, just don't mention you're carrying a weapon."

She pointed at the phone. "I wish Williams would call."

"Me, too. He's aware of the situation, as I left another message in more detail, and he knows where the ranch is located."

Greg entered the office wearing a pair of sturdy work boots. "Will these do?"

"Perfect," Jennifer said, slipping on a navy blue hooded sweatshirt. "Be sure you turn your cell phones to vibrate. The ringing would definitely give us away."

"I'm really nervous," Greg said. "You think my little girl is okay?"

"We think so," Hawkman said, rising from his chair. "The main thing is for us to be cautious. Just remember we're dealing with kids."

He nodded. "It's so hard to believe young people would do such a thing."

"Remember Sarah left home of her own accord. How she got roped into this, we're not real sure. We'll need to hear her story before we can come to any solid conclusions. Right now it appears a big mess."

The three left the office and piled into Hawkman's 4X4.

Sarah stood at the window, her gaze piercing through the darkness. The moonlit sky allowed her to see the top of the woodpile and the outline of the barn. "Christina, did you guys have electricity in the bunkhouse?"

She sat on the end of the cot biting her nails. "No, but we had battery operated lights, which are better than candles. We didn't have to worry about them going out or starting a fire."

"What about running water and a bathroom?" Patricia asked.

"There's an outdoor johnny out back, just like you have, but ours was much closer. We put a bucket in a small closet for night time runs, and took turns emptying it. There's a pump inside a separate room with a makeshift shower that drains to the outside. Someone has to pour water over you to rinse off the soap, and the water is so cold you shiver through the whole bath. Believe me, we didn't take many. Most of the time we just sponged off, unless we got really stinky."

"What about the ranch house?" Sarah asked.

"It has all the luxuries. You can see the electric lines going into the house, plus pipes coming out of the structure. Brenda always stays there when she comes up."

"Did she ever offer to let you take a warm shower?" Patricia asked.

Christina laughed. "Are you kidding? We weren't even allowed to peek in the windows. I can't blame her though, as she told us the place she had for us to stay was very rustic and we all agreed to come. So we knew what we were getting into. It was one hell of a lot better and safer than sleeping on the streets."

"What are you going to do if we ever get out of here?" Sarah asked.

"I'm going to contact my folks and literally beg them to let me come home. I've really learned I had it good, and I want to go back, if they'll let me." Christina glanced at the girls. "What about you two?"

"I know my mom will let me come home," Patricia said.

"My dad is probably worried sick, so he's the one I'll contact," Sarah said, as her gaze turned back to the window. Her body went rigid and she grasped the sill. "The witches are coming."

Both girls clamored to the window, their eyes wide.

"They're in their black hooded robes. What do we do now?" Patricia asked.

Sarah checked the chain around her mid section, making sure it held tight so it wouldn't make a noise, then pulled her blouse down to cover it. "Act like we're expecting them; they told us they'd be back. Just remember they aren't to lay a hand on us."

They moved away from the window and watched as four shadowy figures passed. Then the wooden floors creaked as they trooped through the kitchen. Shortly, they heard the chain rattling and watched with trepidation as the door slowly grated open.

Barbara and Shelby entered, followed by Tammy and Kate. When Barbara raised a hand toward Patricia, Sarah stepped between them.

"Do not touch us."

"We're going to take you to the ritual."

"We can walk on our own."

"Brenda wants us to tie your hands."

"Why?"

Barbara shrugged. "I don't know."

Sarah stared into her eyes. "You mean you don't question her reasoning? Don't you think it sounds a little suspicious, if she wants our hands tied? What's she planning on doing to us?"

Barbara seemed lost for words and Shelby intervened. "She thought you might rebel, but if you'll come with us without a problem, then let's go."

Sarah motioned toward the door. "Lead the way."

The leaders walked out, their long garments making swishing sounds as they hastened through the door. The three girls followed, with Tammy and Kate bringing up the rear. When they got outside, Sarah, Christina and Patricia locked arms as they moved up the slight knoll toward the pile of brush. An owl screeched as it flew from its perch on a nearby tree, and a coyote yelped in the distance, sending a chill up Sarah's spine.

Upon reaching several feet before the perimeter of where the bonfire would be lit, Sarah stopped. "We're not getting any closer if you're going to build a fire."

Barbara and Shelby glanced at one another.

"Are you afraid we're going to throw you into the flames?"

"We're not going to take the chance."

Barbara put her hands on her hips. "The blaze is only a symbol. We don't use it for human sacrifices. We're not mean witches."

Sarah scoffed. "As I said, this is as far as we go. We can watch the ceremony from here." The three girls plopped on the ground."

Barbara spoke to Shelby in a murmur, then whirled around and stalked off toward the back of the bunkhouse. Tammy and Kate, in a measured stroll, left the three girls and sidled up to Shelby, where they huddled in a hushed conversation.

"So far we've got them confused," Sarah whispered. "They're not sure what to do with us."

"Do you think they'll wrestle us down and tie us up?" Patricia asked.

Sarah bent her head toward her friend. "Remember the minute they lay a hand on us, we fight back. There's no way we're going to let them bind our hands or feet. Kick scream, bite, and scratch. Do whatever is necessary."

CHAPTER FORTY-FIVE

Barbara knocked softly on the door of the lab. Brenda poked her head out. "What do you want?" she asked, brusquely. "I told you never to disturb me before a ritual, unless it's an emergency. I'm trying to prepare myself."

"I know, but we've run into a problem."

"Don't tell me the girls have escaped again."

"No, but they're being very stubborn and insisted we don't touch them. So we don't have their arms tied, and they've refused to be near the fire."

Brenda rolled her eyes. "For heavens sakes, can't you overpower them?"

Bowing her head, Barbara scuffed a foot against the hard ground. "I didn't think you wanted us to go so far as to physically put them down. Why do they have to be tied?"

"It's not what I'm going to do. Don't you realize they've escaped once and now they're out of the room? They could run away again."

"They don't act like they will."

Brenda waved a hand and shook her head. "All right, leave them where they are, but stand guard. Get the fire going and I'll be out shortly."

As Barbara stepped away from the room, Brenda closed the door and let out a disgusted hiss. She sat down on the stool and gave a quick look at the ritual book. "I'm definitely past mother's teachings," she murmured, whipping the white robe off the nail and slipping it on. She figured she'd better get out there quickly and take charge.

When Barbara finally made it to the front of the building, she found the other three witches huddled together. Her gaze immediately swept toward the prisoners and she breathed a sigh of relief. She gave her crew orders to stand guard over the captives. They immediately moved to the back and sides of Sarah, Patricia and Christina. Barbara crossed over to a box resting on the small front porch of the bunkhouse and gathered a handful of newspapers. She stuffed it around the edges of the twigs and branches, then set the paper on fire.

The three captives stared as the blaze roared to a head, shooting embers skyward and casting haunting shadows over the area.

Hawkman, Jennifer and Greg Willis drove up the back road leading to the ranch. Eliminating the headlights, Hawkman drove slowly until he reached the halfway mark, then pulled the vehicle to the side and turned off the engine. The three disembarked and hiked through heavy brush with critters scurrying out of their way as they moved toward the cottage. The howling of a wildcat and the twittering of fleeing birds caused Jennifer's heart to pound, feeling thankful she didn't have to do this alone.

The moonlit night made seeing obstacles easier as they tramped through the brambles and detoured around boulders. Hawkman suddenly held up his hand, and everyone came to a stop behind him. He pointed to the outline of a building directly in front of them. He motioned for them to stay low as they cautiously made their way toward it. They came to where the back road doglegged off to the front of the cottage.

Hawkman knelt down and gestured for Greg and Jennifer to move forward.

"Stay here," he whispered. "I can hear voices. I'm going to sneak around the side and see if I can make out where they're coming from."

Greg and Jennifer hunkered down behind a rock while Hawkman ran in a crouched position across the dirt trail. He flattened his back against the building, then inched forward, while keeping an eye on the road for any sign of a vehicle.

Just as he got to the corner, he peeked around the edge and the door opened. He quickly drew back, and waited until he could hear the footsteps fade in the distance, then took another look. Seven girls were marching up the short hill toward the bunkhouse. Four of the girls were wearing flowing dark robes, but the three girls in the middle were dressed in regular clothes and locked arm in arm.

He hurried back to Jennifer and Greg. "I spotted Sarah and two other girls being escorted up the hill toward the bunkhouse," he whispered. "Let's go up this dirt road toward the ranch house and cut over."

Greg grabbed his arm. "You're sure my little girl is among them?"

"Yes, she's alive and apparently well."

"Thank God," Greg murmured.

Before reaching the main building, Hawkman spotted a large propane tank. The three were able to squat behind it without being detected; and even though they couldn't hear the conversation, they could observe the three girls sitting on the ground.

Hawkman recognized two of the witches who'd ordered him off the property. They appeared to also be in charge of whatever was happening. He studied the grounds. The big house set in darkness and he didn't spot Brenda's car parked anywhere on the premises. She must be here, as he didn't think these girls would take on a ritual without her being present. He squinted into the darkness and even raised his eye-patch to search more thoroughly, but no where did he see the convertible.

He leaned toward Jennifer and whispered. "Do you see Brenda's car?"

She scoured the area for several seconds, then shook her head. "No."

"The girl's bound to be here."

"Maybe she had to collect some herbs for her ritual."

Hawkman made a sour face. "I don't think so. She's planned this for a while, and would have everything available."

"Maybe she's mixing her stuff in the bunkhouse," Jennifer said.

"You two keep an eye on things. I'm going to circle the area and see if I can locate her car. Greg, don't make any foolish moves."

Willis could hardly keep his eyes off his daughter. "Don't worry, I wouldn't spoil getting my little girl back for anything."

Hawkman scurried along the side of the big house, and dipped down into the wooded area, praying the squawking of the roosting birds wouldn't arouse suspicion.

When he approached the back of the bunkhouse, he spotted the convertible, then darted behind the outdoor johnny when he saw a flashlight beam playing across the ground at the corner of the dwelling. He peeked around and saw a faint glow flow out of a small door as it opened. The room appeared to be long and narrow. He figured at one time it served the ranch hands as a place to store their extra personal gear. It appeared Brenda had taken it over, as she poked out her head and spoke roughly to the witch he recognized. He couldn't make out what she said, but it didn't sound pleasant.

The girl finally turned away, her shoulders slumped. Hawkman decided to head back to Greg and Jennifer, when he heard a rustling sound come from within the outhouse. He quickly stepped back and his boot landed on a small branch which cracked under his weight. Dropping to the ground, he rolled to his left just as a shaft of light flashed over the outhouse. The door opened and a female stepped onto the ground using a heavy straight limb to support herself.

"Ruth, is that you?"

"Yes," she called.

The other girl hurried to her side and helped her to the back door of the bunkhouse. "You should have asked someone for help."

"I called out a couple of times, but no one answered, and I had to go bad. I hope I haven't hurt my ankle worse."

"Brenda promises to take you to the doctor tomorrow."

"The wild animals must be running in force tonight. I could hear them scurrying around the loo. Should make Brenda happy to have the wildlife supporting her ritual."

The girls disappeared inside, and Hawkman exhaled in relief. "Close call," he murmured, pushing himself off the ground.

Hunched down, he made his way back and whispered to his partners what he'd seen. "Anything happen out front?"

"No, but it seems odd Sarah, Patricia and the other girl are left on their own. You'd think the witches would fear they'd take off."

Hawkman nodded and pointed. "The lead witch has just returned, and it appears she's given them instructions. Looks like the girls are now under guard."

Suddenly, when the pile of sticks erupted into flames, Greg jumped to his feet. "What the hell are they going to do?"

Hawkman grabbed his arm. "Stay down and keep your voice low. We're not going to let anything happen. Don't give us away or we might not be able to catch them in the act."

Greg reluctantly squatted behind the propane tank, wrung his hands and continued to stare at his daughter.

CHAPTER FORTY-SIX

Even though Lea Thompson's agonizing headache made her sick to her stomach, she stripped off her good clothes, dressed quickly in a pair of jeans, sneakers and light windbreaker jacket, then dashed down the stairs to the garage. It was almost midnight, and would take her close to an hour to get to the ranch, but she had to find Brenda. Something terrible was going to happen; she just prayed she could get there in time.

Brenda tucked the recorder into the pocket of her robe. She'd found music which would fit beautifully with the ritual. She picked up the initialed flasks containing the potions she'd concocted for each girl, and slipped them into a velvet bag. The drunken state she'd felt from the brandy earlier had all but disappeared. Glancing around the small lab to make sure she hadn't forgotten anything, she turned off the switch on the portable lamp, closed and locked the door, then slowly strolled around the building, preparing her mind for what had to be done.

The blazing fire pulled her into its trance and she took the recorder from her pocket and placed it on a bench she'd scooted next to the fire. As she turned up the volume, a slow haunting melody penetrated the air.

When Sarah, Patricia and Christina saw Brenda step in front of the fire and then hearing the weird music, they moved close to one another, interlocking their arms. They watched her raise her hands above her head and swirl in a circle. Her white robe lifted and flowed in ripples as her body moved to the strange rhythm. On each turn she'd throw something into the fire, causing it to whip up into a white blaze, then sizzle and spit fingers of flame into the air. Her green eyes took on a bizarre glow as she stared at the three girls.

"She's crazy," Christina whispered.

Patricia put her face against Sarah's shoulder. "I can't watch; she scares me."

"Don't worry, I'll take in her every move and if she advances toward us, we'll fly into action."

Sarah kept her gaze glued to Brenda as she danced around the fire, whirling and throwing the sparklers into the flames. Soon, she slowed and pulled a flask from her pocket. After several pirouettes, she stopped and raised the container above her head while staring at the three girls.

"Bring them to me," she chanted in a high pitched voice.

When the witches reached down to raise the girls to their feet, Sarah slapped their hands away. "Don't you dare touch us."

"Brenda wants you up front," Barbara said.

"I don't care where she wants us. We're not going."

Shelby stepped forward. "Yes, you are." When she bent down to take hold of Christina, she received a hard kick which sent her flying onto her butt.

This gave the three girls time to jump up and position themselves into a fighting stance with their backs to one another which prevented anyone from coming at them on their blind side.

Tammy and Kate tried once to grab Patricia, but got punched in the face, and soon backed away with their hands to their mouths.

Brenda immediately dashed toward the scuffle. "What's going on here?"

"Stay away," Sarah said. "You're not going to cast a stupid spell on us."

Brenda pointed at Sarah. "Get her to the fire."

Barbara and Shelby moved toward her, but Sarah stepped back, whipped the chain from around her waist and whirled it above her head.

"Stand back," she yelled.

Unfortunately, when Sarah moved away from Patricia and Christina, Barbara grabbed Patricia and yanked her arms behind her back. Patricia let out a scream. Christina tried to help, but Shelby tackled her before she had a chance to get to her. Sarah advanced toward Barbara swinging the chain, but the witch kept throwing Patricia in front of her forcing Sarah to guide her weapon so it wouldn't hit her friend.

Brenda had stepped backward toward the fire. Sarah saw her make a quick turn and pick up a burning branch. "Drop it, Brenda, or I'll use this on you," she screamed, whirling the chain.

Hawkman, Jennifer and Greg, jumped up from their haunches and moved to the front of the propane tank.

"I don't like this," Jennifer said. "It's time we intervene."

Suddenly, Greg broke into a run as Brenda flung the burning branch toward his daughter. Sarah jumped away, but it hit her on the legs. She gave the chain a swing above her head and hurled it toward her enemy.

Brenda ducked and suddenly stopped her pursuit of Sarah when she spotted the adults sprinting across the field. She quickly shed the white robe and dashed around the corner of the bunkhouse.

"Sarah, it's dad. Are you all right?" Greg cried, brushing off the glowing embers on her jeans.

"Dad, is it really you," she cried, tears running down her cheeks as she grabbed him around the neck.

Barbara and Shelby dropped their holds on the two girls, and stepped back in fear as the adults moved in.

Patricia and Christina rubbed their arms and smiled as Sarah embraced her father.

Sarah pushed away from Greg and turned toward her two friends. "Dad, I want you to meet two of the bravest girls I've ever known."

At that moment, Brenda gunned her convertible around the building and onto the road leading away from the ranch. Barbara and Shelby attempted to make a dash for the car, but

Hawkman and Jennifer grabbed them before they had a chance to get far.

Barbara yanked away from Hawkman. "You can't keep us here."

"In these circumstances, I can. I'm placing you both under a citizen's arrest."

"What about Brenda?" Shelby asked.

"We'll take care of her later."

Shelby pointed. "She's getting away."

"I know where to find her."

"We haven't done anything wrong," Barbara whimpered.

"I don't think being an accomplice to a kidnapping is innocent," Hawkman said.

"We never kidnapped anyone," Shelby said, her eyes wide.

Hawkman gestured toward Sarah, Patricia and Christina. "It appears to me those three girls weren't here by choice."

"Brenda had them brought to the ranch," Barbara said. "Christina defected and joined them when they escaped."

"Tell it to your lawyer." Hawkman glanced at Greg who gave him a wink and a big smile.

Meanwhile, Jennifer had moved over to Tammy and Kate as they sat on the ground crying.

"I knew we should have left here when Christina did," Tammy sobbed.

"Why didn't you?" Jennifer asked.

"We were scared of Brenda."

All heads turned as a girl stumbled out of the bunkhouse and cried, "Please, someone help me. I'm really sick."

CHAPTER FORTY-SEVEN

"Oh, my God, Ruth," Christina cried, dashing to the girl's aid. She put her hands under the girl's armpits and tried to hold her up. Ruth's eyes were glazed and her body collapsed just as Hawkman reached out and kept her from falling. He eased her down, on the grass, slipped off his jacket and folded it under her head.

"She's burning up with fever. Does anyone know what's wrong?"

Christina kneeled down and pointed to Ruth's ankle. "She hurt it a week ago and when it didn't get better, Brenda promised to take her to the doctor, but never took the time. I guess her thoughts were on other things."

Jennifer hurried toward them, took one look at the swollen, red injury, and pulled her cell phone from her pocket. "This girl needs to get to the hospital immediately. I'm calling an ambulance."

"You better give specific instructions on how to get here. I doubt they've had many runs up in these hills," Hawkman said.

Ruth gazed at his weapon encased in his shoulder holster. "Why do you have a gun? Are you a police officer?" she asked in a weak voice.

"I'm a private investigator. You just rest quietly. Help is on the way."

Before he stood, she reached over and took a hold of his arm. "I hope you've saved Sarah and Patricia from Brenda. She's a horrible person."

"Yes, they're both fine."

"Thank you," she sighed, and closed her eyes.

Hawkman did a double take as the girl's head lobbed to the side. He grabbed her shoulders, but didn't dare shake her. "Ruth, are you okay?"

Her eyes opened a slit. "Yes, I'm just so sleepy."

"Try to stay awake until help arrives." He looked over at Christina. " Keep her talking."

She nodded and moved close to Ruth's head.

When Hawkman stood, his phone vibrated against his waist. He pulled it off and placed it to his ear as he walked away from the group. "Tom Casey."

He listened as he glanced around at the girls. The four witches had shed their robes and used them for cushions on the ground. Jennifer stood guard between them. Greg, Sarah and Patricia moved over and sat next to Ruth and Christina. Greg immediately started a conversation with the girls.

Hawkman listened intently to the party on the phone. "Yes, come as soon as you can. Brenda took off in her car, but I know where to find her."

He patted the toe of his boot on the ground.

"Right, we've called an ambulance. One of the girls is very ill. Looks like a broken ankle, but it didn't have anything to do with tonight. You'll need room to take four girls to the station. We can bring the other three."

His head came up as he listened. "I can hear the siren now. See you soon."

After hanging up, he crossed quickly over to Jennifer and they stepped out of earshot of the girls. "Detective Williams is on his way. He got my message and heard the dispatch for the emergency vehicle." He motioned toward the four seated girls. "Would you be comfortable taking them into the bunkhouse to get their belongings, because they won't be coming back."

"Sure. I don't think they're a threat."

Jennifer lined the girls in single file and they trooped into the bunkhouse. Hawkman lingered behind and spotted a tape recorder on a bench next to the smoldering fire. He picked it up, pushed the on button and the haunting melody they'd heard earlier pierced the air. Punching it off, he placed it back on the stool, and noticed a velvet pouch lying on the ground. When he peered inside, he found three flasks with a different initial on each one. He didn't touch them, but folded the top down and laid the bag beside the recorder. These were items he'd turn over to Detective Williams.

He ambled toward the back to the room where he'd seen Brenda talking to one of the other girls. Finding the door locked with a small padlock, he took his pocket knife, removed the screws holding the latch and opened the door. The small flashlight on his key ring gave him enough illumination to spot the battery operated lamp. He turned it on, and what met his gaze shocked him. The shelves were filled with vials of all sizes. Some held strange looking plants and animal parts. Several sorcerer spell books lay opened on the counter. The walls were plastered with weird scenes from rituals with hags stirring caldrons of bubbling liquids. Hawkman shook his head as he backed out of the narrow room and closed the door. Williams would definitely be interested in this mini witch lab.

Hawkman walked around to the front and lightly knocked on the front door. When he entered, the girls were busy packing their bags as Jennifer looked on.

She glanced at him. "They're very worried about what's going to happen."

"I wish I could ease their minds, but I can't. Three girls were kept captives and they knew it. I don't know how the courts will handle this unusual case."

He wandered through the building and found the small pump. Filling a bucket of water, he carried it outside and doused the smoldering fire.

Greg jumped up. "I'll help you. Would hate to see a forest fire due to flying embers if the wind picked up."

"Exactly," Hawkman said.

They poured half a dozen bucketfuls of water on the blaze until it was completely out, then leaned against the short railing around the bunkhouse's front porch.

Hawkman looked toward the three girls surrounding Ruth. "How's she doing?"

"The girls are keeping her talking," Greg said. "She told us a bunch of scary stuff about Brenda."

"So how's Sarah doing?"

Greg grinned. "To hear Patricia and Christina talk, she's a hero. They said she stood up to the whole bunch and she brought up the idea to wear the chain around her middle. I had no idea my girl had such guts."

Hawkman smiled. "Brave gal." He hooked a thumb in his jeans front pocket. "Get Sarah and Patricia to show us where they were kept as prisoners."

"Yeah, I'd like to see the place too."

The two men approached the girls still huddled around Ruth.

"Sarah, would you and Patricia show me where Brenda had you locked up?" Hawkman then turned to Christina. "Would you mind staying with Ruth while we take the tour?"

"No problem." She glanced at Sarah. "If you guys are going to collect your stuff, could you bring my things? They're all in that black garbage bag. I'll find my suitcase in the bunkhouse."

"Sure," she said, as she and Patricia stood. "Oh, dear, we need a flashlight."

Christina jumped up. "They have some in the bunkhouse. Hold on, and I'll get them."

She returned in a few moments and gave a lantern to each person. Then plopped back down next to Ruth. "Mrs. Casey is having the girls pack your things too. She'll bring them out in a few minutes."

"I'm so glad these people found us," Ruth said, taking Christina's hand.

Sarah, Patricia, Greg and Hawkman, hiked across the grounds to the cottage and entered through the kitchen. Hawkman took a mental note of the surroundings as he and Greg followed the girls down the hallway. When they came to the big wooden door, Sarah pointed out the chain and lock hanging on a nail.

"That's how they locked us in," she shoved open the heavy door and gestured toward the window. Those bars are screwed on the outside of the window, so there was no way we could get them off from the inside."

Greg flashed a beam around the room. "No lights?"

"No electricity or running water, once the sun went down, we were left in total darkness."

"What about bathroom facilities?"

Patricia pointed shaft of light toward the covered bucket. "We used that during the night and during the day, if someone was available, they'd escort us to the outdoor johnny; otherwise the ugly pail sufficed."

Greg scratched his head. "How did you bathe?"

"In the mornings when the witches came over to eat their breakfast, they heated a bucket of water and brought it to us." Sarah laughed. "We managed to stay smell free."

"What about meals?" Hawkman asked.

"We ate when they did," Patricia said. "Usually dry cereal with milk they'd made from powder. Tasted weird, but we ate it. At lunch we'd have whatever they did, mostly sandwiches made with canned chicken or tuna."

Hawkman rubbed his chin. "How'd the food get here?"

Sarah shrugged. "I think Brenda ordered it, and had it delivered."

Greg put his arm around his daughter and gave a squeeze. "I'd say you lived in a dungeon like existence. Did you ever get to go outside?"

"Every once in a while, they'd let us out for a walk, but we were never out of their sight. That ended once we escaped." Sarah sighed. "The kept us in seclusion until tonight."

Hawkman noticed flashing red beams striking the barred window. "Looks like the ambulance is here."

They grabbed the suitcases and Christina's bag, dashed through the kitchen, out the door and jogged back to the bonfire site. Jennifer had taken over, directing the paramedics to Ruth.

Brenda breathed a sigh of relief as she reached the main mountain road without the stupid private investigator taking chase. She assumed he'd parked on the back road, since she didn't see his vehicle, and his group had hidden on the grounds until the fight broke out. Frustrated because nothing had gone right tonight, she hit her hand on the steering wheel in anger. "Damn him," she yelled into the wind.

With the top down on her convertible, she could hear sounds much clearer and the wail of a siren in the distance met her ears. Figuring the police were on their way, she slowed and looked for the driveway that led to a small vacant cabin just off the road. She knew she hadn't passed it yet. Soon, she spotted the dirt lane, pulled off and followed the path to a clump of trees. Turning off her headlights, she maneuvered her car so she could see the road. Oncoming traffic wouldn't pay attention to a vehicle parked in front of a dwelling.

Several seconds passed before the ambulance, with red lights flashing and siren blaring, barreled around the bend within her sight. She stood up and looked over her windshield, gnawing her lower lip. Why an emergency vehicle? I certainly didn't have time to cast my spell, so no one got hurt. Maybe they aren't going to the ranch, she thought, watching their tail lights disappear around the curve. She settled back in the seat, turned on the engine and headed back to the main road.

Once she got on the blacktop, even knowing a deer could dash out in front of the car and cause her to veer off the road, she picked up speed. There wasn't another spot to turn off until she reached the base of the mountain, and she didn't want to meet the police on this road.

CHAPTER FORTY-EIGHT

Detective Williams called in a couple of his officers. "We've located Patricia Riley. Tom Casey, the private investigator found her while looking for another missing female."

"I hope you've called Mrs. Riley. She's driven us nuts," one of the officers said.

"Not yet. Patricia's in good hands under the protective eye of Casey. I'll wait to call her mother when we have the girl safe at the station. Right now, we're headed for this ranch to pick up her, along with four other women connected to this case. So we'll need you both driving your vehicles. He passed out the directions to the men."

One of the officers glanced up after reading the sheet. "This is way up in the hills."

"Yeah, I know. Good place for a kidnapper to hide his victims." He grabbed the search warrant he'd acquired from the judge when he first got Hawkman's message, gave a wave and headed for the door. "Let's get on the road."

Lea Thompson drove at normal speed in town, but once she reached the open highway, she floor-boarded the accelerator. Reaching the turnoff, she almost spun out of control, but righted the car and continued on the two lane blacktop leading into the mountains. She frightened herself several times as the tires squealed while rounding a curve. When she met an ambulance coming from the opposite direction, her heart almost stopped when the right tires of her car went off the pavement and onto the soft shoulder. She sucked in her breath and almost lost control, but jerked the wheel, then exhaled when the car again gripped the asphalt. Never had she driven so fast on this dangerous, winding road with its sheer drop-offs. Spurred by the urgency to reach her daughter, she continued at high speed.

She'd threw on her bright lights so she could see if a deer happened to be in the middle or side of the road. At least it would give her time to come to a stop. Little did she expect traffic on the road at this time of night, and almost screamed as she rounded a bend to see two red reflectors. Lea mashed the brake and burned rubber for several feet before almost hitting the rear end of a trailer loaded with hay, pulled by a Ford tractor.

"What the hell is he doing out on the road at this time of night?" she yelled loudly, and repeatedly hit the steering wheel with the palms of her hands.

Knowing the risk of passing on this mountain road, she stayed behind him for a good half mile before frustration at his slow pace got the better of her. She clicked the bright lights a couple of times, hit the accelerator and lurched out from behind him at a good clip. The tires squealed as she tried to maneuver a very sharp curve. Blinded by the bright lights of the fast oncoming car, she yanked the wheel to the right, but not soon enough. The two cars hit head-on and careened over the side of the mountain, tumbling and bouncing as the vehicles slammed against the trees and rocks.

The old farmer driving the tractor came to a halt, jumped off the seat and headed for the brim of the road. He peered down the embankment as the two cars settled half way down the ridge, leaving behind a large cloud of dust and scattered debris.

He ran back to his tractor and had leaped back onto the seat to go for help, when he spotted a parade of cars coming up behind his trailer. Jumping back down to the road, he waved frantically until the vehicles rolled to a stop. He ran to the driver side of the first unmarked vehicle, but noted the two behind were patrol cars.

"Oh, my, I didn't know the Lord worked so fast, and not only that, he sent police officers." With a trembling finger, he pointed toward the embankment. "Two cars just hit head-on and went over the crest. I don't know how many people are involved." He shook his head. "They were going mighty fast."

Detective Williams immediately put in a 911 call. The officers quickly flipped on the emergency light, and maneuvered their cars to block the road from any oncoming traffic. They removed some high powered lanterns from their trunks, then climbed down the hill to the smoldering pieces of wreckage.

"There's a woman in this car," yelled one of the officers.

The other patrolman went to his aid as Williams dashed for the convertible. He flashed the beam inside the interior. "The persons in this car have been thrown out. Doesn't look like they had on their seat belts. So watch your step." He continued to search the surrounding area, but found no signs of bodies.

Standing under a tree, near the wrecked vehicle, he studied the hill where they'd broke through the barrier. As he tried to calculate the ejection rate, several drops of red moisture fell on his hand. He swung the flashlight ray up into the tree. "Oh, my God," he muttered.

Two bare legs dangled above his head and streams of blood had made its way down to the feet where it slowly dripped to the ground. Williams gripped the lower branch and hoisted himself into the boughs of the oak. He still couldn't reach the victim draped over the large protruding limb. Straddling the rough bark, he inched his way forward. When he managed to grasp the young woman, he flashed his light over her body and grimaced. "I need some help over here," he called.

He lifted her head and looked into the blank face with staring green eyes. Her blond hair rippled through his fingers in the breeze. "What a tragedy," he mumbled.

"Looks like you've got a problem," a voice echoed from below.

Williams shined his light at the two officers. "I'm sure she never knew what happened. Her body is impaled on this branch, and I can't bring her down without help from one of you."

The younger officer shed his gun belt and placed it on a fallen log, then shimmied up the tree. He climbed above the detective, then made his way across a higher branch until he could drop down on the other side of the corpse.

"Oh, man, she's a beautiful girl. What a way to die. This is what happens when you drive too fast and without a seatbelt." The patrolman straddled the branch. "We're going to need a saw to cut off this limb." He called down to his partner. "Jack, look in the trunk of my car, there's a fold-back branch saw in a box. I think it'll do the trick."

The officer brought back the implement and handed it up to the men. Williams shoved his flashlight into his back pocket, then carefully sawed through the branch as the officer held on to the body. Then he folded the saw and tossed it to the ground. "Tell me when you're ready and we'll hand her down to Jack."

At the count of three, the two men lifted her from the branch. Blood dripped from the hole in her back, and splattered their clothes. They gently slid her down to the other man who caught the body and carefully placed it on the ground. He took his lantern and played the light across the face. "Good Lord, she's the spittin' image of the woman in the sedan."

Williams and the officer climbed down the tree.

"What do you mean?" the detective asked.

"Come over here and take a look."

The three men crossed over to the wrecked car and shined the beam over the face behind the steering wheel. The identical blond hair flared around her face, and it appeared the same blank green eyes stared into space.

"Boy, you're right. Run a check on these license plates while we're waiting for the ambulance."

The men were standing around the patrol car listening for the message on the registration of the cars when the ambulance screeched around the bend blaring its siren, its circular lights reflecting off the forest forming an eery illusion of death.

CHAPTER FORTY-NINE

Back at the ranch, while the paramedics loaded Ruth into the ambulance, Sarah, Patricia and Christina hovered around the gurney assuring her they'd drop by the hospital the next day. They waved good-bye and watched the vehicle head down the road, its red light flickering against the blackness of the night.

Hawkman heard the lone howl of a coyote in the distance, and turned to the clan of witches. He noticed they were swatting at mosquitos that had suddenly invaded their territory. "Would you girls be more comfortable in the bunkhouse while we wait for the detective?"

They all nodded.

"Leave your luggage on the front porch," Jennifer said, as the girls hurried inside.

Two hours passed and still no detective. Hawkman moved outside, and punched in Williams cell phone number, only to be transferred to the voice mail box to which he left a message.

He poked his head in the bunkhouse door. "Greg, could you come out here a moment?"

Willis lumbered out the door and joined Hawkman. "What's up?"

"I can't reach the detective. He must have been called out on an emergency. I'm going to walk down the road and bring my vehicle up here. We might end up packing everyone into it to get them out of here."

"Want me to go with you?"

"No, I'm not comfortable in leaving Jennifer alone with these girls. I'll be back in a few minutes. Your presence will keep down any thoughts of escape from the witches."

He nodded. "I'll keep things under control until you're back."

"Thanks." Hawkman took off in a jog toward the back road. He could see the outline of his 4X4 when his cell vibrated against his waist. Slowing to a walk, he put the phone to his ear. "Tom Casey."

He stopped in the middle of the lane, listened, then hung up and continued his journey to the SUV. He drove back to the bunkhouse and went inside to the small living room where two battery operated lights cast strange shadows on the occupants.

He crossed to where Jennifer and Greg occupied the couch. Sarah sat on the floor, leaning against her dad's legs. Patricia lay curled up and asleep on the floor with her head resting on Sarah's leg. Christina offered her chair at the end of the sofa to Hawkman. He waved her off and perched on the arm of the sofa next to his wife. "Everything going okay?"

"Yes, the girls are restless, but they've stayed reasonably quiet."

He studied the four young witches settled on cushions with their backs against the wall on the opposite side of the room. A couple had dropped their heads onto their knees and drifted off to sleep.

"I heard from Detective Williams. He came upon a horrible wreck and had to stay with the victims until the emergency vehicles arrived. He's on his way now."

Jennifer frowned. "Did the accident occur on the mountain road?"

"I don't know. He didn't say and I didn't think it my place to ask him at the moment." He glanced at his watch. "It's three in the morning. A long night for all of us, and it's not over. Once we get to the station, Williams will want statements from our three rescued girls, and he'll book the other four. I don't know what he'll do about Ruth, but I'm sure he'll want to get her account too."

Greg stretched his arms above his head and yawned. "Thank goodness my job has trained me for late hours. I can usually handle them, and this has been a night I wouldn't have missed for the world." He patted Sarah's head and she glanced up with a big admiring smile.

Headlight beams flashed through the windows, and Hawkman rose. "Looks like Detective Williams has arrived. I'll go out and talk to him before we load the girls."

Jennifer stood and handed him a flashlight. "Shall I come?"

"Sure, Greg can take care of things in here."

They walked out to the unmarked patrol car. When Detective Williams stepped onto the ground, Jennifer gasped.

"Oh, my, it must have been a horrible wreck. You're covered in blood."

Williams grimaced. "Sorry I look so gross, but figured you'd waited long enough. I think you're going to be shocked when I tell you what's happened. We haven't been able to locate the next of kin yet, but I'll disclose the names of the victims, only because you're a party in this case."

Jennifer put a hand to her mouth. "Are you trying to tell us Brenda Thompson was involved in this accident?"

"Yes, she was in a convertible and hit head-on by a car driven by her mother, Lea Thompson."

"Oh, my God," Hawkman said. "Were they both killed?"

"Yes, Brenda was thrown from her car and impaled on the dead branch of a tree. The paramedics pronounced her mother dead after they pulled her from the wreckage. Both were driving at a high rate of speed." He sighed and shook his head. "One of the most horrific accidents I've seen in a long time."

Hawkman removed his hat and ran a hand over his head. "Let's not tell any of the girls. They'll find out soon enough. Right now let's haul them to the station so you can get their statements, but first, here's a couple of things you might want to have as evidence." He walked to the small bench in front of the bunkhouse, and handed Williams the recorder and velvet bag. "Brenda had these here when she started the ritual. There's something else I think you'll be interested in."

The detective followed Hawkman to the back where he opened the door and ran the flashlight beam across Brenda's lab. The detective shook his head. "Appears this young woman planned on going into witchcraft big time." They stepped out of the small room and Williams closed the door. "We'll cordon off the whole ranch and come back up here in the next day or two with the lab boys." He let out a loud sigh. "This has been one unusual case. Guess we better load the girls into the cars and get them to the station. Where do you have then holed up?"

Hawkman led the way toward the front and guided Williams into the bunkhouse. The detective waved for his officers to come along. Hawkman introduced them to the group and the officers proceeded to do their job. When the handcuffs were placed on the four witches, Tammy and Kate sobbed.

"Are we going to jail?"

Jennifer moved in front of the two girls. "You'll probably be kept for a few hours until a decision is made on whether to press charges or not. I might add, your parents will be notified."

The girls were then led into the darkness. Two were put into each vehicle, their bags thrown in beside them and the doors slammed shut.

Greg, Sarah, Patricia, Christina and Jennifer climbed into the SUV with their suitcases. Hawkman approached Williams' car. "We'll follow with the three victims, so you can get their statements."

The detective nodded. "Let's hit the road."

When they arrived at the police station, Williams told Hawkman to take his group to number two interrogation room. Then he instructed his officers to take the four girls to the booking area.

Patricia clung to Sarah as they followed Hawkman down the sterile hallway and turned into a room which only contained a table with four chairs. An officer followed, bringing in a couple more seats.

"You girls take a place around the table," Hawkman said, then pointed toward the two chairs against the wall. "Greg and Jennifer, it's best you sit over there. I'm not sure how the detective will want to proceed. More than likely, he'll take the girls one at a time into another room." He glanced at Christina who was gnawing at her fingernails. "You have nothing to fear. Remember, you were the one abused."

She looked up with tears in her eyes. "I know, but I'm all alone. I have no one here who cares or any place to go."

Jennifer crossed the room and put an arm around her shoulders. "Would you like us to contact your parents right now?"

"They live miles away. It would take them hours to get here."

Sarah jumped up and whispered in her dad's ear.

He nodded and grinned. "Sure."

She bounced back to her seat. "Dad says you can stay with us until your folks get here."

Christina wiped the tears from her cheeks and smiled. "That would be great."

Sarah then turned to Patricia. "What about you?"

"I think my mom will be happy to come and get me."

Everyone hushed and stared at Detective Williams when he entered the room.

"Hey, people, I'm not a monster; I'm your salvation."

They all laughed.

"I just need a statement from each of you on what happened and how you ended up at the ranch. I'll take you one at a time to a private area where you can tell your story to a recorder. It won't take long. I'm sure you're all exhausted and would like to get some rest." He glanced at the girls and pointed. "Patricia Riley, I'll take you first, because we've notified your mother you're safe. She'll be down to pick you up in half an hour."

Patricia grinned and followed the detective down the hallway. She came back to the room within fifteen minutes, and just as Christina rose to go with the detective, Mrs. Riley burst through the door.

She grabbed her daughter, tears streaming down her face. "Oh, my baby!" After a few seconds, she held Patricia at arms length and studied her daughter, then frowned. "What happened to your beautiful hair?"

"Don't worry, Mom. It'll grow back. I'll tell you all about it when we get home."

She glanced at the detective. "Can we go now?"

"Yes, but stay in town. I might need to ask you more questions."

Patricia laughed. "Believe me, I'm not going anywhere. I've been away from home way too long."

"You can pick up your things at the front desk."

Arms around each other's waists, Patricia and her mother left the police station.

Once Williams finished with the other two girls, Sarah explained to her dad they'd promised Ruth they'd come by the hospital and pay her a visit.

Greg nodded. "It's a bit early. Why don't we go home, freshen up, get a few winks of sleep, and have a bite to eat before we go."

Sarah laughed. "You're right and I'm famished."

Hawkman and Jennifer watched Greg, Sarah and Christina go down the hallway.

He shook his head. "Those girls were skipping along as if they hadn't been up all night."

Jennifer laughed. "Teenagers are very resilient."

"I wonder how they'll take the death of Brenda."

She shrugged. "Hard to say."

They decided to leave and were headed out the door when Detective Williams called them back. "Could I talk to you two a moment?"

"Sure," Hawkman said, and they stepped back inside and followed him to an interrogation room.

He motioned toward the chairs. "Have a seat."

The detective dropped into the chair across from them. Placing his elbows on the table, he wiped his hands across his face. "Man, it's been a long forty-eight hours."

Hawkman leaned back and crossed his legs. "I think we could all use some shuteye."

"I plan to get a few winks after I've chatted with you two. I'll need statements from you both, but let's do it another day. It might not even be necessary with the deaths of Brenda and her mother. This case hardly holds water right now."

Jennifer leaned forward. "I know those young witches were in the wrong, but I'd hate to see them go to jail for being dragged into something they didn't understand."

Williams nodded. "I agree. So far, all the evidence we've collected points to Brenda."

"Have you contacted any of these girls' parents?" Hawkman asked.

"Yes, we've reached a couple so far, and they'll be up in a few days. Still working on the other two. Another interesting factor. When we did a search on their names, we discovered all of these girls had been reported missing by their folks."

Jennifer sighed. "You wonder what incident in their lives made them run away?"

Williams stood. "Probably something we need to look into." He put out his hand. "I want to thank you both for all your help on this. I doubt we'd have found Patricia Riley if our cases hadn't overlapped. At least we have seven young ladies who are safe and sound."

THE END

EPILOGUE

During the following weeks, Hawkman spoke with Detective Williams on a regular basis, until assured all the girls had been united with their families. On the day of the juvenile court hearing, everyone attended and felt relief when the judge didn't sentence any of the girls or Jerry Olson to jail time. However, he ruled each one would have to do a year's worth of volunteer services and report to a social worker every month. They were to return to school, and finish their high school education. He also gave then a stern lecture about why they should never neglect or ignore the teachings of their parents.

Sarah Willis moved in with her dad as her mother believed she deserved her misery since she'd left home on her own accord. Her dad no longer worried about leaving for days at a time, because his daughter had grown into a level headed young woman.

Patricia Riley's hair would never grow as long as it once had been, but she'd gained self confidence and didn't worry about it. She carried her head high and everyone loved being around this happy girl.

Jerry Olson agreed to talk to high schools about how not to get involved in illegal activities. He went back to school, a rejuvenated young man, and continued his sports with new vigor. It appeared he might be in for some lucrative scholarships if he continued in this vein. He had an eye for Sarah and she didn't mind the attention.

Christina's folks were thrilled their daughter had come home, and secretly admired how gracious she'd become.

Barbara and Shelby had only missed a semester of high school and graduated mid-term before the court hearing. They were very happy with their light sentences as their folks were willing to send them off to college, if they promised never to pull a stupid stunt again.

Tammy and Kate were evaluated by psychological services and referred for counseling while continuing their high school classes.

Greg Willis walked into Tom Casey's office one day shortly after the rescue of his daughter, and placed another five hundred dollar check on Hawkman's desk.

He tried to hand it back. "This isn't necessary. Your daughter's home safe and sound. That's all the payment I need."

Willis shook his head as he pumped Hawkman's hand. "No way. You earned every penny. If it weren't for you, I might never have seen my little girl again."

ABOUT THE AUTHOR

Born and raised in Oklahoma, Betty Sullivan La Pierre attended the Oklahoma College for Women and the University of Oklahoma, graduating with her BS degree in Speech Therapy with a Specialty in the Deaf.

Once married, she moved to California with her husband. When her husband was killed in an automobile accident, she was left with two young boys to raise. She is now remarried and has had another son through that marriage.

Ms. La Pierre has lived in the Silicon Valley (California) for many years. At one time, she owned a Mail Order Used Book business dealing mainly in signed and rare books, but phased it out because it took up too much of her writing time. She's an avid reader, belongs to the Wednesday Writers' Society, and periodically attends functions of other writing organizations.

She writes Mystery/Suspense/Thriller novels, which are published in digital format and print. Her Hawkman Mystery Series is developing quite a fan base. She's also written two stand-alone mystery/thrillers and plans to continue writing. 'BLACKOUT,' Betty's story about a bingo hall (of the Hawkman Series), ranked in the top ten of the P&E Reader's Poll, and won the 2003 BLOODY DAGGER AWARD for best Mystery/ Suspense. EuroReviews recently picked 'THE DEADLY THORN' (One of Betty's stand alone thrillers) for their 2005 May Book of the Month.

Betty Sullivan La Pierre's work is a testament to how much she enjoys the challenge of plotting an exciting story.

Visit her personal site at: www.bettysullivanlapierre.com

2089269

Made in the USA